"Rafe, would you hold me like that again?"

"Francesca..."

"I don't think anything could make me feel more wonderful than that. It was—"

"You understand what you're asking, don't you?" Rafe said huskily.

"I—I think so. I think I want to...that I want you to make love to me."

"You've gotta know that's not possible, 'Cesca." He raised a hand and lightly traced the contours of her face. "I want you to know," he murmured, "that it's not because I don't find you desirable. You've got to know I do!"

"But then why—"

"*Because you're Esteban Valera's daughter.* I'm not for you. My job is to deliver you intact, if you'll forgive my bluntness, to the bridegroom he's handpicked for you. Does that say it plainly enough?"

ABOUT THE AUTHOR

Born in New Jersey, Veronica Sattler has had several career interests, ranging from teaching to selling antiques to her ultimate passion, writing. She has won a number of prestigious awards for her historical romances, but *Wild Cherries* is her first contemporary novel. "I had wanted to write a contemporary for a long time, and one day the name Rafe O'Hara came to mind and I was off and running," she says.

Veronica, who also enjoys gourmet cooking and American folk art, currently resides in rural Pennsylvania with her daughter, Alyssa, and an Irish wolfhound named Brendan.

Veronica Sattler

Wild Cherries

Harlequin Books

TORONTO • NEW YORK • LONDON
AMSTERDAM • PARIS • SYDNEY • HAMBURG
STOCKHOLM • ATHENS • TOKYO • MILAN
MADRID • WARSAW • BUDAPEST • AUCKLAND

To Judith C. Superior—("spelled like the lake")—Kaneff,
one of the loveliest people
I know—with thanks

ISBN 0-373-70612-X

WILD CHERRIES

Copyright © 1994 by Veronica Sattler.

ACKNOWLEDGMENTS

I wish to thank the following people for their help with this, my first contemporary romance novel: Maureen Stonehouse, for being the perfect editor; John Pierce, for assistance in landscaping and populating the Sierra Madre with flora and fauna; Jack Parker and Art Schwedler for telling me about airplanes; Judy Kaneff, to whom this book is dedicated (again), for connecting me to the best agent a writer could have; Nancy Coffey, for being that agent—and loving *Wild Cherries* as much as I do; Connie Rinehold, for her enormous generosity, and for making me join the computer age; Maggie Osborne, for generosity, help, encouragement and friendship; and my daughter, Alyssa, and our Irish wolfhound, Brendan, for putting up with me during the fits and starts of creative insanity.

CHAPTER ONE

"WHAT A *HUNK!*" The postulant nun who'd been sorting the mail clapped her hand over her mouth. She glanced at the photo she'd been holding and dropped it like a hot potato. "Um...sorry, Reverend Mother."

The head of the convent hid a smile and nodded. "That will be all for now, Angelica. I believe Sister Mary Michael has some...less distracting duties for you, now that matins is over. You'll find her in the library."

She accepted the young woman's obeisance and watched her leave, then heaved a sigh. That one would bear careful watching, but already the mother superior suspected little Angelica lacked the otherworldliness necessary to become a member of the order.

"Ah, well," she reflected in her native Spanish, "time will tell."

Her eyes moved to the photograph lying atop a pile of letters and one very significant telegram. Reaching for it, she ran a glance over the handsome, rakishly masculine face that gazed out at her with cool blue eyes.

What a hunk, indeed. She quickly added a silent prayer of thanks to the Virgin that Francesca Valera was a far different sort than the impetuous, flighty Angelica. With the latter, she'd worry no end if a man of such virile good looks were assigned to escort the child on a long journey; with Francesca . . . no, there was no need for concern there.

Twenty-three-year-old Francesca Valera was the pride of El Convento de los Santos, a young woman with both feet planted squarely on the ground. Intelligent, well educated and obedient to authority, yet knowing her own mind, she was the epitome of the kind of young woman their convent school tried to turn out when her time behind its cloistered walls was at an end.

Yet the mother superior was not free of worry for her star charge's future. *Holy Mother of God,* she prayed as she pocketed the photograph and the telegram that had arrived with it, *keep her safe from the world that is about to take her from us. And, most of all, Holy Mother, keep her true to herself!*

While the nun prayed in the solitude of her study, outside early morning sunshine washed the grounds of El Convento de los Santos. The only sounds intruding on the peaceful quietude were the subtle stirrings of nature. Bird song rippled along the hedges that lined the convent's high stone walls. Soft rustlings barely disturbed the bright splashes of color that were the mother superior's pride and joy.

But suddenly the thunder of hoofbeats reverberated around the stone facades of several outbuildings and the whitewashed stucco walls of the convent itself. At the western edge of a wide meadow that flanked the stables, two figures appeared on horseback. Bent low over their mounts' withers, their slender frames moving in unison with the horses, the riders were clearly enjoying themselves. Laughter erupted in a throaty cadence as one rider pulled steadily ahead.

"I've got you now, Maria!" she cried. "Eat my dust!"

"No fair!" shouted the young woman who tried to catch up on her chestnut gelding. "You knew Diablo would shy at that last jump!" But there was laughter in her voice as she issued the protest.

Francesca Valera turned to grin at her companion as she slowed her mare to a canter and then a sedate trot. Sitting tall and erect on her custom-fitted Spanish saddle with its high, tooled-leather cantle, she handled her mount with the ease of a lifelong equestrian.

"No excuses, now, *mi amiga*. If Diablo balks at difficult hurdles, whose fault is that, when you helped train him yourself?"

"Bah!" Maria muttered, but her black eyes answered the amused sparkle in Francesca's as the young women circled back to the stables.

An elderly man came out to take the horses as the pair dismounted.

"Give them an extra half ration of grain this morning, Pedro," Francesca told the groom. "They've earned it."

"Hah!" Maria groused good-naturedly. She threw a mock glare at the chestnut's retreating haunches. "That is up for dispute!"

Francesca chuckled as she tucked a long strand of auburn hair back into the low chignon she wore, then secured it with a hairpin at the nape of her neck.

The two women headed for one of the convent's side entrances, their manner easy, speaking of several years' close companionship. By far the taller of the two, Francesca tailored the strides of her long legs to fit Maria's shorter ones.

Both were lay teachers at the convent, although Maria was older and had been at it longer. She'd been hired as a junior instructor for the younger girls five years before, just as Francesca had begun her undergraduate studies there, via a special correspondence course with La Universidad de Mexico.

But there were to be no classes held today. Madre Dolorosa, the mother superior, had declared a school holiday. Francesca's mood sobered as she recalled why.

"I must finish packing, Maria," she said, switching easily from Spanish to English. Francesca's specialty was languages; she also spoke fluent French and Italian. Maria was Mexican by birth, but her father had been a *norteamericano* businessman, and she'd spent half her childhood growing up in a suburb of San Diego.

"*Sí.*" Maria nodded somberly. She was going to miss this one. She had known, when she'd been given her assignment—not the teaching, but her true assignment, which Francesca knew nothing of, and likely never would—that this day would come. But who would have guessed that Don Esteban Valera's daughter and she would have grown so close? Like sisters, they were, yet each so very different in background and personality.

And looks, Maria added as she glanced at the younger woman.

Where the fun-loving Maria was small, dark and round-faced, Francesca's graceful, long-boned height set off a soft, classical beauty. Her looks were so unique—part fashion model, part angelic madonna— that all her young students attempted to emulate them— with varying degrees of success. Those with long hair wound it in chignons riding low on their necks; those with short hair prayed for the day it would be long enough for them to do the same. Several plucked their eyebrows to imitate the winged curve of the language teacher's. They did their best to copy the easy, floating grace of her walk, tried hard to arrange their facial expressions in some semblance of Señorita Francesca's serene, angelic aspect.

Only Maria knew of the restless, inquiring spirit Francesca buried beneath that ethereal facade. Of the internal struggle she waged on a daily basis to force herself into the mode the good sisters tried to instill in their charges.

And which Francesca's father demanded of his only daughter.

And now the day had come when all of the convent's long years of shaping and pruning would be harvested. Tomorrow Francesca Valera would leave the sheltering walls of El Convento de los Santos forever. To embark on the role for which she'd been groomed all these years: tomorrow she was leaving to be married—to a man handpicked by her father.

To a man she had never met.

Maria suppressed a shudder. Duty and obedience had been as much a part of her life here at the convent as anything else. But to surrender one's entire future—one's very self—to the wishes of a seldom-seen parent without question? *Dios!* It was positively medieval!

But Maria was familiar with the Old World ways that many of the elite adhered to here in Mexico. She had not been born to their class; but anyone who'd spent time at an exclusive convent boarding school like El Convento de los Santos would know this.

In much of Latin America the daughters of the upper crust were as carefully sheltered and protected as hothouse plants. Kept virginal and innocent behind high walls guarded by family and Church, they awaited the day when parent-sanctioned marriages would claim them.

And in El Convento de los Santos, Maria knew, Francesca Valera was the most carefully guarded flower of them all.

"It will be pleasant to see Tía Pilar again," Francesca was saying. "I met her only once, at Cousin Felippe's wedding, when I was eleven. But she was kind to me. She . . . knew my mother."

Maria caught the slight hesitation, knew it had been triggered by the deeply buried pain Francesca tried to hide whenever the subject of her mother arose. Rosa Valera had died when Francesca was only four. The child had been reared by a succession of nurses and housekeepers until she'd been old enough to attend the convent school.

Francesca rarely spoke of the loss. But once, in an unguarded moment, she'd confessed to Maria that she spent most of her childhood in a state of perpetual hunger for details about the mother she barely recalled.

Maria placed a gentle hand on Francesca's arm as they reached the suite of rooms they shared. "She was able to tell you of her, then?"

Francesca gave her a rueful smile. "Some things, yes—but it couldn't begin to be . . . enough."

Maria nodded, her dark eyes compassionate as they entered the sunny sitting room that separated their bedrooms.

"Well, now," said Francesca—her tone became brisk, as if she were determined to break the somber mood—"I've almost finished packing the trunks that will be sent ahead to Rome, but there's still the carryon

I'll be taking with me on the plane. Will you help me decide what—"

"*Idiota!* Of course I'll help!" Maria caught her arm in a conspiratorial manner. "I may never have been a bride myself, Francesca, but with three older sisters, I think I have a good idea of what you'll need. After all, we can't have your Carlo meeting his *novia* when she is anything less than ravishing, can we?"

Francesca's soft laughter accompanied them to her room, but, inside, she was a mass of roiling emotions.

Why did it have to be this way? Why couldn't she and Carlo Pagnani have met, at least once, before they were affianced? Jacinta de Rivera's parents had arranged a party to which her future *novio* had been invited, well before their betrothal was announced. And Cristina Calderon had known she would marry her third cousin from the time they were both hardly more than infants!

Surreptitiously, she studied the silver-framed portrait of a handsome, impeccably groomed young man before thrusting it into a suitcase.

Handsome enough, I suppose, even if he does look a little too much like a model for a toothpaste ad....

Carlo Pagnani, oldest son of Italian industrial magnate, Rudolfo Pagnani, had sent her his portrait last month, when their engagement was announced. With it he'd sent an engagement ring bearing an emerald big enough to choke a horse; Francesca had yet to wear it, and it currently lay in the Van Cleef & Arpels box it had come in, carefully tucked away in her carryon, since she expected she'd better slip it on before landing in Rome.

And with both of these gifts, Carlo had sent what could only be described as a polite, dutiful letter. She supposed he thought he'd described himself adequately in it.

But he hadn't.

What did she care about the degree he'd taken at the University of Bologna? The kind of car he drove? Where he'd vacationed last? Papa could have told her such things—and had, for the most part, in his last phone call.

She needed to know the meat and bones of the man! What made him laugh? Cry?—if, indeed, a twenty-seven-year-old Italian male could be brought to admit such a thing! What were his hopes? . . . his fears? . . . his dreams? What kept him awake at night, on nights when he couldn't fall asleep right away? What made him angry?

Or passionate!

She threw another glance at the perfect smile on the face in the portrait. *Hah! If someone with a face like that even knows what the word means!*

In fact, Carlo Pagnani, she mentally addressed the portrait's even, placid features, *if you have a brain in your head or a depth to your soul, why doesn't it show?*

With a fierce scowl, Francesca clapped a pile of neatly folded underwear over the smiling face.

"*Caramba!* You are not taking *those?*" Maria pointed an accusing finger at the stack of serviceable cotton panties.

"*Sí,* I am."

Drawing herself up to make the most of her five feet three inches, Maria placed her hands on her hips and glared at her. "*Dios!* Haven't I taught you *anything?*"

She shot a scornful glance at the cotton underwear. "Those," she said with disgust, "may be fine for El Convento de los Santos—" she plucked the offending garments from the suitcase and tossed them onto the bed, then indicated the portrait of Carlo "—but for a bridegroom, they are not!"

Francesca raised one eyebrow. "So?" she questioned archly. "Are you telling me that you know something about my *novio* that I don't?"

"I am saying," Maria enunciated with exaggerated patience, "that I know something about the world out there—" she gestured toward the view outside their windows "—which *you* do not! *Niña! Inocente!* Your *novio* is a man, right?"

Francesca glanced at the portrait. *Ah, but what* kind *of a man? Or, more to the point, how* much *of a man?* But she said nothing.

"Well, *amiga,*" Maria went on, "a man, *any man*— but especially a young, virile Italian—wants to see his wife wearing something more...more *feminine!* What's the matter with you? Where have your eyes been when we watched those movies I smuggled in?"

Francesca smiled. Now one of the senior lay teachers, Maria had been entrusted with the convent's Jeep Cherokee, which she often used to go into the town, twenty minutes away, where a video rental store served the needs of tourists who frequented the area.

Unknown to Madre Dolorosa—or anyone else in the convent—a steady stream of Hollywood movies had made their way in and out of their suite during the past year. Late at night, when everyone else slept, Francesca and Maria had surreptitiously viewed videos of films such as *The Prince of Tides, Batman* and *Lethal Weapon 2,* as well as classics like *Casablanca* and *High Noon.*

"They were a welcome, ah, supplement to the language tapes you rented." Francesca's smile became a grin. "I wonder if Ramón ever suspected we'd invent such uses for his gift."

Maria laughed. Ramón was Francesca's older half brother, the son of a mistress Don Esteban had kept before he met Francesca's mother. Although Francesca saw little of Ramón, she was extremely fond of him.

And apparently Ramón was fond of his "baby" sister. He'd sent her generous gifts over the years, for her birthdays and on her saint's days. One of the most appreciated and well used was the video player she pretended to employ solely for "instructional purposes."

"What Ramón doesn't know won't hurt him," Maria said with a grin that was pure mischief. "But, speaking of gifts—wait right here." She ran toward her own room. "*Dios!* I almost forgot!"

Francesca turned back to the suitcase, eyeing Carlo's picture. Then, with a defiant gesture, she whisked the pile of plain underwear off the bed and stuffed it under some things at the bottom of the suitcase. Feeling for a moment like an impudent child, she stuck out her tongue at Carlo's likeness and slammed the suitcase shut.

Maria returned with a wrapped gift she mysteriously refused to allow Francesca to open just then. "Not until you are thousands of feet in the air, aboard that plane," she instructed. "Ah, I wish I were going with you! When you do open it, I'll be lamentably far away. But I'm hoping it will remind you, maybe just when you are beginning to feel a little homesick...or nervous...that I am still your friend...and I love you."

Francesca's eyes welled with tears as she reached for the smaller woman and hugged her. "Oh, Maria, I'm going to miss you!"

FRANCESCA'S LAST FULL DAY at the convent raced by. First, there was a high mass where prayers were offered for her safe journey to Rome, and then for a happy and fruitful marriage.

Several of her young students blushed and fought to suppress giggles at the "fruitful" part. But Francesca maintained the outward serenity for which she'd become known at the school.

Then there was a luncheon in her honor, with songs and farewell speeches from faculty and students alike. Francesca was clearly a favorite of many who resided in this enclave of women. Several times she became deeply moved, pausing to swallow the threat of tears as young girls made their way to her table and whispered quiet words of goodbye.

Many brought gifts, their selections showing the influence of the nuns: a rosary of amethyst quartz crystal; a prayer book bound in soft white leather; a picture of Our Lady in a sterling silver frame...

The afternoon sped by in a blur as the entire convent participated in various games in the shady courtyard. Even Madre Dolorosa joined in, the voluminous skirts of her habit flying behind her as she led a team of nuns to victory over the senior girls in a relay race.

Later there was another trip to the chapel for vespers, followed by a late supper, and then it was over. Yawning and smiling, the students headed for their rooms, Maria and Francesca among them. It was not yet eight o'clock, but the school day would begin early the following morning. The girls would already be in classes while Francesca dressed and readied herself for the car that would carry her to the private plane her father had waiting for her.

"Francesca?"

Both Francesca and Maria turned as they neared the arched doorway of the dining *sala*.

"Yes, Your Reverence?" Francesca met Madre Dolorosa's calm brown eyes while Maria gave them both a nod and turned back toward the doorway.

"No, you, too, Maria," said the mother superior. "I wish a word with each of you."

The middle-aged nun withdrew a pair of envelopes from the folds of her pristine white habit. "A telegram arrived earlier from your father, Francesca. It was addressed to you in my care."

She handed Francesca one of the envelopes, then placed a hand on her shoulder. "We said our true goodbyes in my office after mass this morning, my dear. Therefore I won't belabor what you already know—you are loved here and will be sorely missed. But as you prepare to take your final night of rest at El Convento de los Santos, I ask that you remember the primary topic of our conversation in your prayers. You recall what that was?"

Francesca forced a smile and nodded. How could she forget? *Do not let the ways of the world seduce you, Francesca,* the older woman had said.

Ah, yes, the ways of the world... Francesca did her best to keep her smile from appearing bitter.

Madre Dolorosa was nodding, bidding her good night. "*Vaya con Dios,* Francesca."

The nun's troubled eyes followed Francesca out. She knew Don Esteban's daughter would have a hard row to hoe. Although she had to pretend not to, she knew exactly what kind of international "businessman" the school's chief benefactor was.

With a sigh, she turned to Maria. "I worry about that child, Maria."

Maria shook her head. "Hardly a child any longer, Your Reverence."

"In years, no, but—" The mother superior sighed again. "Well, we have done our part. Now, I suppose, we must leave her in God's hands."

In God's and Don Esteban Valera's, Maria amended silently. "Ah, you wished to see me about something, Your Reverence?"

The nun became all business as she handed Maria the second envelope. "This arrived for us, along with the telegram. It contains a photograph and brief vital statistics of the driver who will be arriving tomorrow to transport Francesca to the plane, along with her duenna."

"The usual security precaution." Maria nodded as she withdrew the photograph from the envelope. She stared at it, feeling her breath catch. *Dios!* She'd never seen a man so—*Dios!*

The nun's observant eyes grew shrewd, and she gave Maria a nod. "Handsome devil, isn't he?"

Still captivated by the stark male beauty of the face that gazed out of the photo with the bluest eyes Maria had ever seen, the younger woman could only nod. Not one of the don's regulars, but then she'd known that. This one was escorting Francesca out of the country, and there could well be paparazzi. Esteban Valera never allowed anyone to photograph his daughter.

But this gorgeous creature didn't even look Spanish—or Italian, for that matter—and that *was* a change. He was an Anglo, for heaven's sake!

And *what* an Anglo!

She flipped the photo over and read the lines typed on the reverse side:

Name: Rafael O'Hara
Born: N.Y.C., 1958
Ht.: 6'4"
Wt.: 220 lbs.
Add'l.: Black Belt, Karate; Pilot's License, U.S.A.,
Mexico, Guatemala, Panama; BS in Engineering,
UCLA, 1985; Self-employed

Maria suppressed a grin as she flipped the photo back over and drank in the handsomer-than-sin features. Reluctantly, she handed it back to the mother superior, wishing for the second time in as many days that she were going with Francesca Valera when she left!

FRANCESCA SLID INTO BED and turned out the lamp. She was tired from the long day, but she knew it would be a while before she slept. Madre Dolorosa's reminder played itself out in her head, again and again: *Do not let the ways of the world seduce you.... Do not let...*

"The ways of the world": deceptively simple words from a circumspect woman. But Francesca had no illusions about what they really meant: Do not let the world of your father become *your* world!

It was clear the nun suspected she knew more than she was supposed to. Perhaps she even knew for sure that Esteban Valera's daughter was leaving these sheltering walls less naive and ignorant than they wished her to be.

Francesca wondered when she'd begun to suspect—or was it only a shrewd guess? She turned restlessly on the mattress as memory called up images of her father from the past.... There was his strong masculine presence as he held her while she wept out her grief at the bewildering loss of her mother. She heard his laughter, and her own, as he swept her child's body onto his broad shoulders and carried her through the hacienda on the morning she'd turned six. She saw his white teeth flash in a grin of pleasure when she presented him with a drawing of the pony he'd given her for her seventh birthday; his proud face as he'd stood in the church on the day she made her first Holy Communion.

Through laughter, smiles, tears—ah, how she'd adored him!

But all too soon that adoration had been tempered by other things ... confusion and shock at first; then deep disappointment. And finally, bitter regret.

The telegram had informed her that it was Ramón who would be meeting the private plane that flew her to Miami International. Papa was already in Italy:

HAVE BUSINESS IN ROME STOP WILL ASSIST WITH
WEDDING ARRANGEMENTS STOP WILL MEET YOU
WITH PAGNANIS AT LEONARDO DA VINCI STOP HAVE
SAFE TRIP STOP LOVE PAPA

Francesca's lips curved into a bitter smile in the darkness. Business in Rome? Ah, yes, she could hardly doubt it! But she seriously doubted whether the business that kept him from flying with her and Ramón out of Miami—as he'd originally promised—had anything to do with a wedding.

"Or anything nearly so *legitimate!*" she said to the darkness as angry tears coursed down her cheeks and she punched her pillow with a clenched fist.

CHAPTER TWO

RAFE O'HARA WONDERED if anyone had ever died of boredom. Pretending to adjust the rearview mirror of the five-year-old rental car, he used it to catch another glimpse of his passenger in the back seat.

The old woman hadn't spoken or moved a muscle since the last time he'd done this, about ten miles back. Señorita Pilar Valera sat, ramrod straight, gazing at whatever she took in through the windshield, past the back of his head and shoulders. In fact, after greeting him back at the hotel, she hadn't said one word. He'd tried to engage her in conversation, just to pass the time. After all, it was a five-hour trip and the radio didn't work, for chrissake. He knew she spoke no English, so he'd used his best colloquial Spanish, but no luck.

But he'd caught the look of apprehension in her dark eyes when he'd first introduced himself, producing her brother's letter of introduction at the same time. The old dame was afraid of him—he'd lay odds on it. Funny...you'd think the sister of one of the world's most powerful crime bosses would be used to a guy like him as an escort.

As a bodyguard, Rafe corrected. *Even if it isn't mainly the old girl Valera hired me to protect. I mean, she's only the kid's duenna. Still, you'd think she'd know my presence means her safety, too. So why the*

hell did her eyes look like those of a deer caught in the
headlights, back there in the hotel lobby?

Heaving a disgusted sigh, Rafe readjusted the mirror
and reached for one of the toothpicks he carried in the
pocket of his denim shirt. He jammed it in between his
teeth, wishing it were one of the Marlboros he'd given
up three weeks ago.

Three weeks and two days, to be exact. Rafe mouthed
a choice expletive, then deftly negotiated a sharp curve
that wound around the side of the mountain. Back on
the straightaway, he glanced at his watch: 2:42, just six
minutes since the last time he'd looked. It was boring
work. No question about it. And likely to get worse.

It was siesta time all over Mexico. He knew this
largely accounted for the lack of traffic on the road.
They hadn't seen more than three vehicles since leaving
Mexico City, where he'd picked up his passenger at the
Marie Isabelle Hotel.

His thoughts jumped ahead to the destination they'd
reach in another hour or so: El Convento de los Santos. He wondered if the nuns in the convent took sies-
tas like everybody else in the country.

Not that Valera's daughter was a nun. He knew his
second and more important passenger had been merely
a student at the exclusive convent boarding school. For
more than twelve years, if McLean's sources were cor-
rect, and he knew they were. The CIA never left anything to chance. The agency's data banks would contain
every last scrap of information available on a family
member of an international Mafia boss, right down to
her hair color and shoe size.

Well, Francesca Valera might not be a nun, but after
spending over a dozen years in a convent, she probably
thought and acted like one.

Helluva preparation for this marriage the don has waiting for her in Rome. McLean says she's never even met the guy! Is that real—or what?

But Rafe knew some of these dons were very "Old Country" in their private lives, especially when it came to their women and children. And Don Esteban Valera was as Old Country as they came. The son of a Sicilian woman who'd done the unusual and married out of her nationality, Valera had been raised by his Italian kin after his father, a Spanish fisherman, died at sea, leaving his mother a young widow. Not too much was known about Valera's early years, but Rafe suspected he'd cut his teeth on everything from smuggled goods to lethal weapons; learned the code of the Brotherhood along with his catechism; developed a taste for power along with his taste for pasta.

The agency had a file on him two inches thick, but Rafe had learned most of what he needed to know about the don in his own years of kicking around Latin America, doing various jobs after he'd left the Marine Corps. He'd made it his business to know such things.

At sixty-eight, Valera was possibly *the* most powerful international crime boss. With an interest in everything from drugs to prostitution, Valera's organization spanned the globe. There wasn't a drug cartel he didn't have major ties with; an illegal gambling operation he hadn't manipulated; an international art-theft ring that made a move without the say-so of Don Esteban Valera.

Although little known by the general public—because the don liked it that way—Valera's family wielded more power than the Calli cartel, the Gambino *cosa nostra,* or the Genovese Family. The only possible rival to Valera's power came from another little-known god-father: Ezio Morano.

Morano and Valera were bitter enemies. A world-wide underground war hadn't broken out between their two organizations yet because Morano was biding his time. Consolidating power. But if Morano needed time to grow before he challenged Valera, time was on his side. Morano was twenty-two years Valera's junior.

Rafe discarded the chewed-up toothpick in the ash-tray and reached for another. Mirages shimmered on the pavement up ahead. It was a hot summer day even at this elevation, and the old Chevy's air-conditioning system labored noisily. He started to ask the old lady if she wanted it turned up, then checked himself and pushed the switch to high without a word.

Remembering Valera's age had him wondering how old he'd been when the girl was born. It was the only thing that hadn't turned up in his own research, and McLean hadn't said.

But Rosa Fiori, later Valera, Francesca Valera's mother, had been a lot younger than her mafioso husband. She'd been one of those sexpot Italian movie stars in the fifties, like Loren and Lollobrigida.

Also like Loren, Rosa had begun to display some acting talent and was in the running for an Academy award when she married Valera in the sixties. But she ended her career to become the don's wife.

Rafe knew much of this from the agency files Mc-Lean had made available, but his curiosity had been aroused, and that's when he'd done some checking on his own.

Apparently the child, Francesca, hadn't been born until much later in the marriage. There were some grainy photos of her in the agency files, taken from a distance, none of them very clear. The don guarded his family's privacy. There was a clipping from a Hollywood fan magazine from the seventies that mentioned Rosa Valera had a baby daughter. But it hadn't said how old the kid was. Then, a few years after that, Rosa Valera was dead, and the don had never remarried.

He'd been intrigued enough by the details of Rosa's background to rent some of her old movies. He smiled to himself, recalling the fabulous figure and sultry features of the woman. No doubt about it—she was a turn-on: gorgeous in an earthy way, unbelievably sexy and— the surprise—intelligent.

He found himself wondering if the daughter would be anything like her, then dismissed the notion at once. Such speculations were not only pointless, they were supremely dangerous. To touch Valera's daughter would mean sealing his own death warrant, and he wasn't stupid.

Besides, he told himself as his vision registered a sleepy peasant village flanking the road down below, the girl had been raised by nuns. An overprotected virgin if ever there was one. Terminally boring. He preferred his women smart, hot and savvy.

And then, of course, there was the job he had to do. He'd never mixed pleasure with business, and he wasn't about to begin now. Hell, even if she weren't Valera's—

Suddenly Rafe caught sight of some children playing with a dog in the dirt at the side of the road. He dropped his speed at once, noting at the same time a rickety old pickup coming toward them from the opposite direction.

But the pickup wasn't slowing down.

"Goddamn kids! Move your skinny little butts!" Rafe yelled as he leaned on his horn. The kids were too damned close to the road, and the fool in the pickup didn't even seem to notice.

But this time, when he hit the horn, the children noticed. He saw them leap back, but the pickup just kept coming.

Then the dog—it was a skinny little thing, just a pup, really—broke loose from the hold one of them had on it. Rafe watched as it ran—

"No-o-o!" Rafe's yell was drowned out by the roar of the truck's engine as the driver stepped on the gas and deliberately ran the dog over. *"Jesus, no-o-o-!"*

Rafe pulled over and his shoulders slumped, yet he clenched the wheel with white-knuckled fists. He closed his eyes, but could still see the twisting body of the dog as it was struck and flung into the air like an old rag doll.

Worse than that, he could still see the filthy, grinning face of the driver while he aimed—*aimed,* for chrissake!—and hit the helpless animal.

And all at once, Rafe saw red. A boiling rage erupted from the pit of his belly and hit his brain.

The son of a bitch had kept right on going! With no more thought of stopping than—

Cutting the wheel, Rafe shot the car into reverse and began the turn.

I'll kill the bastard! Goddamn son of a bitch ran down a helpless animal and came damned close to hitting those kids, too!

Gears shifted as he succeeded in turning the car around. The truck hadn't gone far, he could see, because that hill—

A sudden glance in the rearview mirror reminded him. Slamming on the brakes, he turned and looked at the old woman in the back seat. She was still sitting in that same rigid pose, but her lips were white around the edges as she pressed them together.

The killing rage left as quickly as it had come. He had a job to do.

"Perdón, señorita, por favor," he managed to say. But his voice sounded raw and far from placating.

He saw her nod stiffly and turned his attention back to the wheel. As he pulled out, he was faintly aware of the clicking of rosary beads behind him.

He forced himself to slow beside the trio of sobbing children, where they'd gathered around the dog's crumpled body.

Kids and animals. They'd always been his soft spot.

He braced himself for the unpleasant task of getting out to see about calming the kids and maybe burying the dog.

Somebody had to give a damn.

But at that moment two men came out of what looked like a cantina, and a second later were joined by a large brown-skinned woman. The woman gathered the children together and ushered them toward the shack she'd come out of, talking to them in a steady stream of Spanish the whole time.

Rafe asked the men, in Spanish, if they needed help with the dog.

No, they told him, but it was good of him to stop. They'd seen the whole thing. It was crazy Luis, the sheep farmer's son. A wild one. *"Mucho loco."*

Rafe nodded, glanced back and saw that the old woman was no worse than before, and resumed driving.

As he drove, he wiped the incident from his mind. It was one of the things he'd perfected years ago while involved in one covert mission or another. An undercover agent couldn't afford distractions. Giving in to emotional tangentials could get a man killed.

And whatever else he was, Rafe O'Hara was a survivor. Born in New York City, the son of a Puerto Rican immigrant's daughter and a cop, he'd been orphaned quite young. After that he'd been shuttled through a string of foster homes, one worse than the other. By the time he'd reached his teens, he was a hardened, streetwise tough.

He avoided a criminal life only narrowly, through the influence of a priest who got him to stay in school and even managed to get him scholarship money for college. But Rafe dropped out when the old priest died of injuries suffered in a mugging.

Then he'd joined the marines and seen action in Latin America, where he was involved in various covert activities. After his hitch was up, he stayed on in Central America, largely as a private soldier of fortune, working for groups as divergent as the OAS and the CIA.

A loner, Rafe was the quintessential cynic who believed only the worst of human nature. And above all, he believed in one law: the survival of the fittest. He'd completed a degree in engineering at UCLA a few years back, but only to say to himself that he'd done it. He had little use for society's credentials, trusting mainly to his own skills for survival, and these were largely deadly.

In short, Rafe O'Hara was a highly capable, self-styled maverick—and dangerous.

Rafe's cynicism was in good working order as he reminded himself of the job he'd taken on. When Travis

McLean, his old buddy at the CIA, had first contacted him, he'd turned him down. He was already getting good money for playing nursemaid to Valera's kid, so who needed any complications?

But then McLean had dropped the bomb: the kidnap attempt they expected after the girl left the convent had been planned by Morano, her father's archrival; but, more than that, it would be carried out by Morano's *capo* son, Tony.

Rafe had gone silent on the phone as he digested that piece of news. So had McLean. And he knew they were both thinking of Brad.

Brad Holman was the closest thing to a best friend Rafe had allowed himself to have during his years of undercover work. He and Rafe, along with McLean and Jason Cord, another agent, had been a highly effective team on more than one deadly mission.

But it was Brad who'd always held them together, shaping their divergent, often abrasive, personalities until they functioned like a well-oiled machine. Brad, who made it all work through the persuasive power of his own personality—a combination of strength and easygoing warmth. Brad had been the best of them and had brought out the best in each of the other three.

Until the night Tony Morano broke Brad's cover and had him killed.

And it had been a slow and extremely unpleasant death. Rafe knew, because he'd been the one who found Brad's body.

So now Tony Morano was coming after Valera's daughter. And by a curious twist of fate, Rafe happened to have been hired as her bodyguard. It was too good an opportunity to ignore. He said yes.

The miles slid by as Rafe ran over McLean's instructions in his mind. He was to use the girl to take Morano—alive. Morano knew plenty, not only about his father's operation, but about the whole international crime scene. He was wanted in the U.S. on a number of counts, so he'd stayed clear of the States for the past five years. He generally kept a low profile elsewhere, as well.

They were never going to get a better chance to grab him.

Rafe shoved aside a vivid image of what Tony's body would look like if he did to him what had been done to Brad. Motives of personal revenge had no place here. He couldn't allow himself that luxury. As McLean had known he wouldn't. It would have to be enough that he captured Tony Morano and turned him over to the authorities. And maybe, if he was lucky, McLean would let him in on the questioning.

But meanwhile he'd function as an unemotional machine, capable of carrying out an assignment with ruthless efficiency. He would do his job.

And if Valera's daughter happened to be a means to that end, so what? It was the way life was, wasn't it?

CHAPTER THREE

RAFE'S EYES SCANNED the countryside along the private road leading to the convent. There was no sign of anyone watching while the Chevy made this last leg of the trip, but then, he didn't expect there to be. McLean had told him of the hidden camps Valera had in the hills surrounding El Convento de los Santos, installed the day he'd enrolled his daughter there, but he hardly expected these security outposts to be visible from the road. He doubted the girl—or even the nuns, for that matter—knew they existed.

But keeping his eyes peeled while on an assignment was an old habit that had stood him in good stead on more than one occasion. So he continued his wary perusal as the Chevy chugged along the narrow gravel road. He had no doubt Valera's men were aware of his presence, but he wondered if Morano's little kidnap party was observing, too.

He had no way of knowing when the strike would occur, but he rather suspected it would be well after he left the vicinity with his charge. Morano would know all about Valera's tight security setup here. It was the main reason, McLean had surmised, that a kidnapping hadn't been tried during the time the kid had lived at the convent. Hell, according to McLean's sources, the girl even had a bodyguard with her *inside* the convent, although she probably didn't realize it...a woman named Maria something-or-other.

No, the strike wouldn't come here. More likely it would occur on route to the small private airstrip where Valera's Boeing 727 waited to fly them to Miami. Or maybe at the airstrip itself. He supposed it wasn't even beyond the realm of possibility for them to try it at Miami International; security would be extremely heavy there, but the crowds and mass confusion could provide a good cover.

Rafe's glance shifted to the carry-on bag lying on the floor of the front passenger seat. In it was the Uzi he'd packed, along with several clips of spare ammo. He released one hand from the wheel momentarily and patted the invisible bulge beneath his jacket. The 9 mm semiautomatic was firmly in place in its shoulder holster.

When the strike came, he'd be ready.

"THEY'RE HERE," Maria announced as she peered out the sitting room window. "A blue Chevrolet just passed through the gates. Time to go down, Francesca."

Francesca nodded and mutely rose from the sofa across the room, bending to pick up the Louis Vuitton carryon Ramón had given her for Christmas. She was dressed well, but sensibly, for travel. She had on a navy gabardine Donna Karan suit, worn over a simply tailored white cotton blouse. The suit's thigh-length jacket was buttonless, its overlapping front panels secured by a flat belt of the same material, knotted at the waist. The softly flared skirt fell well below her knees, and on her feet she wore a pair of navy espadrilles.

Maria sighed, giving the outfit a faintly regretful glance. "I still think you should have worn the coral—"

"Maria..." Francesca's voice was soft, but her friend had heard that tone before. Steel encased in velvet. She knew from experience what it meant: there was no use in pursuing an argument; Francesca's mind was made up.

"Okay, okay," said Maria, laughing as she held out both hands, palms outward. "I only thought you'd want to look less like a nun for your *novio* when you arrived."

Francesca smiled and wryly shook her head at her as they left the suite.

Familiar with the response, Maria laughed shamelessly and nudged her with an elbow. "And, *Dios!* Wait till you see this *hombre* who is to be your escort!"

Francesca's laughter joined hers as they headed for the wide, open staircase leading down to the huge entry hall below. The hall was where visitors waited until given audience by the mother superior.

Maria had spoken, last night, of the photo Papa had sent Madre Dolorosa: a picture of the escort he'd hired this time. But she'd listened to Maria's enraptured exclamations with half an ear. It was nothing new. A photo had always arrived, for "security purposes," a day or so before she was picked up and escorted home to Papa's villa. It had happened predictably on those few occasions—Christmas and Easter holidays, usually—when she left the convent to return home for a visit.

And the faces were always the same, as far as she was concerned. Hard-bitten, stony faces, with eyes devoid of human warmth.

For a long time, when she was younger, she had puzzled over these cold, anonymous men who came to collect her for the visits. And occasionally, when she was at the villa, she'd glimpsed their sort as well. Who were they? she'd once asked Ramón—because, for some reason, she'd never dared to ask Papa himself.

Her brother's answer had been smooth, even glib—as if well prepared in advance, she realized now: "Our father is an international businessman, with many jealous rivals. Some are unscrupulous enough to try to use his innocent family to force him to capitulate to their interests. Is it any surprise that he hires tough professional men to guard us, then, Francesca? Do not worry. These men are dangerous, yes, but they are on our side."

She recalled her reasoned acceptance of Ramón's words at the time because they had seemed to make sense. Afterward, although she never liked the presence of such men in her life, she'd endured it. Just as she endured everything else in the life-style Papa had proscribed for her. It was part and parcel of what life at El Convento taught: duty and obedience.

It was what Papa wanted.

But then had come the day when her natural curiosity had gotten the best of her. She'd begun work on her undergraduate degree via the special correspondence course Papa had arranged with La Universidad de Mexico. And, although the arrangement had required that she remain here, she'd been given access to whatever books and periodicals her work required, shipped in from the university's library.

Carte blanche access.

And she'd used it to mount an in-depth, surreptitious investigation—of her father.

Francesca gave herself a mental shake to dislodge the old feelings of shock and dismay that memories of that time always managed to dredge up. No point in going into it all over again. It only renewed the old hurt she'd never really succeeded in dealing with.

But someday... a niggling inner voice persisted, *someday you're going to have to come to terms with these things you feel. Such ambivalence—*

Francesca drew in a rapid breath and stopped short on the last step of the staircase when she felt Maria squeeze her arm.

"Madre de Dios!" Maria murmured under her breath as they watched a tall, denim-clad man flash a grin at Madre Dolorosa. The pair were standing several yards away from the stairs, across the wide expanse of the reception hall's tiled floor. An older nun and an even older woman—not a nun, but wearing black—flanked them.

"There ought to be a law against a man looking that good!" Maria added in a whisper. "Didn't I tell you, Francesca? Hollywood handsome—and sexy!"

Francesca felt herself bristle and wondered why. Maria was only being Maria, after all. But there was something within her that resented the astonishing male beauty her eyes had also taken in.

It was somehow indecent, she thought, that such attractiveness should house what the man really was—a hired gunman. A killer.

At that moment she made up her mind to have as little as possible to do with this man; she feared she almost hated him.

Lowering her eyes, she forced herself to approach as Madre Dolorosa gestured for her and Maria to come forward. Taking a couple of deep, calming breaths, she even began to feel the serene composure her outward form exhibited.

She recognized her father's older sister at once, even though the years had not been kind to her. Tía Pilar reached, with age-spotted hands, to clasp both of hers while the mother superior reintroduced them in rapid Spanish.

Her duenna's picture had apparently been sent to the nun as well; Madre Dolorosa remarked kindly that her aunt looked much younger than her photo. But Francesca rather doubted it. The old spinster's sallow skin was crisscrossed with myriad wrinkles, sagging from a facial bone structure that had never contributed toward great beauty. And the hair she wore scraped back over her narrow skull and knotted tightly behind was more white than the salt-and-pepper Francesca recalled from their single meeting years before.

Still, the old woman smiled warmly as they greeted each other; then, Francesca decided, her face took on a softer aspect, and she did, indeed, look younger.

"Francesca, child," Madre Dolorosa said then in halting, heavily accented English, "allow me to present to you, Meester Rafael O'Hara—your escort.

"Meester O'Hara, your charge—Señorita Francesca Valera."

Francesca kept her eyes lowered as the man bowed— *bowed!* for heaven's sake!—over her outstretched hand. His fingers were warm as they clasped hers, and she felt her resentment grow. These men, with their lethal weapons and hard eyes—they always reminded her of reptiles. His hands should have been clammy and cold, not warm and pleasant to touch!

"Meester O'Hara has surprised us—he speaks Spaneesh, Francesca!" the nun continued. "But I told heem

that I have leetle enough practeece weeth my Engleesh,
so I asked that we speak eet. Weeth your aunt's per-
meession, he kindly agreed to eendulge me."

Francesca saw him bow again—*again*—this time toward the nun. "Whatever pleases you, Reverend
Mother," he said with a smile bracketed by deep
grooves that were male dimples.

Hearing the deep, smooth baritone, Francesca
ground her teeth. And what was so surprising about his
speaking Spanish? All right, so he didn't look like a
Latino despite his black hair; she herself had already
noted his Anglo appearance. "Blue, blue eyes," Maria
had said. She wasn't going to give him the satisfaction
of gazing into them herself! And, of course, there was
his Anglo surname...O'Hara...Irish, actually, although the denim and Reeboks he wore, even coupled
with the battered "Aussie" hat he held at his side, pro-
claimed him conspicuously *norteamericano*. And that
was another thing about him that was different: the men
hired to escort her previously had always worn neat,
conservative business suits.

Where did Papa ever find this one?

But what had her seething inside was the way he
seemed to have charmed his way around the mother superior. None of the others had *ever* done that! Stealing
a glance behind the head of the convent, she discovered that even Sister Ignatius, Madre's elderly secretary, seemed smitten. How *dare* he? Had the man no
shame?

Only Tía Pilar seemed impervious to his charm.
Francesca immediately felt herself drawn closer to the
old woman, respecting her for her good sense.

Rafe let his eyes travel briefly over the slender figure
of the girl as he released her hand. He wasn't sure, ex-

actly, what he'd been expecting when he met Rosa Fiori's daughter, but it sure as hell wasn't what he saw now.

Francesca Valera looked, for all the world, like she could be one of the novices at the convent. There was a soft, gentle quality about her—ethereal, he wanted to call it—that immediately set her apart from any female he could recall meeting. Oh, some of the old masters had captured that quality, in renderings of exquisite madonnas on canvas, but who'd ever have thought a sexpot movie star and an underworld godfather would produce *this?*

He murmured a greeting and turned his attention back to the pair of women wearing habits. He'd known nuns like this mother superior before. Canny old girls who let very little escape their notice. No sense in letting this one know how stunned—and, yes, intrigued—he was by the kid's unusual beauty. Besides, she had to know she'd been harboring a special little looker all these years. Even nuns had eyes.

He gave himself over to the second introduction the nun was making... *Ah. The bodyguard...* a little heller with know-it-all-eyes. When a quick glance told him the others weren't watching, Rafe caught Maria's gaze— and winked.

He grinned when he saw her blush. *Not so know-it- all, after all, then.* Of course, living in a convent for five years had to have a dampening effect on any woman... And the Valera kid had been here for twelve. *Hell! No wonder she looks like a nun!*

After the final farewells, Rafe saw his two passengers to the car. It was hot, even at this elevation, and he immediately turned the air-conditioning on high. The two women were quiet as he put the Chevy in gear and headed for the gates.

As he drove, he wondered at their silence. Hell, you'd think two females who hadn't seen each other in a long while would have *something* to say to each other!

He thought back to the moment they'd all approached the car, when he'd offered the girl the choice of sitting up front if she wished. Of course, he hadn't expected her to accept, but he'd somehow adopted a gallant air when meeting the nuns—it was the kind of role-playing he often fell into to keep boredom at bay while on a job.

The little nun had acted predictably, of course. She'd shaken her head without a word and, keeping her eyes downcast, had joined her aunt in the back seat.

Suddenly Rafe realized he hardly knew what her voice sounded like, she'd spoken so little since they met—and then only in a whisper, her eyes on the floor. Hell, he didn't even know what color her eyes were!

Well, the assignment was what he'd expected, wasn't it? Boring.

But there was another assignment he was here to carry out. Then his boredom could be readily challenged—and damned soon, too.

Jamming a toothpick between his teeth, Rafe settled in for some heavy surveillance on route.

But wherever Morano was, he did not appear on the drive to the private airstrip. Rafe thought there were several spots where a strike might have been made, and he kept his attention attuned to the possibility while cruising past all of them.

Yet nothing happened.

In between these places, when the terrain along the road lay wide open, he let himself relax a bit. But then the boredom threatened again.

He decided at one point to try for a little conversation with the kid—if only to learn what she sounded like. Was the temperature in the car to her satisfaction? he asked in English, because he knew of her language skills. Also in English, he asked if she was looking forward to flying. Had she ever been to Miami before? To Rome?

And each time the answer had come back to him in Spanish—from her duenna! The girl would translate for the old lady in a soft murmur, then let the aunt reply for her!

Hell, you'd think he was Jack the Ripper, the way the two of them were carrying on!

Rafe soon gave up on asking his questions, and by the time they reached the airstrip, he was steaming. Who the hell did these two dames think they were, anyhow? He was their *protection,* for chrissake!

Francesca wanted to laugh out loud at the obvious annoyance of O'Hara over the little game she had devised with Tía Pilar. But she didn't. The essence of her plan was that it be carried out with a straight face.

And it was too perfect that her aunt had fallen right in with it. Of course, it was altogether quite possible that her duenna merely thought of it as doing her duty.

Still, Francesca didn't care. Rafe O'Hara's irritation had increased with every stilted Spanish response to his inane questions. She could see it by the stiffening of his shoulder muscles and a tightening of that square jaw when he'd turned his head once or twice. Well, it served him right. Plying his charms on two old nuns! Mister

Tough Guy was due for a comeuppance, and she was here to give it to him!

Smiling to herself, Francesca settled back to enjoy the trip.

THEY MADE THE AIRSTRIP by late afternoon. Clouds rolling in from the east had helped lower the temperature somewhat, but the humidity was still high. When they left the car's comfortable interior, Francesca felt as if she'd stepped into a sauna.

Several men were waiting beside the jet. One was the pilot; another was a man hired to drive Rafe's rental car back. But it was the other three and the cargo they were in the process of loading that made Rafe's annoyance soar.

"What the hell is going on?" he asked the short, middle-aged Mexican whose face he recognized as their pilot's from a photo Valera had given him.

The pilot shrugged. "Our employer owns racehorses, *señor.*" He gestured toward what Rafe now saw was a horse van, parked behind the jet. "Apparently he decided not to allow the cargo space to go to waste on thees treep."

"Racehorses!" Rafe eyed the pair of Thoroughbreds prancing gingerly before a gangplank one of the three extra men was lowering from the body of the 727.

Of course, he knew all about Valera's involvement in the "sport of kings." Accordingly to the agency file, it had never actually been connected to Valera's more nefarious activities, but Rafe suspected it provided more than enough opportunity for money laundering, if nothing else.

Moreover, his highly honed instincts, which had always served him well in the past, were telling him to be wary of this glitch in the plan. It wasn't like Valera—or McLean, for that matter—to fail to apprise him of something like this.

"Nobody said anything about a pair of nags coming with us," he told the pilot. "And who the hell are these guys who brought them? Do they have clearance? Did they show you any papers or—"

"*Perdón, señor.*" One of the trio with the horses had approached. Somewhere in his early thirties, he was dark and slender, with a wiry build, and wore a mustache.

He pulled a wrinkled envelope out of his hip pocket as he addressed Rafe. "We are *mucho* sorry for thees eenconvenience, *señor,* but Don Esteban deed not expect these *caballos* he purchased to arrive so soon. Perhaps thees weel explain." He handed Rafe the envelope.

Rafe opened it and studied the typed letter bearing what looked like Esteban Valera's bold signature. The letter seemed to bear out what this man—one Franco Ortez, according to the accompanying photo—was saying: Valera's manager had purchased the horses for the don's racing stables in Florida.

It also said that if O'Hara had any further doubts about the orthodoxy of such a procedure, he was to check out the plane's cargo hold; he would see it was outfitted with two specially padded stalls that had obviously been used for such a purpose in the past.

Rafe matched the features in the other two photos in the envelope to the faces of the pair holding the horses. These men were handlers, the letter said, and, unlike the groom, they would be returning to Valera's villa with the van.

Everything seemed to fit, yet Rafe still felt uneasy. He tapped the backs of his fingers against the envelope in agitation, running over the details of the situation in his mind. Out of the corner of his eye he saw Valera's daughter approach the horses and begin running her hands over one of them—the mare. He noted her movements had the look of someone experienced with horses.

He still didn't like it.

He checked his watch and knew he'd have to make up his mind soon. If the plane didn't take off by four-thirty, the kid wouldn't make Miami International in time for the flight to Rome.

It was four-twenty.

Rafe heaved a disgusted sigh and strode purposefully toward the plane. He had just verified the existence of the padded stalls when he heard the rumble of thunder in the near distance.

Checking out the lowering sky, he knew it could be only a matter of minutes until the storm broke. Weather moved fast here, in the foothills of the Sierra Madre.

"Señor?" the pilot asked in a tone that came close to pleading that he tell them what to do.

Checking his watch again, Rafe cursed furiously in Spanish under his breath. A second later he was repeating the same oath at the top of his voice as a loud crack and a bolt of accompanying lightning frightened the mare Francesca was holding, and it reared.

Growling orders to the pilot and Ortez to get things under way, Rafe charged straight for Francesca.

"You little fool!" he barked as the mare's front hooves crashed to the ground within inches of her espadrilles. "Give that nag back to someone who's paid to take chances and move your little butt onto the plane!"

He grabbed the mare's halter out of her hand, gesturing for one of the handlers, but his attention was still focused on Francesca. "Come on, little nun, move it! Your bridegroom's waiting!" He dipped his head in the direction of her aunt, who was being helped into the passenger cabin by the pilot.

Then Rafe blinked, as if to clear his vision, and looked at the girl again. She'd said nothing, but for the first time, Francesca Valera was looking directly at him, and her eyes flashed.

Rafe's breath caught in his throat.

Suddenly he was reminded of her actress mother. Francesca Valera's eyes were the same sensuous, feline green.

Stunned, Rafe ignored the fury blazing there and sought to cover his reaction. Sweeping his Aussie hat from his head in a broad, exaggerated gesture, he bent grandly toward her with a wide, mocking bow.

"After you, little nun," he said, and there was no way to tell which mocked her more—his words, or his blatant grin.

CHAPTER FOUR

FRANCESCA TOOK HER SEAT beside Tía Pilar, buckling herself in as the pilot prepared for takeoff. A quick glance at the cockpit when she'd entered told her the pilot was flying unassisted, but then she saw O'Hara join him up front. Realizing O'Hara would be acting as copilot, she found herself mildly surprised. The men her father usually hired as her "escorts" had been skilled, as far as she'd been able to determine, in only one thing: killing. O'Hara had definitely begun to exhibit more complexity than his predecessors.

But then she remembered the brittle anger in those blue eyes as he'd ordered her aboard the plane, and she nearly snorted. *Little nun, am I? I wonder what he'd say if I asked him what a hired gunman could possibly know about nuns!*

The pilot taxied for takeoff while Rafe familiarized himself with the controls. He'd never flown one of these babies, but he'd once had a stint on "Air Force 1," and they weren't all that dissimilar. What worried him more than the possibility of having to take over for the pilot was the storm breaking overhead. Fierce winds buffeted the fuselage as they approached liftoff, and the sky had taken on the color of night.

And here comes the rain, Rafe thought as sheets of the stuff reduced visibility to nil. He cast a glance at the pilot, who was so thoroughly absorbed by what he was doing with the controls he didn't seem to notice Rafe was even alive.

But then the sensation of wheels bumping along the ground disappeared. They were airborne and climbing, and a second glance at the man beside him produced a thumbs-up sign from the little Mexican. Grinning, Rafe returned the sign and settled back in his seat. He still didn't like the weather, with the dark sky streaked by lightning, but at least there was no question of the pilot's competence.

Of course, he reminded himself, there really shouldn't have been a question in the first place: Valera always demanded the best—and got it. The little nun would make it to Rome, after all.

Meanwhile, Francesca tried to ignore the storm crashing overhead, but it was hard. Tía Pilar was white-faced and rigid with fear beside her, except for her hands, which trembled violently as the old woman clutched her rosary and attempted to mutter a Hail Mary between clenched teeth.

Francesca tried to calm her by patting her gently on the shoulder, but her aunt behaved as if she weren't even there. Deciding she could best offer support by appearing calm herself, Francesca began to talk casually about mundane matters, acting much as if they were sitting in someone's parlor.

Did she have much luggage? she asked, mentioning her own pair of enormous trunks, which had been sent ahead to Rome. There was no answer from the terrified spinster, but Francesca kept up a gentle, steady patter.

"I wonder if I remembered to pack my toothbrush,' she said, reaching under her seat, where she'd stashed her carryon. Opening the bag, she made a great show of casually perusing its contents. Then she was glad she had.

Lying beneath her hairbrush and comb was Maria's beautifully wrapped farewell gift. She'd forgotten all about it! Withdrawing it carefully and laying it atop the bag on her lap, she darted a sideways glance at her aunt. *Bueno.* She had the old woman's attention.

But a minute later, she almost wished she hadn't. Amid the folds of the pink tissue paper she'd just parted was the filmiest piece of lingerie she'd ever seen. At least, she *thought* it was lingerie; the thin spaghetti straps and exquisitely wrought, sheer, sheer lace said so, but she'd never known a piece of underwear to come in such a deep shade of green.

Another quick glance at her aunt told her Tía Pilar was of a similar mind, but at least her attention was diverted from the storm. Lifting the garment from its box by the fragile-looking straps, Francesca held it aloft and couldn't help the gurgle of laughter that broke from her throat. It was a teddy! A sexy, see-through, "cut high on the thigh and low on the bosom" piece of outrageous nonsense that only Maria would have thought of. Or dared to send along.

"Ah, Maria," she murmured, laughter escaping, despite her attempt to restrain it, "no wonder you wanted me to wait until now to discover this!"

She was still fighting laughter as she tried to explain to her aunt the nature of the gift, attempting to pass it off as a private jest between schoolmates. Tía Pilar nodded with a small smile, recollecting aloud similar incidents of shared mischief from her own convent-school days.

Francesca laughed again, delighted that the old woman understood. But then the laughter died as she chanced to look up, and she blushed from the roots of her hair to her toes.

Rafe O'Hara was standing in the doorway of the cockpit. And the unnerving grin plastered across his handsome face made her want to crawl beneath her seat and disappear.

Rafe watched her fumble with the pink tissue paper on her lap as she hastily stuffed the dark green lacy thing out of sight. He knew by her blush, more than by what he'd been able to see of the garment, that it had been designed with more physical intimacy in mind than Francesca Valera had ever thought of.

But that wasn't what had made him grin. Rather, it had been the throaty sound of her laughter. It was what had lured him out of the cockpit in the first place.

He now had the answer to another of the things he'd wanted to learn about her. Her voice had a low, husky quality that put him in mind of a French chanteuse, and when she laughed, the sound thrummed and vibrated in the air like chords played on some exotic instrument. He'd felt those chords reaching into the center of him a moment ago, felt them singing in the marrow of his bones. Trouble was, he was hard put to relate them to the virginal schoolgirl he saw now, blushing furiously as she stashed her carryon under her seat.

Shaking his head in bewilderment, he was just turning back toward the cockpit when a monstrous crack of thunder threatened to split his eardrums. It was immediately followed by a flash of blue-white light, and then another. More thunder boomed overhead, and the plane's interior lights failed briefly.

He had to brace himself against the doorway of the cockpit as the plane began to buck and lurch like an untamed bronco. There was a scream from behind him, in the passenger cabin, and he had just a second to turn and see it was coming from the old woman when it was lost in the boom of another belt of thunder.

The floor beneath his feet seemed to steady, if only a little, and he made his way toward the two women. Francesca, he noticed, wasn't reacting much at all, only gripping the arms of her seat as if to brace herself, but her aunt was shrieking hysterically amid ongoing cracks of thunder.

The turbulence that had caused the craft to lurch had abated now, and the rolls of thunder seemed a bit more distant, but the old woman continued to scream in between bursts of half-intelligible Spanish. Back in the cockpit, he heard the pilot curse loudly in the same language and then call to him in English.

"See eef you can shut her up, eh, *señor?* I require *mucho* concentration right now."

"Roger," Rafe called, and squatted beside Francesca, who was closer, but focused his attention on the old woman. *"Señorita, por favor..."*

Francesca listened to his carefully enunciated Spanish as he spoke to Tía Pilar and was nothing short of amazed. For all his hard and ruthless appearance, O'Hara addressed the frightened woman with utter courtesy, and in soothing, softly modulated tones. Again and again, with great patience, he assured her of the safety record of planes such as this, of the jet's ability to withstand much more than it was being subjected to, which was, after all, "just a lot of wind and noise."

All to no avail. Her aunt appeared as if she were about to listen to such reasoning for a moment, but then immediately lapsed into another round of ear-piercing shrieks, her thin frame shuddering.

The pilot swore again, louder than before, and Rafe met Francesca's eyes, looking as if he'd like to do the same. An enormous rumble of thunder drowned out pilot and spinster alike, and the look on the American's face told Francesca that something had to be done, and quickly.

Grabbing her aunt firmly by the shoulders with both hands, Francesca turned the old woman toward her until she had her attention. "Dearest Tía," she said in Spanish, "I am asking for your help. Yes, help, for how am I to keep my own fear at bay if I do not have your brave example to follow? You are my duenna, after all, and..."

Rafe saw the transformation take place in the old woman, but still didn't half believe it. In seconds she was like a different person. The stiffness went out of her, her features softened, and, of course, the screaming had stopped. Hell, she even managed a weak smile when Francesca mentioned a novice at the convent who hid under her bed during thunderstorms that weren't half as bad as this.

Retreating to the cockpit, Rafe mused on what he'd just seen. The kid had handled the old woman like a pro. By appealing to the old lady's sense of duty, she'd struck just the right chord, and Tía Pilar had fallen into line like a well-trained soldier. Hell, to watch them, you could've wondered just who was the duenna and who was the kid!

IN THE COMPARTMENT of the jet where the horses were stabled, the man who traveled with them swore a fervent string of oaths. The damned stallion had nearly trampled him during that last rough spell. The man eyed the riding crop someone had left in the corner, then caught the big horse's wild-eyed glare and decided against it.

The stupid nags were going to die, anyway, so why risk his neck for a little satisfaction now? Grinning to himself, Morano's man checked his watch and then the pair of parachutes resting beside the bag he'd carried on the plane. The *only* working parachutes on the plane.

Checking his watch again, he nodded smugly to himself and settled down to wait. It would be a while yet before the pilot noted the loss of fuel from the slow leak they'd engineered. Then, in what he hoped would be enough confusion and panic in the cockpit and passenger cabin, he'd make his move.

His eyes traveled to the M16 he'd assembled after removing the parts from his bag, and he grinned again, then spat into the straw at his feet. *Sangre de Christos,* even if they didn't panic, he held the upper hand.

His eyes went cold as he thought of the gringo bodyguard. That one promised trouble, but he figured he'd be able to handle it. He'd hit him first. The element of surprise was on his side, and that should make all the difference. The pilot and the old woman would present little difficulty. Nor would the girl when the M16 persuaded her to put on the second parachute and bail out with him.

A monumental crack of thunder resounded, drawing his attention away from his plans. The jet began to pitch and roll, sending the horses into another frenzy.

"*Madre de Christos!* You miserable beast!" he cried as the stallion tried to take a chunk out of his arm. "For two pesetas I'd finish you off now!"

Nursing the arm where the stallion's teeth had likely left marks right through his jacket sleeve, Morano's man satisfied himself with visions of the horse being burned alive in the wreckage of the plane.

SEEING THE OLD WOMAN settled, Rafe made his way back to the copilot's seat. He sat and nodded briefly at the pilot's appreciative grin, a little too aware the man was assigning credit to the wrong person. Rafe scanned the controls, and then the view outside the windscreen. They were flying above the storm now, but that didn't mean they were free of the danger of turbulence, of air currents churned up by the roiling air mass below.

They were flying thousands of feet above the Mexican Sierra Madre, a wicked mountain range that Brad used to call the Fear-a-Madre when they—

Brad... His mind tripped on the name, yet kept coming back to it like a tongue worrying a sore tooth. He wondered how Brad's parents and sister were taking the loss. Unlike himself, Brad and the others had families living, and Brad's had been the most closely knit of all.

He'd seen them at the funeral, of course, but aside from the usual brief words that are spoken on such occasions, he hadn't really talked to them. Travis and Jason had gone back to their house with them afterward, he knew; he'd been invited, too, but, somehow, he just hadn't had the stomach for it at the time. He wondered how Travis and Jason had managed it.

But then, Travis McLean was a different kind of *hombre*—different from himself, at any rate. And Jason Cord...hell, who knew what went on in *that* dude's head! Though in some ways, despite his closemouthed manner, Cord was the easier of the pair to figure out.

Jason Cord came from a long line of military men, the histories of his ancestors stretching back to the days of the American Revolution. There had been a Cord who fought with Francis Marion, the Swamp Fox, for chrissake! No wonder ol' Jason knew what he wanted to do before he was old enough to talk about it. It was in his blood. A career in the navy, and from there to naval intelligence before an uncle of his drafted him for the agency.

Something about the agency was eating at Cord, though. They'd talked once after the funeral, and Rafe had heard a certain...ambivalence in Jason's voice when the subject came up. He'd tried to feel him out about it, but naturally ol' Clam-Up hadn't admitted to a thing. But then, that was part of what made him a good agent. Yep, Jason Cord was a career man, through and through.

Not like himself—or McLean, either, for that matter. Oh, Travis liked to pretend he was in for the long haul, but Rafe just wasn't buying it. The guy had gone all the way through med school, for God's sake! Harvard, no less! Nobody with any sense threw all that away. Not permanently, anyhow.

But he knew that, like himself, McLean was a rebel, and, also like himself, he needed to be his own man. Well, no one who was a career man in the CIA was his own man. Like it or not, they owned you, body and soul.

Rafe smiled sardonically to himself, wondering if Travis had figured that out yet. Or was he so busy avoiding the constraints of the family he was rebelling against, he hadn't had time to realize he'd simply exchanged them for a far more heavy-duty keeper?

Like Jason, Travis came from a long line of professionals. Only in McLean's case, the line of work was medicine. A great-grandfather had fought malaria and yellow fever during the building of the Panama Canal. Both of Travis's grandfathers were physicians, too, not to mention his father and brother and a baby sister who was pre-med at Georgetown right now.

But that was exactly the problem: at the last minute, Trav had up and decided he wasn't going to allow himself to be pushed into that pre-fab mold.

Rafe shifted in his seat, frowning. He'd heard McLean's old man hadn't spoken to or seen him since he'd quit med school. And Travis claimed he didn't give a damn.

Wasn't that just the way of it, though? Some people had it all, everything anybody could ever dream of, and they just up and threw it away...a place in life, security...family....

A sudden bout of turbulence yanked Rafe's attention back to the cockpit, and he gripped the arms of his seat to avoid being bruised by his seat belt. The pilot seemed to be on top of things, though, and there were no more screams from the passenger cabin.

Rafe grinned as his thoughts returned to Valera's daughter. *Like a little pro.* Still grinning, he wondered if she had any more surprises in store for him. He was beginning to suspect there was a lot more to Francesca Valera than met the eye.

CHAPTER FIVE

FRANCESCA CONTINUED holding her aunt's hand as she watched the older woman nod and begin to doze. It had taken some time to settle her after that last bout of turbulence, notwithstanding the mild sedative Tía had swallowed. Francesca had suggested she take it after her aunt admitted to having some in her purse.

Francesca sighed, wishing she felt drowsy enough to take a catnap herself. Instead, she closed her eyes and allowed her mind to wander.

Ever in the forefront of her thoughts these days was her relationship with her father. Papa had always been the biggest single entity in her world, regardless of the months and years spent away from him while she was at the convent. Vital, handsome, completely engaging, Esteban Valera was a figure larger than life. Or so it had always seemed to a young, impressionable child who hungered for a source of love and stability in her life after losing the mother she barely remembered.

Oh, the convent with its world of women, and Madre Dolorosa in particular, had provided mothering of a sort, but Francesca couldn't kid herself; it had been Papa, always Papa, who'd been the rock upon which everything rested.

She still possessed the myriad letters he'd sent her over the years, written in the big, bold script that was so much like the man himself. Months giving way to seasons, seasons melting into years, their communication had forged and anchored a bond she felt could never be broken.

Only now, God help her, she knew that it could be broken, after all. The first cracks had appeared the day she began to discover exactly who, and what, her father was. She felt as if he were two men: one, the warm, laughing hero who was both father and mother to her at a time when her world had threatened to fall apart; the other...

Francesca shivered, refusing to give that stranger who lived within her father a name. Instead, she dealt with him in her mind as she always had since those terrible days of discovery. She clung desperately to the Papa she knew, doing all she could to nurture and sustain that one remaining tenuous tie that bound her to him.

But a small, still voice inside her whispered insistently that this was the coward's way out, and she would have to face her dilemma squarely before long.

She forced her mind away from this troubling line of thought, the soft snores of the woman beside her reminding her of other things she had to ponder.

Carlo, for instance. She was on her way to marry the man who belonged to that blandly smiling face in the photo, and she thought it might serve her very well if she could drum up some enthusiasm for the venture.

Venture? Was that how to categorize it? A venture was an undertaking involving implications of unknown risk. Was that how she approached her union to this young Italian, her *novio?*

She grinned wryly to herself, almost breaking into a chuckle. There were a lot of things she might think of in connection with Carlo Pagnani's smiling countenance, but risk wasn't one of them. Doubt, yes, but not risk. Risk was the sort of thing she associated with another kind of man, a man like— *Speak of the devil!*

Rafael O'Hara again stood in the doorway to the cockpit—slouched against it, actually. How long had he been there? she wondered. She swore the man could be part cat, the way he moved around so noiselessly. A big jungle cat, she amended, eyeing the long panther-black hair that brushed his collar.

"Like what you see, little nun?"

Francesca felt herself go beet-red. And as if the realization that he'd caught her staring at him wasn't bad enough, that infuriating grin was back. He was actually enjoying himself!

"What I see," she replied tartly, "is a man who could benefit from some lessons in manners!"

The grin merely deepened, the grooves that bracketed it calling attention to the whiteness of his teeth against the tanned face. Francesca looked away, wishing she had bitten her tongue. Answering him simply fed the fire—or whatever it was that made him enjoy baiting her. *Patán,* she mouthed, savoring the Spanish word for boor.

Out of the corner of her eye, she caught the slight lift of his eyebrows, telling her he'd seen, and of course he understood Spanish. *Well, let him know exactly what I think of him and his kind!*

Francesca had been right about one thing; Rafe was certainly enjoying himself, although he currently found himself wondering why. It wasn't as if overprotected schoolgirls had ever held any attraction for him, even if they *were* long-legged with faultless profiles.

That was probably it, of course. This was a whole different number. Not what he was used to in the world he ran in. And while Valera's daughter was off-limits, there was nothing that said he couldn't look. She was easy on the eyes even if she tried to bury her attractiveness under shapeless clothes that had "convent" written all over them, or by snagging her hair back in that dumb bun.

Still, he had to admit there was something else that had made him wander back out here to get another look at her. It was the things that didn't add up, like when she got riled and those green eyes flashed fire.

And then there was the way she didn't seem the least bit intimidated by him—not that he wanted to scare her, but given what he was, what his line of work was . . . It wouldn't have been the first time some innocent he'd been assigned to guard thought *he* was the bigger danger!

Rafe shrugged, reaching for one of the toothpicks in his shirt pocket. He was just about to jam it between his teeth when they hit another patch of turbulence—a humdinger. He dropped the toothpick as both hands latched on to the frame of the doorway to keep the bucking jet from heaving him to the floor. Then a shout from the cockpit claimed his attention.

"¿Qué pasa?" he shouted over a resounding crack of thunder. *Thunder?* Godalmighty, they were losing altitude!

He lurched into the cockpit to discover the pilot manipulating various controls in a purposeful but rapid fashion. Too rapid.

Lightning flashed amid deafening booms of thunder. They had descended fully into the storm now.

He thought he heard the pilot shout "Not responding!" in reply to his question, and then Rafe looked at the gauges and felt his stomach clench.

"Take over and see what you can do, *señor,*" the pilot told him, even as Rafe was maneuvering into the copilot's seat.

As he began to repeat with his own controls the same manipulations he'd seen the pilot making, out of the corner of his eye, Rafe saw the Mexican fiddle with his headphones and grab the microphone in front of them. He didn't need to guess why. Unless they could conjure up a miracle, it was time to radio a Mayday.

In the passenger cabin Francesca had both arms wrapped around the frail figure of her aunt while doing her best to master her own fear. She knew the situation was far worse than the roughness caused by the earlier turbulence. For one thing, they were back in the storm, and they were descending rapidly. But it was far too early to prepare for landing. Miami, even by her untutored calculations was a couple of hours away, and—

Suddenly Tía stiffened in her grasp, and she looked up to see Rafe O'Hara's tall, denim-clad form looming over them.

"Take these," he said, handing her a pair of pillows from the storage rack, "and get yourselves into crash positions. The pilot says you've been instructed in the procedure, so let's go—heads down...come on, *come on!* We don't have much time!"

Francesca did what he told her, wondering whether to be concerned about the ease with which she succeeded in getting Tía to comply. Was it the sedative? Her aunt was strangely silent and docile now, while her own composure hung by a thread.

Her stomach felt as if it were about to slam into her chest, and her heart was beating like a giant drum. Her fear was building into an enormous pressure inside her, and she felt the only way she could release it was to scream and scream....

Scenarios of earlier flights raced through her mind, especially those from when she was younger that had allowed her fears to conjure up disasters.... *What if...*

In later years she'd come to laugh at those childish imaginings, but now she had good reason to be afraid and the potential for disaster was all too real. Again, she felt the urge to scream, but she didn't. It was as if by containing her fear she could somehow contain the danger and cheat fate.

The storm was all around them now, a maelstrom of wind and noise. Somewhere there was the sound of screaming that wasn't human, and she pressed her face harder into the pillow when she realized it was the horses. *Oh, sweet holy Mary, the horses...*

And then she began to pray in earnest....

Rafe heard the pilot announce his intention of trying for a "soft" crash landing, which meant zeroing in on some trees to cushion the impact, if he could. He listened to the Mexican's steady, matter-of-fact Spanish and nodded. He had to give the man big points for his cool.

They were totally without power now, the pilot's guess being that they had sustained damage during their earlier encounter with the storm and that the subsequent turbulence had finished the job. There was no way of knowing, even, if their Mayday call had gone through.

Of course, a Mayday would only do any good if there were survivors.... The thought made him lurch to his feet. Survivors meant maybe Valera's daughter, and it was his job to see to it that if anyone survived, it was the girl!

THE MAN IN THE CARGO hold staggered against the side of the stallion's stall. *Sangre de Christos,* they were going down, and it was too soon! It wasn't supposed to happen this way!

A curse tore from his lips as the terrified stallion tried to kick him. He'd decided to vent his ire on the beast, after all, and had just entered its stall when the plane began to plummet.

"Diablo! Miserable..." he snarled, raising the whip in his hand. "I'll show you!"

The horse screamed as the whip landed across its withers. Not in terror now, but in rage. It lunged for the man as he raised the whip again.

Luis Carrera screamed as the stallion's teeth sank into his flesh. In a single instant he knew he'd been a fool to indulge his cruel whim. Knew he should have tried to get to the girl before they crashed. But the storm's ferocity had wreaked havoc on his plans, had driven reason from his mind, and now it was too late.

The stallion ripped the whip from his hand. Luis screamed, the sound lost in the noise of howling wind and the mare's shrill neighs, as the big horse reared above him.

The last thing Luis Carrera saw was a blur of thrashing hooves above his head, and then he saw nothing at all.

GROPING HIS WAY THROUGH the plane's lightless interior as much by memory as by touch, Rafe stumbled toward the passenger compartment. He didn't bother calling out to the women; through the combined sounds of rushing wind, thunder and screaming horses, they wouldn't hear him, anyway.

Finally, when the toe of his Reebok made contact with the base of the jet's designer lounge seat, he flung his body over the huddled figures of the two women.

The silken texture of Francesca Valera's chignon was the last thing he remembered feeling before they hit.

"FRANCESCA...*FRANCESCA!* Can you hear me?" Rafe felt the steady thrumming of her pulse under his fingers at the side of her neck, so he knew she was alive. Whether she was out cold or injured in some way, he couldn't tell yet.

Which was still more than he could say for the old woman. Her lifeless body bore a streaming head wound, sustained when she'd struggled out of his grasp with a superhuman strength at the last second and hit her head against the window on impact. Adrenaline, of course. It supplied extra strength in times of great stress, to sustain even the weak in life-threatening situations. Only in Tía Pilar's case, it had helped to end a life.

The crusty little pilot was dead, too. He'd checked.

He concentrated on the living.

"Francesca!" he shouted again, giving her a little shake. On the periphery of his vision he caught an ominous flickering of light that told him the plane was on fire. *"Francesca..."*

Francesca groped her way out of an engulfing darkness, vaguely aware of a dull pain at the side of her head. She heard her name called in a demanding voice, a male voice.... *Where...?*

And then she remembered—the unreal descent... the blackout inside the plane—all of it. "M-Mr. O'Hara...?" she questioned carefully, bringing a hand to the side of her head.

She thought she heard a relieved outpouring of breath, but couldn't be sure. It was hard to be sure of anything right now. The sense of disorientation...

"Yeah, it's me. Now, listen carefully, Francesca. We need to get out of here—*fast*. Can you move? Tell me if you're hurt—hurry!"

"I—I don't think so...." She tested her arms and legs. She was able to move them. "Just a bruise, I think, on the side of my head...I think Tía's elbow—*Tía! Santa Maria, mi tía!*—my *aunt!* I—"

"*Muerto.*" The single Spanish word drove home the reality as nothing else could.

"I'm sorry," she heard O'Hara add as she cried out softly. She twisted in the seat, tried to get a look in the flickering light that—*flickering light?*

"Dear God, we're on *fire!*" She felt the American pulling her out of her seat as the realization sank in.

"Exactly what I've been trying to tell you." His voice sounded grim. "Now, let's move!"

The floor was tilted sharply, with the downside near the exit door. The door appeared undamaged, but there were tongues of flame licking toward it from the blazing doorway of the cockpit.

"The pilot—" Francesca began, but Rafe cut her off as he shoved something bulky at her.

"Dead," she heard him rasp, and she closed her hands around her carryon while O'Hara half dragged, half carried her to the exit.

At least, she assumed it was the exit; the enclosed space had begun to fill rapidly with smoke, and her eyes teared, blurring her vision entirely in the dim interior.

O'Hara heaved a shoulder against the exit door, which seemed to be jammed, but it finally gave way, letting in a cool rush of rainswept air amid the light of gathering dusk. As she took in deep gulps of air, Francesca noted briefly that the rain had stopped, but then there was no time to think about anything else.

"Move!" Rafe shouted, his eyes on the flames, which had picked up strength from the increase in oxygen. Then he was on the ground below her, not too far a leap because of the angle at which the plane rested.

"Jump!" Rafe commanded, and was relieved to see her obey without a second's hesitation.

Then he had her in his arms, her carryon sandwiched between them as he turned and headed away from the crippled aircraft.

Francesca had a second to realize they were in a small, densely wooded area, mostly pines, when she heard a high-pitched, pitiful neighing over the noise of crackling flames.

"The horses! They're *alive!*" she cried, and struggled to get down.

Rafe hesitated for the briefest of instants, then kept moving, tightening his hold on her as he made his way through some dense underbrush. "Forget it. That plane's about to—"

"No!" she cried. Twisting in his grasp, Francesca used all of her strength to shove away from him and free herself. "We can't just let them die!" she added as she hit the ground running—straight for the rear of the plane.

"Like hell we can't!" Rafe raced after her, catching up easily. Seizing her by the shoulders, he spun her around to face him.

"You little fool! That fire's about to reach the fuel tanks any minute, and when it does, the whole thing's gonna blow sky-high!"

Francesca gave him a murderous look and resumed struggling.

Rafe heaved an exasperated sigh, then tried to sound more reasonable. "Look, I love animals just as—"

"There's also a human being in there, Mr. O'Hara! Or have you forgotten about the groom? I tell you, we've got to—"

Again, she broke his hold on her, using a maneuver Ramón had once shown her when she cajoled him into a minilesson in self-defense. He wasn't expecting it, and she tore free, racing toward the burning plane.

Grating out a particularly colorful oath, Rafe gave chase and caught up with her again. Once more he spun her to face him—and this time none too gently.

"Okay," he growled, "you win. But *you're* staying away! *I'll* go after the goddamned horses and whoever! Got that, little nun? In fact, if you do anything but walk carefully in that direction—" he pointed to a clearing beyond the trees and well beyond the plane "—I'll turn right around and drag you there...if I have to knock you cold to do it!"

Francesca nodded, heaving a little sigh of relief as she watched him turn and sprint toward the rear of the plane, removing his jacket as he ran.

She took another second to eye the advancing flames, which were now blazing from the exit door through which they'd emerged just minutes before, wondering if he hadn't been right—and whether she'd just sent him to his death.

Then, recalling the look on his face when he'd warned her off, she turned and headed for the clearing.

Rafe approached the cargo door amid streams of acrid smoke. He clutched the lightweight jacket he'd been wearing over his denims, wrapped the garment around his right hand and used it to grab the door handle—and swore.

The handle didn't feel hot beneath the jacket material, as he'd feared, but neither did it turn. Locked.

Another vivid oath competed with the sounds of terrified horses as he took a backward step, reaching for the semi in his shoulder holster at the same time.

The air exploded with sound as he aimed and fired in one fluid motion. He used only a few bullets from the clip, but it was enough. The noises of frightened horses were louder now, a high-pitched whinny likely belonging to the mare, with the stallion trumpeting an alarm that eclipsed it a second later.

Rafe sprang forward and tore open the door. Because of the angle of the plane and the terrain, it was closer to the ground than their exit door had been. Good. He needn't waste time with the ramp.

He pulled himself up and into the cargo bay. There was some smoke, but it wasn't too bad. His eyes went immediately to the stall where the larger of the two horses had succeeded in kicking out all but the top two planks of the door.

And he took in the badly trampled body of the groom lying under the stallion's thrashing hooves.

Rafe wasted no time on the man, who was clearly dead, but went straight to the mare, figuring she'd be the easier horse to handle. He opened the door to her stall, placing his hand gently on her rump to let her know that what was behind her was no threat. Keeping a hand on the jittery animal, he spoke to her in soothing tones as he advanced toward her head. It was what he'd been taught as a very young boy by the father who'd been a mounted policeman, one of New York's finest.

The mare snorted when he reached for her halter, but she calmed down quickly after he ran his hand over her face and stroked the velvety soft muzzle. But Rafe was wasting no time; even as he stroked, he was backing her out of the stall.

Beside them, the stallion worked himself into a frenzy as Rafe handled the mare, seeming more angry now than afraid.

"Good fella," Rafe murmured to him as he led the mare past the damaged stall. "Stay that way, boy...mad as hell, and maybe I'll get you out, too." *That is, if any of us get out alive.*

Rafe registered the doubt, then dismissed it. In his line of work, if you faltered you were finished. A man just went ahead and did what was necessary. No second guesses, no equivocating.

With that in mind, he deftly blindfolded the still-nervous mare with his jacket and led her out the exit.

Once outside, he retrieved the jacket and gave the mare a slap on the rump that sent her running. He didn't wait to see where she ran—her good sense would take her away from the smoke and the flames. Then he turned and headed back into the plane to get the stallion.

The smoke was thicker now, and the noises coming from the big horse said he didn't like it. Again, Rafe spoke in a calm, gentling voice, but even before he'd reached the all-but-slatless door to the box stall, he knew the big chestnut was going to be a lot harder to handle than the mare.

He'd just succeeded in pulling the door away when he caught sight of something he hadn't noticed before: lying at his feet, just outside the stall, were two parachute packs. A suspicion began to form in his mind, but he stashed it away for future consideration.

If there was a future. No time to think of that now. "Easy, big boy," he crooned. "Easy, now..."

Using exactly the same technique he'd used with the mare, Rafe eased his way around the dead man's body and approached the stallion's head. But the big horse wasn't buying any of it. He rolled his eyes until the whites showed, pawing the ground and shaking his head so vehemently, it was impossible to catch hold of the halter.

Sweat had broken out on Rafe's forehead and was running down his neck after the third try. Time had become a ticking bomb in his brain, and he knew they didn't have much left. Swearing to himself, but softly so as not to further alarm the stallion, he seized on an idea.

Inching his way back along the wall of the stall, he came even with the dead man. Then, careful to avoid the chestnut's dancing hooves, he grabbed the outstretched arm, lying atop a riding crop, and dragged the body out of the stall as fast as possible.

The gamble—worth the extra seconds if it worked—was that the dead man's presence was as much to blame for the horse's nervousness as anything. Rafe had already caught sight of whip marks on the animal's withers, and that told him plenty.

He turned back to the stall. Almost as an afterthought, he bent to grab the pair of parachutes. Out of the corner of his eye, he glimpsed something in the far corner of the cargo bay that had him snarling an obscenity, but that, too, would have to be sorted out later.

He approached the big horse using the same soothing procedure as before, but moving a bit more quickly.

The stallion was definitely calmer, but the smoke was a lot thicker.

The stallion allowed himself to be handled to the point of being blindfolded, but when Rafe tried to back him out of the stall, he balked. Forcing himself to remain calm, Rafe gave it another try. No go. Again, Rafe tried to move the animal, and on the third try, he succeeded—only to have the beast refuse to move a step farther once they were outside the stall.

The smoke was bad now, and as he coughed with it, Rafe thought he might have to abandon the animal, after all. But an image of the magnificent animal dying in a blazing inferno intruded, and with a stubborn set to his jaw, he dismissed the notion. He'd be damned if he'd give up now!

Swearing mightily, he looped the handles of the parachute packs over his arms, grabbed hold of the stallion's mane and swung himself up on its back. The animal danced nervously, but Rafe held on, hunching over its withers.

"Move, boy!" Rafe rasped on a cough, and with just the right amount of pressure to the horse's sides from his thighs, he urged it forward and out the door.

Air, sweet air! It was all Rafe could think of as he tore his jacket away from the stallion's eyes and gave him his head. It didn't matter that they weren't moving all that fast because of the dense underbrush. It didn't matter that his eyes were tearing so hard from the smoke that he couldn't see. They were out of that hellhole, dammit, and he could breathe!

It didn't even matter when, less than a minute after he made his escape, the plane exploded with a force so great it nearly knocked him off the stallion's back.

CHAPTER SIX

FRANCESCA HIT THE GROUND with the force of the blast. Then, ears throbbing from the deafening sound, she barely had time to wrap her arms over her head before a second explosion rocked the ground, and then a third. It was as if the gates of hell itself had opened, and for a second she wondered if she were alive or dead.

But a high-pitched whinny behind her told her she'd survived, and so had the mare. And the explosions had stopped.

Her next thought, as she pushed herself to her knees, was for the horse and rider she'd seen emerging from the plane. Emerging, yes, but had they come far enough to—

She scrambled to her feet, straining to see through the billowing black smoke that stung her eyes, even at this distance. *O'Hara... Where was O'Hara?*

The mare, somewhere close behind her now, whinnied again, and this time there was an answering call: the shrill, clarion trumpet of a stallion.

Tears strung Francesca's eyes, not entirely from the smoke. She made the sign of the cross and choked out a barely audible prayer of thanks to the Virgin, and then another to Saint Francis.

And that was how Rafe found her as he let the stallion, drawn by the sound of the mare, take him to the clearing.

At first, of course, he could see nothing; the surging mass of dark, oily smoke had effectively blinded him. But a stiff breeze had begun to build from the west, blowing the smoke back toward the burning wreckage; and once he'd used his sleeve to swipe away the cleansing tears streaming from his eyes, he could make out the slender figure several yards away, head bent, hands clasped in prayer.

There was something about the pose that both touched and angered him, and he found himself taking a second to try to figure out why.

The kid was convent bred, so there should have been no surprise at discovering her in prayer, not after what she'd just been through. But he knew the realist in him rejected that simple, open faith...the man who'd long ago relegated God to the backwaters of hope and memory...the man who'd begun his apostasy on the day big Mike O'Hara died and had let it culminate on the day Father Tomás—

Rafe bit down hard on the old anger, surprised it still survived in the deep place where he'd buried it too many years ago to count. Giving his face another swipe with his sleeve, he drew the stallion to a halt a few yards away from Francesca and pointedly cleared his throat.

Francesca's head jerked up and Rafe saw the green eyes widen before a dazzling smile tilted their corners upward. The effect was twofold and oddly contradictory; while the smile lent her face an angelic, almost beatific appeal, the green-eyed tilt was decidedly feline.

And sexy, he found himself adding, then almost snorted at the absurdity of it. Valera's daughter looked exactly like what she was—a scared kid from a convent who'd just come through her first scrape with death and couldn't quite believe it.

"You made it," Francesca said softly, and wondered at the frown this brought from O'Hara. His only acknowledgment was a grunt as he slid from the stallion's back.

She took in the soot-blackened denims, the dark smears on his face and forearms, and wondered what she herself must look like. A downward glance told her the navy Donna Karan suit was hopelessly rumpled, and she could feel her heavy chignon drooping onto the back of her collar.

"You all right?" Rafe asked when he saw her hand go to the back of her neck.

"I—I feel fine," Francesca replied, noting to her surprise that she did. Her eyes had stopped smarting now that the wind had shifted, and the dull pain that earlier had throbbed at the side of her head was gone. "But the groom—didn't he—?"

A swift, negative shake of the head was her only reply as O'Hara turned to the stallion. Francesca made the sign of the cross and mouthed a silent prayer, then watched O'Hara run his hands over the chestnut's flanks and legs with an assured hand that said he had more than a passing familiarity with horses.

But of course she already knew that.

"It—it is fortunate you were able to ride Fuego out of there bareback," she ventured. "How—"

"Fuego?" Rafe frowned at her over the back of the stallion.

Francesca felt herself flush. "I—I heard one of the men call him that, back at the airstrip."

He nodded, giving the horse a final stroke along its sleek, muscular back. Then his eyes strayed toward the blood bay mare that was nuzzling some vegetation on the ground a few yards behind Francesca.

"I don't suppose you caught the mare's name while you were at it?" he questioned as he moved toward the bay. "We'll need all the help we can get if we're gonna have a prayer of managing these two, and—"

"Mr. O'Hara, you're not—"

"Rafe," he said bluntly before lapsing into a soothing cadence of semi-intelligible Spanish as he approached the mare.

"I beg your pardon?"

He didn't bother looking at her, but answered in tones that continued to soothe the bay as much as the hand he ran gently along its neck. "I said to call me Rafe, didn't I, pretty red girl? Whoa, now, baby... nobody's gonna hurt you.... That's it, easy now...."

He glanced back at Francesca as he continued stroking and soothing, checking the mare for injuries as carefully as he had the stallion. "No sense in being formal, is there, pretty baby? The way I see it, we're gonna be stuck out here together for a while, and formalities—"

"Mr. O'Hara..." Francesca began, her tone sharper than she'd intended and earning her a scowl from the man she addressed. "I—I mean Rafe...."

She watched him nod approval, as if she were a student who'd performed appropriately. She stifled her resentment and made herself continue addressing the man, but wondered why he had the ability to make her feel so callow. "I was asking about something you said a moment ago...um, Rafe—about managing the horses? Surely you're not thinking of riding these high-strung animals? Not for any appreciable distance, I mean."

Rafe set down the hoof he'd been examining and straightened to his full height, which brought his head and shoulders into view above the animal's back. Francesca had a moment to marvel at how he managed to look "drop-dead gorgeous," as Maria would have put it, despite the streaks of oily soot on his face or the way the wind churned his hair.

And for some reason, she found herself wishing she hadn't asked that question when those penetrating blue eyes met hers in a frankly assessing look.

"We may have no choice," he told her. "And if we don't, are you up to it, little nun?"

Francesca felt herself bristle. "I can ride, if that's what you mean."

Giving the mare a final pat, he circled the animal and walked toward her. "That's only part of it, lady…only one *small* part of it."

"You mean—"

"What I mean," he said, stopping a few feet in front of her, his prepossessing height making her feel smaller than she could remember feeling in years, "is this. We are stranded some—"

"Oh, but—"

"Listen to me, Francesca, because what I'm about to say may be necessary to our survival. ¿Comprende? Survival."

Chastened, and hating the feeling despite an instinctive knowledge that he was right, she nodded.

"We are stranded," Rafe went on, "somewhere in the Sierra Madre, well north of Mexico City—or hundreds of miles from any point of civilization, for that matter."

He paused long enough to see that she was taking in what he had to say with sober intent, then went on. "It's early summer, so we don't need to worry too much about exposure—in the daytime."

He acknowledged the question in her eyes with a nod. Then he glanced westward. In that direction the sunset was painting the distant peaks of the mountains with a vivid splash of color. Magenta and orange streaks washed the jagged horizon, and the lowering sun crowned the snowy tips with fire.

"Pretty, isn't it?" Rafe continued. "But once that sun sets, the temperature will plummet. The nighttime temperature in mountains like these can be thirty degrees cooler than in the daytime."

He eyed her navy suit, then glanced at the lightweight tan jacket he'd left lying on the ground near the stallion.

"We're not exactly outfitted for that possibility." His eyes shifted briefly to the carryon near her feet as he ambled toward the stallion. "I don't suppose you have anything warmer in that bag?"

He'd grabbed it, figuring they could use all the help they could get. God knew, women carried all kinds of things in these bags, and some of them might prove useful.

Francesca nearly smiled, recalling Maria's gift, which was the only article of clothing in the carryon. The rest was various toiletries. "N-no," she manage to say with a straight face.

Rafe grunted, as if to say he'd figured as much, then bent to retrieve his jacket. She watched him shrug into it, wondering how such a simple act could be accomplished with such fluid grace.

He turned toward her as he zipped up, and Francesca had a moment to wonder about the outline of something bulky under the denim of his shirt before it disappeared from sight.

It was as if he'd read her mind, Francesca thought as she watched him smile sardonically and pat the spot, which was slightly below his left shoulder.

"Yeah, I'm packin' a piece, little nun. 'S'matter? Didn't figure I'd be carrying some protection?"

I'd have to be a fool to think anything of the sort, Mr. Hired Killer! But the fact was that she *had* forgotten somehow...had been taken aback by the presence of the weapon. She shot him a look that said she wouldn't forget such a thing again.

"Well, you'd better be damned glad I have it," Rafe went on. "It might just make the difference between starving and survival out here. I've never enjoyed killing animals for my food, but I've done it before, and it looks like I'm about to have to—"

"Oh, but surely you don't believe we'll be here long enough to—" Francesca paused, seeing the patronizing look he gave her. "Well, I mean, there will be search planes, won't there? And rescue parties, or whatever? Didn't you—didn't the pilot radio some kind of distress call or something?"

The look he shot her before she saw him unbuckle and remove a leather belt from his jeans bordered on the contemptuous.

"Oh, there'll be a search-and-rescue effort, all right." She watched him remove a Swiss army knife from a hip pocket and begin applying it to the belt as he answered her. "Even if the Mayday didn't get through—which might be the case. We were losing power when the call went out."

"Then when the plane fails to ar—"

"Bingo, little nun. When we fail to show up at Miami, the inquiries will begin, and I have no doubt your father will turn them into an all-out search, pronto. But how long do you think that will take? Long enough for us to get a little hungry, maybe?"

He was right, she thought as she watched him slice the leather of his belt into yard-long strips. The questions wouldn't even begin until a reasonable amount of time had passed after their ETA. And then, once it was finally established that their plane had disappeared... *Dear God, Papa will be frantic! And poor Ramón—*

"I see you get my point," said Rafe. He had completed severing the four long strips of leather from the belt buckle and was tying them together, in pairs.

"Even if they start tonight," he went on, "which isn't likely, given the fact that darkness makes an already difficult procedure nearly impossible. But even if they do start the search, got any idea how many miles they'll need to consider, trying to pinpoint the site of the crash?"

Francesca merely shook her head. Tired of conceding how right he was, she focused her interest on what it was he planned to do with the pair of long, joined strips of leather.

She had her answer a moment later, when she saw him take the first one and begin to fasten it to the stallion's halter as a set of reins.

"Ever ride bareback, little nun?" Rafe questioned with a grin she didn't like. It was more than simply teasing; it was baiting, and she'd had enough of that from him already.

"Once or twice," she murmured uncomfortably, knowing it had been strictly forbidden at the convent.

"For reasons of modesty," the nuns had obliquely put it, but she, as well as most of the older girls, knew it had mainly to do with preserving their hymens.

And she had a pretty good idea O'Hara's grin said he knew this, too. *Patán*, she found herself mouthing again.

But Rafe wasn't even looking at her as he moved toward the mare with the remaining set of reins. "You never did tell me if you happened to catch this one's name."

"No, but she reminds me of a filly I once—"

"I was thinking of Flama," he said with an unbelievably sweet smile for the mare. He looked back at Francesca as he fastened the improvised reins to the blood bay's halter, and the smile became a grin. "You know...Flame...sort of goes with her coloring...."

Yes, it meant "flame," Francesca mused. It could also mean "ardor" or "passion."

But to Rafe she said none of this. There was something about the way he was looking at her, even though he was discussing the mare, that made her wonder if it was really the horse he was describing....

Vaguely uncomfortable, she nodded and looked away.

Rafe led the mare over to Francesca, then heaved a sigh. He sounded exasperated.

"Is something wrong, Mr.—Rafe?" Francesca gave him a brief glance, then began to stroke the horse's neck.

He was eyeing her lower torso—and frowning. "Nothing that couldn't be fixed by a pair of jeans and some boots."

Francesca glanced down, took in her muddied espadrilles, the wide run in her panty hose, and barely suppressed a sigh. Was he about to fault her for her attire now? Really, the man was becoming infuriating! It had been the worst day of her life. Her aunt was dead and Francesca herself had barely escaped with her life. Now she was stranded in this wilderness. And here he was, criticizing her choice of clothes! She'd had enough.

"I'm sorry if I came unprepared for a plane crash!" she snapped.

Rafe threw her a penetrating look, and at once, his features softened. He gave his head a little shake, and when he spoke, his voice was patient and forbearing.

"Easy, little one. No one's blaming you for anything. As a matter of fact, maybe someone oughta be complimenting you on a few things." His smile echoed the softness of his words, catching her totally by surprise.

"Wha—what things?"

Rafe gazed back at the smoldering wreckage. "Ever been this close to so much devastation?" he asked quietly.

Francesca surveyed the site and shuddered. A huge area around the point of touchdown lay scorched and denuded of the trees that had cushioned the crash. A scattering of smaller fires still burned on the periphery, but they were on the wane. She realized the heavy rain from the storm had probably inundated the site enough to contain them, and it appeared they would soon die out.

"No," she whispered, relief mingling with awe in her voice as she continued to stare at the wreckage.

Rafe nodded. "And yet I've watched you come through the whole thing so far without flinching. No tears, no hysterics...just a rock-steady handling of what had to be done." He met her eyes as she turned toward him with mild surprise on her face. "A steadiness, I might add, that could put a lot of older, more experienced people I've known to shame, Francesca."

"Like poor Tía," she murmured tonelessly.

Rafe sighed. "I'm sorry about your aunt. And while it's true she might have had a better chance if she'd remained cool, it wasn't really her I was thinking of just now. She was older, yeah—but more experienced?" He gestured at the devastation. "In things like this? Nah.

"But in my line of work," he went on, "you meet people who've been around some, y'know? Seen stuff...yet sometimes none of that makes a damn bit of difference when the chips are down. Hell, I've seen grown men with combat training who—"

He shook his head, as if to dislodge some memories that were no longer important. "The way I figure it, it all comes down to what you've got inside...the 'right stuff,' as somebody's already neatly termed it. Experience helps, but mostly, I figure you're just born with it. And sometimes," he added, "you find it in the most unexpected places."

He grinned at her then, and gave her a mock clip on the jaw with his knuckles. "Like in a skinny kid, fresh outta some convent south of the border."

Francesca threw him a mock scowl. In truth, the backhanded compliment felt good, though why praise from him should matter, she wasn't certain.

Feeling momentarily confused, she forced her attention back to the horses. "What happens now, O'Hara?"

Rafe ignored the less personal form of address, more tuned in to the gruffness in tone that accentuated the throaty timbre of her voice. He scanned the distance, noting the fiery glow that bathed the craggy peaks, indicating the sun had just dipped below the horizon.

"Dressed as we are, I'd say we need to keep moving to stay warm." He eyed her lower torso again and grinned. "Think you can sit a horse in those without cussing me for wishing out loud that they were jeans and a sturdy pair of boots?"

Francesca felt her face flush. "I never cuss," she managed with some asperity.

"So I've noticed" came the dry reply, and he handed her Flama's makeshift reins.

"But I would like to ask a question."

"Shoot."

"Why ride at night—on high-strung horses, in dangerous mountain terrain that's completely unfamiliar? Why leave the site at all? Couldn't we try to build a—a campfire or something? We might be able to start one from some of those—" she gestured toward the scattering of small blazes "—before they go out, and...."

"And there you've just pinpointed the problem, smart little nun that you are," he replied with light sarcasm. "So you've noticed those fires are dying, right?"

Francesca nodded impatiently, irritation evident in her stance as she waited for him to set her right on yet another minor, but crucial, detail. It seemed like the umpteenth time this had happened.

"Well, the same thing that keeps them from burning out of control—the wetness—would make it unlikely that we could keep a friendly fire going all night. And as for leaving the site, we need to find better shelter and at least head toward civilization. Anyone searching for us will be able to follow our trail if they need to. *¿Comprende?*"

Sighing, Francesca nodded. She should have thought of that. And the fact that she hadn't—and that *he* had to point it out to her—made her even more irritable.

"As for riding these babies in the dark—" he ambled over to the stallion "—we won't. Much too dangerous."

"Then . . . ?"

"We ride them, or try to." His tone said *she* would be the one doing the trying; he had already succeeded. "But only until the light fails. Then we walk them. But we keep moving. It's our best chance against the cold."

He scooped up the pair of parachute packs from the ground, where he'd flung them when dismounting earlier, then paused to eye the sky overhead. "Besides," he added as he led Fuego toward her and the mare, "the sky's clearing and there oughtta be some light from a moon that's heading toward full."

He handed her Flama's makeshift reins. "Need any help mounting up?"

Francesca threw him a scornful glance, then spoke a quiet word to the blood bay, grabbed fistfuls of the horse's mane, and swung herself gracefully onto her back.

Rafe nodded approvingly. The little nun had strength as well as that elegance of movement he'd noted hours earlier. And she sure as hell knew her way around horses. Good. Maybe they had a chance.

The chance he was thinking of had to do with more than a need to keep moving to stay warm. He wanted to get as far away from the area as possible. While it was true that, come daylight, rescue copters might be able to spot the site of the crash from the air, it was also true that Valera's people might not be the only ones looking for them.

It was entirely possible that their Mayday *had* gotten out, and if it had, Morano and his people would be homing in on the area as fast as anyone else. Maybe faster. And Rafe wanted to be on terrain better suited to dealing with them.

He knew the difficulty of his mission had increased tremendously. He no longer had his Uzi, nor even the spare clips he'd carried for the semi; they'd all been blown to hell in the wreckage.

So now he had to avoid being caught by Morano's men while trying to lure Tony with the girl at the same time, but with far fewer resources than he'd anticipated.

And on top of all that, he also had to consider a genuine, safe rescue, or he and the kid could wind up dead from the dangers inherent in being stranded in these damned mountains . . . the Fear-a-Madre. . . .

Christ, how he wanted Morano's ass!

Morano had stashed the "groom" on the plane. Rafe was sure of it. He recalled the object he'd seen through the smoke, lying in the corner of the cargo bay. An M16. Every bit as effective as the Uzi Rafe had lost in the wreck. And the pair of parachutes . . .

It all made sense. The creeps had sabotaged the plane somehow.

One of the things that Rafe and the pilot had noted during the furious checking of gauges had been a curious depletion of fuel. At the time he'd merely wondered if the gauge was registering improperly, and he'd gone past it, too caught up in trying to get some response out of the controls to give it enough thought.

But even though there were explosions when the jet finally blew, Rafe knew they could have been much greater than they were. They were minimal because there had been far less fuel to feed them than there ought to have been. The fuel gauge had been right.

Morano had probably engineered a leak in the fuel tank, or maybe the line, although Rafe suspected the former... less dangerous. Especially to a thug who had to be on the plane himself—waiting for just the right moment to bail out with his kidnap victim.

Yeah, it all made sense. The creep had been biding his time—only the storm had precipitated things a bit and done its own damage to the plane. And, along with Fuego, more than enough damage to keep the creep from acting.

Rafe smiled to himself and patted the stallion's neck. Then he eyed Francesca, who was moving the mare around in a circle, obviously trying to get a feel for the animal, for what she could get it to do for her.

The navy skirt was flared enough to allow her to sit astride the horse, but it had ridden up high—almost to her hips—revealing a smooth expanse of shapely thigh. The kid had long, knockout legs, and Rafe couldn't suppress a grin as he checked them out with the thoroughness of a connoiseur.

"Something amuses you, O'Hara?"

"Thought I told you to call me Rafe."

Francesca threw him a smile that was overly sweet. "I might, if you tell me what has you grinning like the Cheshire cat!"

The grin grew lopsided, accompanied by a slight lift of the eyebrows and a teasing look in his eyes before they shifted back to her thighs. "Just wondering how you'd take an apology... for calling you skinny."

Francesca felt the telltale flush creeping upward from her collar as she struggled for words to form a suitable reply. *"O'Hara..."*

Low, teasing laughter cut her off as she watched him turn and stride toward her carry-on bag, which lay on the ground a few yards away. "Here," he said, laughter still lurking in his blue eyes as he gently set the bag across the mare's withers. "See if you can manage this while you ride. I know it won't be easy, given the fact that you've got no saddle to attach it to, but it's not very heavy, and— Hey, how come it's so lightweight? Aren't you females always lugging around tons of—"

"I'll manage," Francesca told him between gritted teeth. She settled the flexible bag within the cradle formed by her thighs and the horse's neck and gave Rafe a look that said she dared him to say another word.

He merely offered a cocky salute, then sauntered over to the stallion. In one effortless movement, he was on the big chestnut's back, the pair of parachute packs slung over his arm.

Francesca couldn't resist a little baiting of her own. "Are you planning on having to *bail* out of these mountains, O'Hara?"

Rafe's eyes went to the rough, uncertain terrain beyond the clearing, with the deepening shadows of early evening already stretching out across its features. "Out of the mouths of babes..." he muttered.

"I beg your pardon?"

He glanced at her, then turned Fuego's head westward. "I couldn't have put it better myself, little nun. Not one iota better. Now, if you're done making inane small talk, let's ride, okay?"

Mouthing the word *patán,* for the third time that day, Francesca pressed her knees against the mare's sides and mutely followed the irritating figure on the stallion.

CHAPTER SEVEN

THEY RODE WITH EXTREME care, largely letting the horses pick their own way over the unfamiliar ground. It was slow going. The failing light and uneven terrain compounded the difficulty of maneuvering a pair of highly charged, sensitive Thoroughbreds with bitless bridles and no saddles.

Rafe took the lead, which was fine with Francesca. The mare had clearly accepted the stallion's dominance, so she was relieved of the need to guide the bay, which followed docilely. This left Francesca free to continue building a rapport with her mount—difficult enough, given the mare's clear dislike of the carryon slung across its withers.

They were able to proceed this way for barely half an hour before it grew too dark to see where they were going. They had just crossed a little arroyo devoid of vegetation, but full of scattered rocks and rain-washed debris, when Rafe decided it was time to dismount.

Francesca heaved a sigh of relief as she slid off the mare's back. She'd ridden horseback from the time she was old enough to know what a horse was, but always under near-perfect conditions. She'd had the best saddle mounts, custom-made tack, carefully selected instructors—and turf ideally suited to whatever level of ability she'd reached at various points over the years.

None of which applied to their present circumstances.

The geography of the Sierra Madre was as harsh and forbidding as it was beautiful. And the parts of it they'd been forced to cross were the last places on earth a sane person would choose to ride a horse, she thought as her feet met the ground and dislodged some loose stones, which she heard tumble downward.

But loose stones and screed slopes were only part of the problem. Vegetation covered much of the ground, some of it hiding dangerous cavities where a horse could snap its leg like a matchstick. Gullies and ravines had crisscrossed their path with stomach-wrenching regularity. Trees ranging from wind-bent scrub oak to tall pines and other conifers had suddenly loomed out of the fading dusk.

Francesca shivered, recalling one particular image of a clump of evergreens that had seemed like specters waiting to snare hapless prey. She shut out the image with a determined shake of her head, but she continued to shiver. Only then did she realize it was from the cold.

The temperature had dropped severely, just as O'Hara had said it would. She'd been so preoccupied with the dangerous terrain, with her slowly dawning realization of just how precarious their situation was, she actually hadn't noticed.

Until now, when her body, trembling like a leaf in the wind, forced her into awareness. Exhaling warm breath over hands that had grown so numb she could barely feel Flama's reins, she stamped her feet, which were equally icy. Then she dropped the reins and wrapped her arms around her waist, trying to hug in what little body heat remained beneath the inadequate material of her jacket.

"Here." Rafe's disembodied voice reached her through the darkness. The night had grown inky, unrelieved as yet by the promised light of a moon. "Take this and wrap it around you."

Something solid, yet oddly soft, was thrust into Francesca's hands, but their icy numbness kept her from discerning what it was for a moment. Then she realized she held the folded mass of one of the parachutes. O'Hara had taken it out of its pack, and she was supposed to use it for warmth.

She started to do what he'd said, but between the stiffness of her fingers and an all-over trembling that had set her teeth to chattering uncontrollably, she only managed to drop the folded bundle on the ground.

"S-Santa M-Maria—" she swore before sucking in breath to stop herself. It was a mild-enough oath, but unlike her in the extreme. She'd never given in to such lapses of speech in all her years at the convent, and—

"Don't stop there, little nun." Rafe's words came from a spot so near, she felt the warmth of his breath on her ear before she sensed him bending beside her to scoop up the silky bundle.

"Or then again, maybe you'd better wait until you're warmer," he went on as she felt him straighten beside her in the darkness. "There's nothing like chattering teeth to take the guts out of an oath."

Then, before she could think of a retort, she heard a rustle of silk and Rafe was wrapping the enormous swath of lightweight material around her.

"Hold still," he ordered when she made a move to take over the process herself. "You're shivering like a rabbit in a trap."

Francesca had an immediate sense of the size of the man beside her in the darkness. She was fairly tall, but next to O'Hara, especially this close, and in the dark, she felt dwarfed. It was also impossible to ignore the sheer solidity of the man. She was keenly aware of strong, capable arms performing a task she should be doing for herself. It suddenly seemed too personal, somehow.

"Wh-why aren't you sh-shivering, t-too, O'Hara?" she questioned as he succeeded in fashioning an enormous stole out of the fabric and cocooning her in it. "D-don't you f-freeze and b-bleed like the r-rest of us m-mortals?"

She'd tried for flippancy, but suspected it had merely come out accusingly. It was hard to control such nuances of tone when your teeth were rattling like a set of old bones. And when a man you'd already decided was too dangerous by far was briskly rubbing your arms and shoulders while you were swaddled like a helpless infant.

"Me?" She heard him step away from her in the dark and immediately felt the loss of his body heat. "Just too tough and ornery, I guess," he went on. "But I'll take whatever help I can get."

She heard him speak in low, soothing tones to Fuego. Then there was a whisper of silky fabric, and she knew he was wrapping himself in the second parachute.

"As soon as you feel the blood get going a bit," he told her from a short distance away, "do whatever you need to, to rewrap that thing so it's functional. You know . . . toga-style, or whatever, so your arms are free enough to guide the mare and all."

Already feeling considerably warmer, Francesca did as she was told, rewrapping the cloth around her as best she could. Suddenly she had a flash of one of those odd little recollections that crop up from time to time: she saw herself at about thirteen or fourteen, when she and several of her classmates had wrapped sheets around themselves for a performance of *Julius Caesar*. She remembered she'd played Brutus.

The incongruity between her present situation and that one suddenly struck her as ridiculous, and she had an urge to giggle. *That had been so mundane. Now here I am surviving a plane wreck, only to be lost and in danger of freezing to death somewhere in the Sierra Madre. And with a hired killer as my only hope of getting out alive.*

And suddenly she giggled. She tried to suppress it, but merely succeeded in turning it into a long, rippling peal of laughter.

She sensed Rafe's presence before she actually felt his touch. He was beside her in an instant, giving her shoulders a rough shake, saying in a tight whisper, "Whoa! You're not gonna go to pieces on me now, are you, kid? Take it easy!"

The urgency in his voice quelled the laughter more than anything else, and she stopped. Then she was looking up into O'Hara's sternly set features, taken aback by the fact that they were suddenly visible.

By the light of the newly risen moon she could now discern their sharp, chiseled contours. Harsh, almost forbidding in the unforgiving light, they were thrown into high relief by the juxtaposition of light and shadow. She had the impression of some nameless, primitive god... carved out of onyx... limned in silver.

Francesca gave her head a little shake. "I—I am not going to pieces."

Rafe eased his hold on her shoulders, but it was his eyes that pinned her where she stood. She knew they searched her face for evidence of her emotional state. There was nothing of blue in them now. Only chips of obsidian, glinting quicksilver in the moonlight. Francesca resisted the urge to shiver, and not from the cold.

Apparently satisfied, he released her shoulders, giving her face a final scrutiny. "Okay," he said. His voice had a faintly sarcastic edge to it. "Guess I'll have to accept the fact that you're just prone to fits of giggles for no apparent reason. I can live with that."

He turned abruptly and headed for the stallion, leaving Francesca to debate the wisdom of trying to explain herself. Deciding she owed him no explanations for her behavior, she chose silence. Besides, what would a man like O'Hara know about costumes and school plays anyway?

With Rafe again in the lead, they resumed traveling. In some ways it was easier than before now that they were on foot. Certainly, without a pair of unpredictable mounts to control, they were better able to focus their attentions on the terrain. And the moon rising above the mountaintops in the east gave enough light for them to avoid the most dangerous pitfalls of the topography; they no longer had to worry about narrow defiles that suddenly veed into dead ends, or giant boulders that not only blocked their path but seemingly rose out of nowhere to do so.

But the footing was still treacherous, the shadows cast in the moonlight often obliterating more than the silvery glow revealed. And Francesca soon found herself wishing for the sturdy pair of boots Rafe had mentioned. Each step she took made her painfully aware of how inadequate her flimsy espadrilles were for such a trek.

Of course, her feet were a lot warmer now, thanks to the increased circulation gained by walking. But since they were no longer numb, she could feel the sharpness of every rock, the painful thrust of each wayward twig, through the thin cloth of the shoes.

Hours passed. Francesca knew without once looking at the illuminated dial of the Rolex her father had given her as a graduation gift; the moon climbing ever higher in the sky was evidence enough. She found herself glancing at it whenever it seemed safe to take her eyes off the ground for a while, and then she sometimes gazed at the stars, as well.

Myriad constellations crowded the midnight sky, their crystalline brilliance greater than she could ever recall observing before. Perhaps, she thought, it had something to do with the isolation of the mountains; this far from civilization there was none of the pollution hovering around cities to obscure them, no competing light from buildings or street lamps, or the garish flare of neon that marred the night in the places like Mexico City.

Not that she'd been exposed, personally, to such things as cities after dark. Papa had occasionally allowed Ramón to escort her on a shopping spree in Mexico City or Puerto Vallarta, but always in the daytime; afterward, there'd be a luncheon at some extravagantly expensive restaurant, and then she'd be whisked back to the convent by limousine under the watchful eye of yet another "escort."

Recollections of those sumptuous meals in elegant dining rooms proved a mistake; she was suddenly aware of how hungry she was, realizing it had been at least a dozen hours since she'd eaten—and then it had been merely a handful of grapes, shared on the plane with Tía.

The sudden stab of grief she felt recalling the dead woman did not surprise her, despite the fact that she and her aunt had been barely more than strangers. She'd truly begun to develop a fondness for the old woman. Especially after observing how immune she was to the blandishments of a certain *norteamericano* "escort."

Ah, Tía, if only—

The unexpected sting of tears brought Francesca up short, and she hastily brushed them aside and focused her thoughts elsewhere. Time to mourn would have to come later, when she was alone. She would no more expose her grief to a man like Rafael O'Hara than she would any other of her most private emotions. Like her suddenly gnawing hunger, she would tuck it away, pretending it didn't exist.

It was a technique she'd developed for dealing with impossible yearnings a long time ago. A technique that had served her well over the years. She would make it serve her equally well now.

Forcing her attention back to the tall figure leading the stallion, just a few yards ahead of her and the mare, Francesca concentrated on the invisible trail they seemed to be following.

More time passed, and Francesca couldn't remember ever feeling so tired. But, as she had with her hunger and her grief, she made herself ignore the silent screams of unused muscles, the leaden feeling that invaded her body and seemed to weigh her down with each step. Instead, she kept her focus on the man lead-

ing the stallion; if he could do it, she told herself again
and again, so could she.

Through all the slowly passing hours, Rafe remained
utterly silent, and Francesca followed suit. At times she
wondered about the direction he'd chosen—roughly
north by northwest, she guessed by calculating from the
position of the moon—and was tempted to ask why
he'd selected it. But there was something about his silence that made her hold back.

He would pause from time to time, holding up a hand
in a gesture that quickly became familiar, signaling her
to halt. At such times he reminded her of the stallion
that stood poised beside him, ears pricked, nostrils
quivering, testing the air.

It was as if he was listening for something—or someone. Which was silly, she chided herself. The idea of
someone out here in these mountains was as improbable as it was fanciful. As he'd pointed out, not even her
father's rescue crews could be expected this early.

Of course, like the stallion, he could be on the look-
out for four-footed company, Francesca thought with
a sudden tightening of her fingers on Flama's halter.
What had she read about these mountains in those geography textbooks so long ago? She frowned, trying to
remember.

There were mountain lions, she recalled, and timber
wolves, too, although they were becoming scarce—she
thought she remembered reading something about their
being put on the endangered species list. And . . . what
else? Were there bears? Vaguely she remembered reading about black bears, but she couldn't be sure if they
were supposed to be here or in the more northern—

Francesca's scream tore through the night. Rafe's
mind formed a split-second image of the banshees he'd

imagined as a child. Pivoting sharply about, he had another fraction of a second to catch the terror in her eyes as the face of the escarpment on which she stood gave way, pitching her sideways and over the edge.

"Christ!" Rafe's shout eclipsed her scream as he threw himself forward, chest against the ground, arms straining for the slender figure that was no longer there. He was dimly aware of the frightened neighing of horses from somewhere nearby, of the damp feeling of water-logged clay against his palms as he maneuvered himself closer to the edge, but his eyes were riveted on the steep slope below where a moon-washed figure tumbled downward like a limp doll.

Rocks and pebbles bounced past her, here and there hitting a patch of vegetation or a gnarled scrub pine that had managed to cling to the slope. He saw several lodge in a scraggly looking manzanita bush about twenty feet away, but the kid continued to tumble helplessly downward.

"Francesca!" he yelled, hoping she was conscious and could hear him. "Grab for something—one of those bushes, anything! Grab and try to hold on!"

Suddenly she seemed to come to life. Hardly daring to breathe—or hope—Rafe watched with frozen, heart-stopping apprehension as Francesca stretched sideways and collided with a clump of scrubby vegetation. Then he saw her twist to clutch it with both arms, and some-how—miraculously—hang on.

"'Atta girl!" he shouted. "Now, hold on and don't move! I'm coming for you!"

Francesca hardly needed to be told. She was breathless and slightly dizzy from tumbling, but soberly aware of the necessity of clinging to the damp clump of greenery that had broken her fall.

She was also aware that it had been O'Hara's shouted instructions that had cut through her shock and made her act. In the agonizing seconds before she'd heard his voice, she'd been numb with fright, not even daring to open her eyes or think beyond the terror that had lodged itself in her chest.

And now he was coming for her. She had a second to savor the sense of safety this gave her before the impossibility of that promise struck. Coming for her? In God's name, how? She was dozens of yards down the near-vertical face of an escarpment that had already proved too fragile for her own, far lighter weight. How on earth—

She knew it was a mistake the minute she moved. Even the slight adjustment of posture required to turn her head and shoulders. As she tried to get a view of what was happening above her, she must have redistributed her weight, and it was enough to send rocks and pebbles tumbling downward. Worse, it was enough to dislodge the root system of the bushy plant she clung to, and she felt it begin to give.

"Dammit! Didn't I tell you not to move?" O'Hara's voice, some distance above, but sounding closer than it had before, held a mixture of alarm and fury.

Well, she could hardly blame him, Francesca thought as she prayed for the branches in her grasp to stop inching away from where they'd been anchored moments before. She tried not to think of the dry gully that waited hundreds of feet below, forced herself to concentrate.... *Hail, Mary, full of grace...*

The choice of words in Rafe's muttered incantations was far less holy as he hugged the face of the escarpment and slowly inched his way toward her. The slope wasn't entirely vertical, as anyone who'd done a bit of mountain climbing would see, and Rafe had done his share. But what worried him and had him cursing under his breath was that the kid had no such experience. If that bush tore loose, in all likelihood she'd go crashing downward again.

But maybe he could prepare her...teach her what to do from where he was, until he reached her. She hadn't panicked yet, from what he could tell, and...hell, he'd give it a try.

"Francesca," he called. "Listen to me. Don't move, if you can help it...."

It probably took less than an hour—but could have been years, for all Francesca knew—until Rafe reached her. She had unconsciously measured out the time with the agonizing slowness accorded those who can do nothing but wait. But she had long since relinquished her grasp on the fragile clump of vegetation that had started to give way. She had traded it, under O'Hara's watchful eyes, for her present, improbable hold on the slope.

Improbable, because she'd never have believed it could be done. Not this flattened, uncertain clinging to barefaced rock, with no more than a precarious toehold, a clutching at stone with fingertips, to keep her in place.

But here she was, and O'Hara—

She felt him ease into place beside her, even before she heard his voice. He'd been silent as a cat, with only the occasionally loose pebble marking his descent. But now, here he was, his solid, undeniable presence beside her on the moon-washed slope...solid, yes, and utterly comforting....

Francesca released the breath she hadn't realized she'd been holding since the last pebble had tumbled past her.

"How ya doin', kid?" Spoken carelessly, as if he were asking the time of day, the casual words made Francesca smile.

"Oh, I'm in rare form," she quipped, "although not nearly as rare, I suspect, as I'll be when we get back to the top of this scenic marvel."

Rafe's answering grin was a flash of white she caught out of the corner of her eye. "You okay otherwise? No broken bones? Nothing sprained, that sorta thing?"

As she had after the crash, Francesca made a quick check and found herself surprisingly sound. "I'll live," she told him.

There was another quick grin, gone before she could think about it; then he was supporting her with an arm around her waist while he calmly issued instructions. She would move only when and how he told her to, placing a foot here, a hand there, until they reached the top. He would remain beside her, guiding her every inch of the way. She was not to look down, not to give in to the temptation to do anything other than what he said.

"*¿Comprende?*" he questioned when he was through.

Francesca not only understood, but actually felt she'd be able to do it. She had a moment to realize she was seeing a new dimension to Rafael O'Hara; whatever else he was, he was a man who was able to inspire confidence. The sudden realization took her by surprise, but before she could examine it further, he was issuing instructions in a quiet voice and she had to concentrate on what he was saying.

They reached the top—not the spot where Francesca had fallen, Rafe having determined it too unstable, but a place a few yards distant from it—a grueling half hour later. Under O'Hara's scrupulously careful guidance, there'd been no mistakes, not a single misstep, but Francesca had been white-knuckled and grim the entire time.

But now, suddenly, it was over—*over!*—and she slumped to the ground with relief.

"Easy, there, kid," Rafe murmured as he pulled himself up beside her. She was huddled against the stony surface, not making a sound, but he could see she was shaken. "It's okay now. You're safe. Go ahead and cry if it'll make you feel better."

There was no response, and Rafe leaned closer, prepared to offer what comfort he could. But he hoped she wouldn't need much. His experience with kids of the female variety was zilch. Hell, even his work with teenage boys—those kids at the settlement house back in New York—had happened so long ago, it was like part of another lifetime.

Then she shifted position slightly, allowing Rafe to see her lips moving to form silent words. She was praying.

Feeling suddenly more out of his element than if she'd turned to him for a shoulder to cry on, Rafe pulled away and rose to his feet, his mouth set in a hard, angry line. *So she's praying again. So what? What'd you expect, stupid? Tears of gratitude?*

He strode toward the horses, which had wandered several yards away, ostensibly to check them out. But his real reason was to cool his anger, which, as he saw it, should never have materialized in the first place.

Why the hell should he be bothered by Valera's daughter? She was nothing more than the kid of a slimy crook, for chrissake. No—more than that: she was a means to an end, as far as he was concerned. Bait, god-dammit! Valera's daughter was no more than a piece of bait he would use to get that scum bag, Morano, and he'd damn well better not forget it!

Francesca crossed herself, her prayers at an end for the moment. At the convent she'd been accustomed to lengthy periods on her knees—they all had, scholars and nuns alike. It had been a part of her way of life for years, and although she had never felt a religious vo-cation, she'd easily assumed the various duties and dis-ciplines required by someone growing up in such a place.

So praying at the end of an ordeal such as the one she'd just been through was as automatic as breathing, and she'd probably still have been at it, except that—

Her gaze swung sharply to the tall figure standing beside the horses. Why was it that she had the impres-sion he was angry? Had she done something? Surely he couldn't be annoyed with her for having caused him the trouble of rescuing her. He'd been more than positive in his attitude during the entire business. In fact, she had the impression of having heard a comforting tone in his voice while she was at prayer—or had she imag-ined it?

Francesca sighed, deciding to leave the matter alone. Trying to figure out a man like O'Hara was harder than trying to ride Flama without the standard equipment. At least the mare shared common ground with other horses she'd ridden. In the case of the man hired to protect her, she suspected there was no common ground at all; what he was, where he came from, was as alien to her as something from another planet, and she had just better accept it. Besides, once they got out of this mess, she'd never see him again, so why worry about it?

She heaved another sigh and pushed herself to her feet. She was bruised and scraped in several places, but in surprisingly good shape, considering what she'd been through. Of course, her clothing was in tatters, but—

The parachute! It was gone! When had she—

"Looking for this?"

Francesca's gaze swung from the ground she'd been scanning and came to rest on the jumbled wad of cloth in Rafe's outstretched hand. He was close enough to hand it to her, yet she hadn't seen or felt him move.

"I wish you wouldn't keep doing that," she told him, avoiding his eyes but snatching up the parachute with a brisk motion.

"What, hand you that thing?" Rafe eyed her with a mixture of annoyance and the kind of condescension she recalled all too well from before. "Listen up, little girl. The only reason you're not shivering now is because you've still got lots of adrenaline pouring through you. But any minute now, you're gonna—"

"*Mr.* O'Hara, I am neither a *little girl* or a *nun,* and I was speaking of the habit you have of sneaking up on people and—oh, never mind!" Francesca looped the parachute over her shoulders and stalked off, heading for the horses.

Rafe raised an eyebrow in sardonic appreciation as he watched her stride away. "Helluva temper for a little girl, I'd say," he said to the stallion as it wandered over to him. "Not to mention a nun. I wonder if she'd buy me calling her Pita."

Fuego nudged his arm, and Rafe grinned at the horse. "What's a Pita, you ask? Oh, you know, fella...*P-I-T-A*. It stands for *pain in the—*"

Rafe's laughter rang out as he gave the stallion an affectionate slap on the rump. Still laughing, he turned the horse in the direction they'd been headed earlier.

Behind them, Francesca gritted her teeth and fell in step. The word *patán* echoed in her thoughts.

THE BALDING, muscular man with the beard held the stump of a Cuban cigar clamped between his teeth as he settled himself into the passenger seat. He glanced at his pilot, who was busy checking the controls.

"You ever fly this thing in the dark before, Bruno?"

Bruno, a thin, wiry man with weathered skin, didn't bother to look at him as he answered. "The big boss says we go out and have a look, we have a look. Night...day...makes no difference t'me. Day might be better, but I done plentya both."

The man beside him grunted while the helicopter's third occupant, seated behind them both, coughed from the cigar smoke. When he spoke, it was over the sudden roar of the engine, in a raspy voice. "This is some whirlybird, Bruno. What's it called?"

The pilot was busy engineering the lift-off, and the bearded man answered for him. "It's a Bell Jet Ranger!" he shouted over the noise of the engine and whirring blades overhead. "*The best.* Only the best for the Old Man—ain't that right, Bruno?"

Earphones in place, Bruno still didn't answer, whether from lack of hearing or attention to the details of lift-off.

The man in the rear seat laughed. "Yeah, well it better be the best if he thinks we're gonna locate the spot in the dark!"

The bald-headed man turned his head and sneered at him. "He just wants us t'have a look around, stupid! Besides, this bird has the latest equipment on board. If that Mayday was from the girl's plane, we've already got a good fix on the general area where it went down."

"Yeah, boss, I know. But not on where Lou an' the kid bailed out. How the hell—"

"Shut up, Vito! The orders were t'look, an' that's what we do, *capisce?* Now, keep your eyes peeled. When that baby went down, there hadda be one hell of a bang. She could *still* be burnin', now that the rain's stopped."

Vito shook his head but held his peace. He would have liked to say something about that damn Cuban stogie, too, but he didn't. The boss had a nasty temper—worse than the big boss's any day.

Vito shivered. The boss had a mean streak a mile wide. He *enjoyed* hurting people. No way was Vito going to cross him. But privately he had doubts about this scouting mission. Doubts about the whole business, period. If Lou and the boys were successful, how come they hadn't picked up anything from that beeper Lou was wearing? It was supposed to let them know where him and the girl were, wasn't it?

With a sigh, Vito shrugged and turned to look at the moonlit terrain below. Who knew? They could get lucky. Valera's daughter could be stranded somewhere right down there, underneath them. Just waiting for the boss to get his hands on her.

CHAPTER EIGHT

FACING THE BANK of telephones that had been set up for him in his hotel suite, Ramón Valera checked his watch for the third time in a minute. Where in the name of all the demons in hell was the call?

Ramón slammed his fist on the table, angry frustration evident in every line of his angular frame. Behind him a pair of burly bodyguards glanced at each other but said nothing. Ramón wasn't known for his patience, and his temper ran hot, even when things were going okay.

But now nothing was going okay, to put it mildly. And it looked like the big boss's *capo* son was ready to explode. Not that they blamed him. The boss's private jet was missing, and the girl with it. Nobody knew much more than that, except that Ramón still hadn't gotten through to the old man.

The phone directly in front of Valera let out a shrill ring, and he picked up the receiver before the sound ended. "¿*Sí?* No, Barbero, I *haven't* left yet! They still haven't located my father, and you know we can't make a move until— What? No, he left Palermo yesterday, right on schedule. But he's not at the villa or at the town house, either. Guiseppe thought he might be with the Pagnanis, and that's where—"

Another phone rang, and Ramón told Barbero to hold while grabbing the second receiver. "*¿Sí?* Yeah, it's me. Never mind, what— Put him on!"

The bodyguards shared a look that said they wouldn't want to be anywhere near Esteban Valera when he heard what Ramón was about to tell him. Everybody knew how the big boss felt about the girl. It was like the sun rose and set on the kid. Rumor was, he'd felt the same about the kid's mother. Valera was hard as nails, but if anything bad had happened to his daughter...

"Hello, Papa?" Ramón's voice was tightly controlled as he spoke, but he'd lurched from his chair when the final connection was made. His knuckles showed white under the tanned skin of his fingers as he gripped the receiver. "Papa, listen...."

Less than ten minutes later, Ramón was in action. The two bodyguards flanking him looked relieved as he barked out orders into two telephones simultaneously; the younger Valera was at his best when there was something that needed to be done and he could act on it.

Ramón slammed down the receiver on his left after telling his secretary to complete arrangements for his flight to Mexico. He continued with instructions for Barbero, who was still on the other line.

"I don't *care* if it's four in the morning! Get the son of a bitch out of bed personally if you have to! No two-bit Mexican official's more important than my sister! And while you're at it, call in Luis Mendoza. What? Yeah, I know he only does sea searches, but I want all bases covered. That plane had some water to cross before it landed, didn't it? Now, you got everything, Barbero? Good. Oh...Barbero?" Ramón's voice suddenly became silky-smooth, but with a menacing undercurrent. "Be very, very sure there are no screwups, hear? Because if there are, *compadre,* I'm comin' after you—*personally!*"

Ramón hung up and reached for his suit jacket, which he'd slung over the back of a chair hours earlier. He'd have preferred changing into something more casual and he needed a shave, but it would have to wait. His father had put him in charge of directing a search operation from the Mexican end, and he had a plane waiting.

Ramón handed a sleek, imported leather valise to one bodyguard while the other picked up his suitcase, which had been packed almost twenty-four hours before, in readiness for the trip to Rome. The bodyguards preceded him out the door of the suite, and at their signal, he followed.

He was anxious to get going but made no complaint when the two men made him wait while one checked out the stairs. Sure, the elevator would be quicker, but it could also be deadly. More than one hit man had come blazing out of one as the doors opened, automatic spewing ammo so fast the mark never had a chance.

And something about this whole business had the smell of that sort of trouble, Ramón decided as one of the bodyguards signaled him toward the stairwell. *Morano* trouble, unless he was way off base, and he seldom was in these matters. He'd always had a sixth sense about such things. It was one of the reasons Esteban Valera had decided to groom his son for the spot he held in the organization, right under the old man. That, and the fact that he had brains, of course.

Not, he secretly suspected, that he was as smart as Francesca. His little sister could run circles around anybody he'd ever met when it came to smarts. Too bad they didn't let women into the organization, because if they did—

"Ramón!" The first bodyguard, who'd reached the lobby ahead of Ramón and the other man, came running back toward them. "Your secretary called—must've happened just after we left the room."

"Yeah?" Ramón hurried down the last of the steps.

"She left a message with the desk." The man handed him a slip of paper.

Francesca's brother scanned the note, then nodded grimly.

"Trouble?"

Ramón's eyes revealed nothing as they met the bodyguard's, but the man knew that didn't mean anything; the younger Valera was as likely to hide his feelings as he was to let them explode. It all depended on what was at stake.

"Could be," Ramón finally answered. "There's been a call from the police in Mexico City. Some guy in a private plane caught a Mayday while he was busy trying to fly clear of a storm in the mountains. He just reported it a little while ago. They're pretty sure it was from the 727—my sister's plane."

FRANCESCA AWOKE SLOWLY, at first not realizing where she was. Then, as she started to move and felt the protest in every muscle of her body, she remembered all too well. She was shrouded in a parachute somewhere in the Sierra Madre.

They had stopped moving shortly after her rescue from the fall. It had quickly become evident that the accident, not to mention the plane crash and the long trek that had followed, had taken its toll on Francesca.

She'd begun to lag behind Rafe and the stallion, and when he saw her faltering, he'd called a halt.

What had happened after that was mostly a blur to her. She'd been so exhausted, she could barely stand. She vaguely remembered O'Hara scraping together some leaves for them to lie on, and there was something about the horses...he'd hobbled them, yes, that was it—but that was all she could recall before she'd bedded down.

The last memory she had was of sinking onto a damp pile of leaves, her parachute still around her, and gazing up into a sky full of stars. She'd been dirty, hungry, bruised and exhausted, but it had felt like heaven.

But now it was no longer night, she realized, even before opening her eyes. She could feel the sun's warmth on her face, and the air was filled with bird song. What time was it?

Pulling an arm free of the parachute silk, she squinted at her watch. Good heavens, it couldn't be—

"Quarter past ten, little nun, but my timepiece is just your garden-variety Timex. Could be that fancy Rolex keeps better time, of course." Rafe's voice cut into her thoughts from somewhere behind her head, and Francesca twisted sharply—then groaned.

"Better take it easy. Yesterday you used muscles I'll bet you didn't know you had." Rafe hunkered down beside her makeshift pallet.

She looked up at him. The first thing she noticed was that he now wore his weapon outside his clothes, having refashioned the gun belt to hold the holster low on his hip. His dark hair was disheveled, and a thick stubble covered the lower part of his face. Somehow this drew her attention to the eyes that gazed directly back at her. They had to be the world's bluest, she found herself thinking, then quickly glanced away.

Now, what had brought that on? It wasn't as if she'd never seen him before. She wondered if she was light-headed from sleeping in the sun. Or perhaps from hunger, she amended as the aroma of something delicious stole into her awareness.

"Hungry?" It was as if he'd read her mind.

Francesca's gaze swung sharply back as he reached for something beside him on the ground. Her eyes widened as they fastened on a pile of limp and steaming, partially charred leaves that Rafe held out to her on a thin slab of stone.

"Food?" she murmured disbelievingly, even as she felt her mouth water. "Good God, O'Hara, where on earth did—"

"It's not much, kid, believe me. Just some edible mushrooms I scared up and steamed together with a little wild onion. Here."

He set the slab on the ground between them, then gingerly began to pull away the fleshy, steaming leaves. "I found these leaves to wrap everything in. Don't know what they are, exactly... some kind of agaves, I think, but they made a good— *Ouch!*"

He snatched his fingers away, giving them a hard shake, then tossed her a wry grin. "Guess I oughta let 'em cool a little. Besides, these are yours. 'Fraid I already ate my batch...uh, sorry. I'd have given you first dibs, but you looked like you could use more sleep at the time, and—"

"O'Hara..."

"Yeah?"

"If you think for one minute I'm anything less than grateful, you're crazy. *Food!* I can't believe it!"

Francesca pushed herself to a sitting position, ignoring her aches and pains as she began unwrapping where he'd left off.

"Yeah, well, like I said, it's not much." Rafe rose to his feet, drawing her attention away from the food, which was still hot enough to burn her fingers, she discovered.

"In fact," he went on, "you may feel even hungrier after you've finished it. Mushrooms are mostly water, and—"

Francesca had suddenly abandoned the food. She also had a rather pained look on her face, although he could see she was trying to hide it; she was squirming as she glanced away.

"'S'matter? They're not poisonous, if that's what's worrying you. Besides, since I ate some first... Hey, kid, what's wrong?"

Francesca closed her eyes, fighting embarrassment. For some reason the call of nature hadn't presented a problem until now. She'd trekked all those miles without once having to... Well, she finally had to—and soon!

"Um..." She could feel the heat rising to her face, but there was no way of getting around it. She glanced around, noting they seemed to be camped at the edge of a thicket of yellow pine. At least the trees would provide some privacy. Thank heaven for small favors.

Searching for some polite way to phrase her need, she happened to glance up. O'Hara stood there, hands on the low-slung waistband of his jeans, eyeing her oddly. Then she saw his gaze shift to her lower torso where, underneath the folds of parachute, she had been trying, surreptitiously, to cross her legs.

"Think I'll go check on the horses," he told her abruptly. "I moved them down that way—" he gestured over his shoulder "—where I found a stream they could drink from. You . . . take care of things here till I get back, okay?"

Francesca uttered a tiny sigh of relief as he swung away and began striding in the direction he'd indicated. She was certain he'd understood her discomfort, and his discretion surprised her; it almost had her apologizing for all the times she'd called him a boor.

She had just risen to her feet, her eyes on the pines, when Rafe suddenly turned around. "Don't wander too far into those pines, okay, kid?"

Then he gestured toward her carryon, which she now noticed resting near the small fire he'd built inside a ring of stones. "But if you have any tissues in that thing, I'd bring them along." A sudden grin shone white against the dark stubble on his face. "Pine needles can be murder on a tender hide!"

He gave her a cocky salute and, with a wink, turned and resumed his stride, whistling some insufferably cheerful tune.

Having turned a deep shade of pink, Francesca gritted her teeth as she scrambled for the trees. As she ran, she racked her brain for a more caustic term than *patán*.

Rafe found himself in an oddly buoyant mood, despite their situation, and he wondered about it. Was he going soft? Maybe he was getting too old for this sort of thing.

Nothing about the dangers he faced had changed. He was still stranded in these damn mountains with the kid, still had a job to do, still faced the complications stemming from the plane wreck. So why the hell was he feeling so up, despite too little sleep and hardly anything to eat? Why the hell was he whistling, for chrissake?

The answer came to him as he reached the horses, and he stopped dead in his tracks.

Valera's daughter.

Unbelievable as it seemed, there was something about that wet-behind-the-ears kid that intrigued him. Made the job he'd taken on not nearly as boring as he'd figured it would be. But for the life of him, he couldn't put his finger on what that something was. Her looks had been a surprise initially, but he was past that now. Of course, another surprise had come with the steady way she handled herself.

The kid had guts.

Hell, he could have wound up with a spoiled, pampered hothouse plant, considering who she was. But the little nun had kept up with him for much longer than he'd had a right to expect, now that he thought about it. By the time she caved in last night, he'd been close to calling it quits himself.

And then there was this thing that made him tease the hell out of her. Despite the fact that it made no sense. He kept telling himself to lay off, that it was stupid kid stuff. And she might be a kid, but he sure as hell wasn't, and he had a job to do. Hell, the last time he'd indulged in that kind of stuff was when he *had* been a kid, so what was it with him, anyway?

An image of those wide green eyes flashed in his mind—and he sensed the keen intelligence behind them. Not to mention the way her face revealed almost everything lurking in that quick brain—including just what she was thinking each time she rose to his bait.

Giving his head a shake, Rafe wiped the grin from his face and told himself not to be stupid. *She's Valera's daughter, got that, wise guy? And you're here to—*

Francesca had just finished repinning her chignon with some hairpins from her carryon when she heard the shots. She froze at the unexpected sound, both hands hovering above the nape of her neck. She was still in the trees, having decided to make some emergency repairs to her toilette before going back to eat the food, so she could see nothing from where she stood.

Slowly she lowered her arms, hardly daring to breathe. She was suddenly acutely aware of every danger that had lurked since the crash. She was aware, too, that she had somehow pushed those thoughts to the back of her mind since awakening this morning. Even when she'd spied that gun on O'Hara's hip, she had somehow failed to remember how precarious their situation was. How he might have to use it.

And now he had. On what? What had—

She thought she saw something move, out beyond the trees. She took a cautious step forward, then stopped, thinking better of it. If whatever he'd shot at had gotten O'Hara, instead of—

"Hey, little nun! You can come out now!" O'Hara's voice carried clearly to where she stood, and she sagged with relief.

"I—I'm coming!" she called, then stooped to grab her carryon and hurried toward him, her curiosity as strong as her apprehension seconds earlier.

Rafe was standing near the cook fire when she broke from the trees. He held aloft something feathery and brownish-red in color for her to see. "Breakfast—second course," he announced grandly. "Wild turkey, kid. Wanna help me pluck it?"

He held the bird aloft by its feet. It had three dark stains on its bronze-tipped feathers, and it was dripping blood. Francesca tried to summon up the proper enthusiasm, but succeeded only in eyeing it doubtfully. "Help...pluck it?"

Rafe smothered a grin, well aware he was doing it again. "Yeah, but that's after we remove the entrails, of course. For that, we'll need—"

Amusement won out over discretion as Rafe's laughter exploded. The look on her face—

"Not funny, O'Hara!" Francesca's face burned as she realized she'd been had. "I may not be a back-woodsman, but at least my father saw to it that I was taught some mann— Oh, *here*—" she marched toward him "—*give* me that thing!" She snatched the fowl from his grasp.

The laughter ceased abruptly as Rafe looked at her. There was surprise on his face, but something else as well. His eyes ran over her as if taking her measure for the first time.

She stood, holding the fowl, with an adamant look on her face, and her eyes flashed a warning. Lit with green fire, they met his with an unflinching certainty dominating her face.

She was completely disheveled. Her wrinkled clothes betrayed the fact that she'd slept in them; several long strands of hair had pulled loose from the bun that rode crookedly on the back of her neck; there were smudges of dirt on her nose and chin; her hose were full of runs; and there were gobs of caked mud on her shoes. But in the split second it took him to assimilate all this, Rafe was looking past it. Looking at the stubborn tilt of her chin and the proud, willowy stance that was daring him to object—and telling him to go to hell if he did. He was looking at a fragile, feminine package, but seeing instead a bundle of grit and determination.

He suddenly had the oddest perception. It felt as if he was looking at a female, years-younger version of himself.

Francesca saw the look of surprise replaced by a frown, but was too angry to care what it meant. "Get out that knife of yours, O'Hara, and tell me what to do."

The frown was gone as quickly as it had appeared. Francesca thought she glimpsed an odd light in his eyes before they shuttered and he gave her a careless shrug.

"Follow me, little chef." Pivoting abruptly, Rafe motioned her forward and headed back the way he'd come.

BY EARLY AFTERNOON Francesca found herself back on the mare and glad of it. She was still feeling dirtier than she could ever recall, and she still had aches and pains from abused muscles, but she no longer felt exhausted, and her stomach was full.

She was also possessed of a crash course in culinary crafts in the wild. It had taught her, she realized, more than she ever wanted to know about such things. Even now, she wondered at her ability to consume a single bite of that miserable bird, given what she'd had to do to get it to the eating stage.

Still, she mused with a half-formed smile on her face, she'd done it, hadn't she? Eviscerated it and skinned it because there'd been no pot to boil water for plucking. Then she'd roasted it on a crudely fashioned spit over the fire, and it had proved edible.

The whole business had been accomplished with the barest minimum of words between them. At least, on

O'Hara's end, she amended. He'd been unusually taciturn, telling her only what she needed to know to prepare their meal. No small talk. Not even any of that reprehensible baiting—not that she missed it, of course.

But as she gazed at the denim-clad back of the man riding ahead of her, Francesca couldn't help wondering what had prompted the latest change in him. One minute he'd been relaxed and full of that bantering he seemed to relish; then, without any apparent reason, he'd become this silent enigma with a face that gave nothing away.

It was when he was like this that he reinforced her foremost impression of him—a dangerous professional, a trained killer who hired out his deadly skills to someone who could afford them and was willing to pay his price...someone like her father....

Francesca shivered, despite the warmth of the sun. It was the first time she'd allowed herself to make a conscious connection between O'Hara and the parent who was responsible for the ambivalent emotions that sometimes threatened to tear her apart.

But the link was there, wasn't it? Rafael O'Hara and Esteban Valera lived in the same world...a world ruled by violence and fed by unholy greed.... *Do not let his world become* your *world, Francesca....* The parting admonition of Madre Dolorosa echoed in her mind with a brutal clarity.

Well, she had no intention of living in that world, she told herself adamantly. She might have been forced, by circumstances utterly beyond her control, to brush up against it, but she would never walk its corridors—*never.*

She would survive this wilderness with her life and soul intact, just as she'd survived the plane crash. Then she'd be free of the need for men like Rafael O'Hara and their "protection."

Furthermore, she was going to Rome to marry, and once she did, she would no longer be under her father's charge; she would have a husband, and a normal life with that husband.

And if the husband should turn out to be part of their world? a niggling voice asked, but Francesca banished it with ruthless determination. She would deal with one devil at a time.

And that particular devil, she found herself musing several hours later, was Rafael O'Hara.

The man seemed bent on riding until they dropped. They had traveled for miles without stopping for more than brief minutes at a time, mostly to water the horses. Although their pace was moderate and careful—again, to spare the horses, Francesca suspected—it was relentless, and she soon found herself hot, achy and tired.

In many ways it was worse than the night before; while daylight freed them from the worry of not being able to see their way around dangers in the terrain, the sun had driven the temperature up to a level that had perspiration soaking her undergarments and trickling down her neck. And without a hat, she knew her face was courting a sunburn, despite frequent applications of the suntan lotion she'd found in the carryon.

"You sure packed a helluva lot of stuff in that bag," Rafe said at one point when he saw her using it.

Francesca nearly jumped when he spoke. He hadn't said a word to her for hours, although why, she couldn't ascertain.

"*Sí,*" she replied, seeing no reason to tell him it was Maria who'd packed it so thoughtfully. "We women like to travel well prepared."

Rafe snorted. "I've never seen a woman yet who didn't pack five times as much stuff as any reasonable man would take along. And probably *six* times as much as needed."

Francesca bristled. "I thought you said my bag was light!"

"Yeah, for a woman's."

"Oh, really! It seems to me, Mr. *Macho Hombre,* that I saw *you* carry a bag onto that plane—and it looked extremely heavy to me!"

Rafe thought with regret of the bag that held the Uzi and all those spare clips. "Yeah, well, that was different."

"Hah!"

"Whaddaya mean, hah?"

"It is always 'different' if it's the man we speak of, isn't it?" She couldn't help thinking of all the freedoms Ramón had been granted while they were growing up. Even if he was years older, she knew the true reason was because he was a male.

Rafe had reined Fuego to a halt, and he turned to look at her. "Listen up, little girl. That—"

"Well, at least it's not *little nun* anymore!"

The blue eyes narrowed. "That bag you saw contained *hardware.* And the time might come when you'll be wishing we had it!"

"Hardware?"

"Guns and ammo, *little nun,* and don't you dare wrinkle up your delicate little nose in disgust!" That said, he turned Fuego's head and rode on, leaving her to fume in his wake.

They rode in silence again for hours, with Francesca eyeing the progress of the sun overhead, willing it to move westward. She could only assume—and hope—

that his plan was to stop by nightfall. A fire would be possible then, wouldn't it? Things had dried out since the storm.

It was only midafternoon when he next stopped, and of course it was only to water the horses again. They had just had to double back a distance to avoid some kind of treacherous mudhole he called a *ciénaga*. The sluggishly moving stream where they halted was swarming with gnats and mosquitoes.

"Got any insect repellent in that bag of tricks?" Rafe asked as he slid off Fuego's back.

Francesca snorted, something she'd never done in her life. "Don't tell me Mr. Macho Hired Killer actually wants protection from a few insects! What's the matter—haven't you got the right gun to shoot them?"

Rafe's jaw tightened as he shot her a withering look. "Hired Killer, huh? And just who hired this killer, little girl? It wasn't Santa Claus, I can tell you."

The adamantine brilliance in the green eyes faltered, and Rafe saw her look away. Had he seen shadows there, or was it just a trick of the light? Well, damn it, if she insisted on jabbing with a sharp tongue, she'd better be ready to get some back! *Dine with the devil, you'd best use a long spoon,* the old man used to say....

Francesca did her best to hide her reaction as she slid off Flama's back. He was right, of course. Again. Papa had hired him, and Papa was no saint. *Dios,* sometimes she wished she didn't know what he truly was! Life would be so much simpler—*had* been simpler before she'd opened that Pandora's box!

"Well, got any of that stuff in there or not?" Rafe asked as she rummaged in her bag.

"Here!" she said, thrusting a small plastic bottle at him. Maria had remembered to pack the repellent as well.

He ignored it and turned toward the stallion. "Not for me, little nun. You're the one with the tender flesh."

Francesca gaped at him. "Not for... *You* were the one who asked about it!"

He continued with his back to her, busy picking burrs out of Fuego's tail. "Hell, I figured you could make use of the stuff if you had some."

"And *you...?*" She was still flabbergasted, never more aware of how he always managed to keep her off balance.

"Me?" He turned toward her then, hands on the low-slung waistband of his jeans. "Oh, mosquitoes hardly ever touch me. Gnats, either. Guess my blood's just too nasty and mean for 'em." A cocky grin spread across his face as he ran his eyes over her. "Now, in your case, I can see they're just hungry for a sweet little snack of—"

"Oh, do shut up, O'Hara!" Francesca cried as she swatted a fat mosquito on her arm. She had never in her life told anyone to shut up, either, and she gritted her teeth at the sound of his mocking laughter as he walked away. She wondered how many other bad habits she was in danger of accumulating in this man's company.

They remounted and rode on. Rafe had again turned silent, and Francesca occupied herself with the wild, fierce beauty of the landscape. For a while she was content with this. The Sierra Madre seemed to fill her senses, dominating her consciousness with a majestic presence.

But as the afternoon wore on, she began to weary of it all. It was beautiful, yes, but as her energy began to flag, the mountains seemed to press in on her, their looming presence a weight she could almost feel.

She began to study the sun's position in the sky again, intermittently eyeing the broad shoulders of the man on the stallion and grinding her teeth. Easier to will the sun to set than to will O'Hara to stop and let them rest.

She had the odd feeling he was testing her somehow. How, or for what, she couldn't say, but she felt it. Well, whatever he was doing with this relentless pace he'd set, she'd match him. She would not—*would not*—give him the satisfaction of seeing her weaken!

Besides, he was too full of himself, anyway. Him, with his superior knowledge and vast experience! Not to mention those rugged good looks that probably had women falling all over themselves for him! There was no way she'd add to that smug self-image.

But "smug" was no way to describe Rafe O'Hara that afternoon. Smugness implied certainty, and he had little of that at the moment. In fact, he'd have been hard-pressed to say what made him drift into these long silences on the trail—except that Francesca Valera was at the heart of it.

What the hell was it with him? If he'd reminded himself once, he'd done it a dozen times: he had a mission, a job to do, and forget anything else.

But with each reminder, the resolve quickly waned, replaced by disturbing images of the kid. Valera's daughter, who was nothing like what he'd expected.

Nothing like it at all.

And he was an ass to let it matter. So from time to time in the late hours of the afternoon he'd hit on her with a few well-chosen words to show it didn't.

"You don't need to stay ten paces behind me at all times, y'know," he told her as they came to a high mesa, lush with coconut grass from the spring rains. "Bet you wouldn't if I told you about Indian squaws I heard of once."

"Indian squaws?" She was scowling.

"Yep. They always kept ten paces behind their men. They knew their place, all right."

"Then they should have paid more attention to the deer."

"Yeah, how's that?"

"I've been watching them as we've run across them," said Francesca, gazing at a small herd of whitetail deer in the distance. "The does always move *ahead* of the stag."

Rafe laughed, enjoying himself.

"And what is so funny?" she asked, fuming.

He knew she wasn't going to like this, and his voice grew smug. "Oh, but that's no pecking order," he told her. "The male *makes* them go ahead of him—so if there's a predator waiting, they'll get caught while he gets away!"

"*¡Excellenté!*" she spat. "Be sure to tell me when danger comes, then, Señor Stag. I assure you, I'll not hestitate to make my escape!"

Later, when he saw her wrestling with a long strand of hair that had come loose from that old maid's knot at the back of her neck, he couldn't resist another taunt.

"You could always just let it hang, like most normal women," he offered dryly.

"And they could always hang *you,* like most normal killers!" she shot back.

"Oh, so we're on that again, are we?"

"We're on *that* because *you* were on *me!*"

"Well, well, well . . . *Touché,* little girl!"

She placed her free hand on her hip and glared at him. "I am not fencing with you, O'Hara. I'm *enduring* you!"

"Heck, I'll bet you say that to all the boys," Rafe mocked in a falsetto.

"No," she returned with dripping sarcasm, "only those with lovely manners, kind hearts—and the decency to know when to lay off!"

Well, she was a feisty little nun. He'd give her that. He just wished he could stop thinking about it. About her. The images persisted... feline eyes spearing him when he'd given her those marching orders back at the airstrip... silent fortitude and straight, slender shoulders as she'd trudged for miles the night before in the dark.

Was she scared? He'd bet on it. But she did it anyhow, without a whimper... and then that gut-wrenching tumble—and her, *wisecracking* over it when she had to be half out of her mind with fear, down there on the face of that escarpment....

The recollections were relentless... the curve of her neck as she bent in prayer... the flawless way she moved, even when she had to be half-dead on her feet... the stubborn tilt of her chin when she'd—

Damn! The picture of her calling his bluff this morning was the most potent of all. Unsettling. But in the end, it was the one that put his uncertainty to rest.

So she reminded him of himself when he was a kid. So what? He'd always been a sucker for kids, hadn't he? Kids and animals... the only uncorrupted things in a world bent on corruption. If something was good and pure, it was finished, as he saw it. Headed for destruction in one way or another. Life was hell on innocents, so either they changed or they didn't survive.

Valera's daughter had survived this long without being corrupted only because she'd been walled off from the world. But now she was taking that first giant step into it, and his job was merely to see that she lived to take the next step. Beyond that, the little nun wasn't his problem, he told himself, and he relaxed for the first time since they'd ridden out that morning.

But the corruption will come, a voice nagged from somewhere deep inside. *Yeah,* Rafe answered with a ruthless certainty born of his own odyssey of survival, *but not on my watch.*

CHAPTER NINE

FRANCESCA NOTICED the change in him immediately. It was late afternoon, and Rafe indicated a small stream she had also spotted, sunlight glinting off its waters as it wound its way through some trees downslope from them.

"Let's water up down there," he said, pointing toward it, "but this time maybe we oughtta take a longer break. How about it? Ready for some time out?"

Francesca's mouth dropped open; she had to consciously snap it shut as she recovered from total astonishment. It was more than he'd uttered all afternoon, and he'd actually asked her. *Asked!*

Dumbfounded, she could only nod her assent as he flashed her one of those crooked smiles she'd seen all too rarely and clucked the stallion forward.

Her mind awhirl with possibilities as to what had prompted this sudden about-face, she followed eagerly. But by the time they'd dismounted and were leading the horses to drink, she still hadn't a clue and gave up trying. She'd never figure him out, she reminded herself—*common ground, remember?*—and the promise of a rest in this cool, shady spot beckoned like a visible piece of heaven.

As the horses drank thirstily, Rafe pointed to a spot upstream. "You can catch a drink and cool yourself off over there without running afoul of the sediment these guys are churning up. Go on. I'll keep an eye out here, then hobble them so they can graze"— he indicated a grassy verge downstream "—and then I'll join you, okay?"

"O-okay," Francesca murmured, wondering at the way his smile and the deep grooves bracketing it had suddenly made her feel as if she'd been given a lovely gift. *I must have had too much sun.... It's O'Hara, for heaven's sake!*

She gave him a smile tinged with uncertainty and turned to go. Then she felt a playful tug on a lock of hair that had escaped her chignon. She glanced at him over her shoulder, surprise evident in her eyes.

His smile had become a grin. "You look as if you've gotten a good dose of sun," he told her. "Better get out that stuff you've been using and put some more on."

The grin deepened and he tapped the tip of her nose lightly with his forefinger. "Wouldn't want a burn on that pretty nose. And, uh—" he trailed the finger upward to trace the curve of her ear, lightly, with the same, almost careless insouciance "—better make sure you cover these this time. Ears can be particularly susceptible—y'know?"

Francesca felt an odd ripple of pleasure along her spine, and for several seconds, she couldn't move. Or speak. She could only stand there, wondering if there had ever been anything bluer than Rafe O'Hara's eyes. Wondering if there was some inverted natural law that gave certain men those thick, lush eyelashes, while women spent a fortune on makeup trying to replicate them.

She later realized she might have gone on standing there even longer if Flama hadn't chosen that moment to raise her head from the stream and whicker at something in the foliage. As it was, this broke the spell, for which Francesca was immeasurably grateful. She quickly dropped her eyes and managed a small murmur of assent before turning to pick up her carryon and hurrying upstream.

Rafe's eyes remained fixed on her as she headed away from him. She had the natural grace of a dancer, he decided, and he never tired of watching her move. Long, lithe and clean-limbed, she moved over the ground like she wasn't even touching it. And she might be young, but he could tell, even beneath the shapeless clothes, that she had the body of a woman. Imagine all that coming out of a convent!

He frowned as he thought of the husband Valera had waiting for her. It was just like those Old Country Italians to marry a daughter off before she'd even lived a little. Before she found out what life was all about. A kid her age ... hell, how old could she be? Eighteen?

The frown gave way to a wry twist of his mouth. But that was exactly the idea, wasn't it? March 'em off to the altar when they're young and stupid—too young and stupid to know what they're getting into—and then they're the husband's problem. A problem that's usually handled by keeping them "barefoot and pregnant."

A jolt of anger sluiced through him at the thought of Francesca Valera being forced to submit to that process. It was wrong. The kid might be young, yeah, but she sure as hell wasn't stupid!

An image formed in his mind, of Francesca bending over that turkey, skinning it with surprising dexterity, while she muttered a steady stream of rapid-fire Spanish under her breath, and he grinned. Whatever he was like, this Carlo Pagnani that Valera had handpicked as her bridegroom, he'd better be someone who could handle her. Rafe somehow couldn't see her submitting meekly to...

But she'd just spent twelve years doing exactly that kind of thing. Submitting meekly to a rigidly circumscribed life-style. That's what life in a convent was all about, from what he'd heard. It was why Valera had put her in a place like that. He *wanted* her meek and submissive.

But what about the kid? What did *she* want?

Rafe's eyes strayed to the slender figure splashing water on her face several yards upstream. Hell, even doing a simple thing like that, she was graceful... and ephemerally beautiful, in the way of things that are exquisitely lovely in the moment, like a young doe he'd seen drinking from a mountain stream once, years ago....

Rafe gave his head a shake, this time succeeding in suppressing the surge of anger at what Valera had in store for her. Maybe it was exactly what she wanted, after all. Could be she had no wish to be anything but this young Italian's wife and all that went with it.

But somehow he didn't think so.

Glancing at his watch, he saw it was a little after four-thirty. Early enough to take a half-hour break and still travel a couple of hours before making camp for the night. Early enough to draw the kid into conversation and learn a few things. Like how she felt about being Esteban Valera's sacrificial lamb, led to the altar of her not-so-nice father's dirty pride, and maybe his ambition, too. Only he wouldn't put it that way, of course.

A slow smile spread across his features. He knew exactly how he would put it....

Some minutes later they were sitting across from each other, each propped against the bole of a tree. Francesca had found some more of the tissues that had already proved so useful and was using them to wipe her face dry. She saw Rafe use his sleeve to perform the same function, then rake his fingers along his beard-stubbled jaw.

He paused, glanced over at her, and grinned before giving the stubble a final rub. "It gets itchy when it starts to grow in, especially in warm weather."

Francesca's eyes registered mild surprise, and then he thought he caught a wash of color on her face that was deeper than the tint it had taken on from the sun. Rafe took a second to ponder her reaction, then grinned as he figured it out. Of course. In the female world she'd lived in, she'd never encountered a simple phenomenon like beards, or the creatures who wore them. This was brand-new knowledge to her. He wondered exactly what was running through her mind with the discovery. What was causing that intriguing blush.

"I remember once," he went on when she didn't say anything, "when I was on an assignment in Italy, and for reasons I won't go into, I had to grow a beard. It was mid-August, hot as—ah, Hades, and a lot of what I was required to do kept me outside... no air-conditioning, if you get the picture."

Francesca watched him rub his thumb and fingers thoughtfully over the square jaw as he paused. The simple action had a sensual quality about it. He reminded her of a large cat preening itself in the sun.

"Well, let me tell you," he continued, his eyes lifting to meet hers, "there were times during that first week or so when I thought I'd go nuts from the itching. Rome in August is no picnic. No wonder the natives—those who can afford it, anyway—leave the city in droves by mid-July and head for the seashore."

Francesca nodded. The Pagnanis, she knew, had a villa on Capri. That was where Carlo and she would be spending August, after they returned from their July honeymoon off the Greek island of Santorin, on Papa's yacht.

Thoughts of the honeymoon to come made her blush again, and the realization that Rafe was watching this made her look quickly away. But as she did, she also realized her blush had little to do with her intended bridegroom and the intimacies expected of her. And everything to do with Rafael O'Hara.

Because she also realized she knew next to nothing about what those intimacies were like. Oh, she had some vague idea of the preliminaries, thanks to Maria and their smuggled videotapes, but it was a far cry from something one experienced firsthand. Seeing someone like Mel Gibson make love to an actress on screen didn't tell her what it *felt* like. Kevin Costner's filmed caresses weren't touching *her* body. She was hopelessly ignorant of such things, and there was something about feeling helplessly aware of it while under the watchful scrutiny of Rafe O'Hara that was utterly unnerving. She all too often felt like a callow schoolgirl in his presence, and never more than right now.

Rafe didn't miss the deepening blush and wondered at it, but only for a second. He was more interested in steering the conversation around to his objective.

"Yeah, that was some uncomfortable week, that time in Rome," he ventured. "Of course, if we get outta this place in time, that's where you'll be heading, isn't it?"

Glad of the small talk to cover her discomfort, Francesca glanced at him and nodded. "But with any luck, it will still be June...not too warm yet, I hope."

"You've never been there before?"

She shook her head. "A couple of times when my...when I was a baby, but I suppose they don't really count. I don't—I was too young to remember them."

Rafe thought he saw a brief flash of pain in the green eyes, but before he could consider it, it was gone, leaving him to wonder if it had been his imagination or some trick of the light. Giving a mental shrug, he pursued his objective.

"Well, I hardly think you'll have any worries when you get there," he said. "I mean, even if our little side excursion postpones things into the heat of the summer. You'll hardly be staying where there's no air-conditioning."

Francesca responded to the light smile with one of her own. "No, I don't suppose I will."

Rafe leaned back against the trunk of the tree and stretched lazily. It was a casual gesture, but it drew her attention to the sinew and muscle beneath the bronzed skin of his arms, the taut stretch of fabric across the breadth of his chest and shoulders. For a moment she found it impossible to take her eyes off him.

"Yeah," he went on, "you'll be doing the Eternal City in style, kid. There'll be cool, shady courtyards...air-conditioned limos...most likely a swimming pool. They'll have it all set up for you."

Suddenly Rafe's eyes seemed more intense to her as he made a seemingly casual remark: "It must be nice to have your life all laid out that way.... Y'know, never having to worry about where you'll live, how you'll travel, that sort of thing."

Francesca gave a small shrug and smiled. "It's convenient, I suppose. And nothing new. I've lived that way all my life."

Rafe nodded. "Yeah. I guess your father knew what he was doing when he arranged this marriage for you. Not a bad idea when you look at it that way. Sees to it that you go from your old life-style to the new one with hardly a ripple."

The blue eyes were fastened on hers intently now, and Francesca was again conscious of how vivid they were. Vivid and penetrating. Framed by those thick, inky lashes, they seemed to reach into the center of her, where something unfamiliar, something sweet and pleasurable, was curling and unraveling.

"It—" she had to clear her throat "—it has its merits, I suppose."

Rafe effected another lazy stretch, and Francesca's eyes followed, taking in the corded muscles of his neck, the muscular strength implicit in the curling and uncurling of the wide, denim-clad shoulders.

"Yessir," he said, "that must be the life. Never having all those worrisome little decisions to make, never having to lift a finger to... 'S'matter? Something wrong?"

Francesca was suddenly frowning as the things he'd been talking about began to penetrate. The life he was extolling, the one she'd lead with her marriage to Carlo, was one of the very things she'd chafed about after Papa had given her the news of her engagement. Still chafed about, when she allowed herself to think about it. It was part and parcel of the anger she felt whenever she focused on this marriage to a man she'd never met.

Where was *her* say in it? *Any* of it! Did O'Hara, with his effusions of approval for such a carefree life-style, stop to think of that? Did *any* male who'd never lived the restricted life many women led?

"No, it is *not*," she blurted out with no further thought.

Rafe cocked an eyebrow at her, stifling the grin that tugged at the corners of his mouth. He knew he was about to receive a confirmation of his guess as to how this arranged marriage sat with her. It was all he could do not to shout, "'Atta girl!"

"Not what?" he asked as innocently as he could.

Two bright flags of color rode Francesca's cheeks as she let fly with emotions long-suppressed. "It is not 'the life,' as you so grandly put it!"

Rafe blinked in feigned surprise, still fighting a grin.

"How would *you* like to know exactly what you will be doing, and exactly *how* you will be doing it, day after day, year after year, O'Hara? You talk of never having any worries? What about never being *allowed* to worry? And then there are those tiresome 'little decisions' you spoke of. What about having all your decisions made *for* you? And not just the *little* ones! I mean *all* of them!"

Francesca was on her feet now, the force of her words feeding a restless emotional energy that had been trapped inside her for months. She vaguely realized she was looking down at him through eyes swimming with tears, but she was too far gone to care.

"Do you really believe you'd be living 'the life' if you'd been stripped of every decision, large *or* small, regarding how you lived that life? *Do* you?" she asked angrily.

Stunned by the depth of her reaction, Rafe was instantly sobered. He'd intended merely a lighthearted probing, but now he knew he'd struck a nerve.

"No," he told her seriously, "I don't."

The solemnity of his gaze took her aback for a moment. She realized she was better prepared to deal with his bantering and teasing than with this unexpected show of open sincerity. The effect was to make her suddenly aware of the tears wetting her cheeks. Embarrassed, she swiped at them with her fingers and looked away for something to occupy her.

Spying her carryon, she bent to retrieve it. But as she made a show of rummaging through its contents, she managed to deliver a final retort. "Then I suggest, Mr. Rafael O'Hara, that you cease commenting on subjects you know nothing about!"

Pushing himself to his feet, Rafe let the remark pass, too intrigued by something that had just occurred to him. What did it say about her, that in all she'd been through in the past twenty-four hours she hadn't cried once—not a whimper; yet an oblique reference to her upcoming marriage, to the future it implied, could reduce her to tears?

He felt like a heel. Wishing he'd never brought up the whole sorry business, he stared at her back and shook his head. Kids and animals. Would he ever learn? They were his Achilles' heel, and if he didn't watch it...

Inexplicably furious with her as well as himself, Rafe whirled toward the horses. "Mount up!" he growled.

The sun was dropping toward the tops of the mountains when Rafe finally allowed them to stop again. The shallow ravine looked like a good place to make camp. The recent rains had fed the stream at its base, so there was water for all of them and plenty of forage for the horses. Moreover, the area immediately surrounding the ravine was free of thick trees and other natural features that might provide cover for someone stalking them. He'd finally made up his mind to build a signal fire, but if this drew Morano, he wanted it to be on *his* terms. Here the advantage would be in Rafe's favor, not Tony's.

He glanced at Francesca as they dismounted and wondered if he'd pushed her too hard. She swayed momentarily on her feet after sliding off the mare's back and now leaned tiredly against the animal. She was exhausted, but he still hadn't heard her complain. Yeah, the little nun was a trooper, he'd say that for her.

He gestured toward the stream as he came forward to take Flama's halter. ''You look like you could use a rest, maybe some freshening up. Why don't you head for the stream while I take care of things?''

She looked up at him gratefully, nodded and headed down the slope. He noticed she walked slowly, with a tired cast to her shoulders. But there was no letup of that innate, unconscious grace.

Rafe hobbled the horses near the stream. He noted they were in surprisingly good shape, considering the distance they'd traveled. Satisfied that they had access to all the water and grazing they required, he set about making camp.

A fire was no problem. There was plenty of deadwood and other debris that various rains had washed into the gulch. Food, however, was another matter. The turkey he'd bagged that morning was history, and he had only the one clip in the semi.

Better make it count, he thought, then glanced at Francesca. She was sitting on a large flat rock in the stream, her bare legs dangling in the water. Next to her was her carryon, which he'd brought down to her before he built the fire. She'd washed her hair and was now wringing water from the long, dripping mass that lay heavily over one shoulder.

Wet, her hair was the color of old wine, except where the last of the westering sun's rays caught it. Then it glinted copper, like a brand-new penny. He was surprised at how long it was, now that it wasn't in that stupid bun.

"Sure you haven't got any dry threads in that bag?" he called, noting the clothes she hadn't removed—her blouse and the plain white slip under it. They were as wet as her hair.

Francesca recalled his seeing the green teddy on the plane, but she wasn't afraid to refer to it. "Only—only some spare underthings, I'm afraid."

"Well, get out of the wet stuff and put on something dry together with those—" he pointed to her suit jacket and skirt resting on the embankment, along with the shoes and hose she'd removed "—before I get back. Remember, it'll be cold once the sun goes down."

Francesca nodded and watched him move off with the gun in hand. She wondered if he'd get anything with it. The wild turkey, as he'd explained at one point, had been pure luck.

Eyeing the horses greedily cropping the short, lush grass along the streambed a short distance away, she forced her thoughts away from her own hunger. If Rafe was successful, they'd eat; if not, how bad could it be? Their failure to appear in Miami had been noted by now, even if the pilot's message hadn't gotten through. Surely there'd be search planes and rescue parties soon. Papa wasn't likely to spare a moment finding out what had happened—or in finding *her*.

Shivering with the breeze that had begun to build as the sun disappeared below the mountains, Francesca hurried out of the stream. She peeled off the wet blouse and underwear, which she'd lathered and rinsed along with her hair and body. Thank goodness Maria had packed that shampoo! She hadn't realized how truly gritty and dusty she'd been until she began to bathe. Or maybe she'd been too exhausted to care.

She found the teddy and hesitated only a moment before putting it on, then her suit jacket and skirt. They were travel-stained and wrinkled, but warm.

Her hose were hopelessly shredded, so she slipped on the espadrilles without them.

Considerably warmer, but feeling tired again, now that the exhilarating effect of the cold water was wearing off, she made her way up to the fire. She saw Rafe had again spread the lengths of the parachutes over some leafy branches and piles of loose grass to cushion them. Smiling, she sat down on the makeshift bed and began to comb the tangles out of her hair while the fire dried it.

The smile remained while she continued to think of Rafe O'Hara. He was such a strange one, this gringo bodyguard of hers. The smile broadened when she considered the term she'd used: gringo. She realized she must have picked it up from some movie.

But Rafe O'Hara fit the image. Hard and lean, looking like one of those gunslingers populating old American westerns, O'Hara seemed the epitome of the lone hero who lived by his wits to survive. And like a Clint Eastwood or John Wayne character, he was hard-edged and dangerous.

Far handsomer, though, she found herself thinking with a blush she was glad he wasn't there to catch.

Yet his looks had a severity to them, too. She thought of the photo of Carlo Pagnani. The man she was to marry might be very handsome in a neat, manicured way, she supposed. But his pretty looks were a far cry from Rafe's rugged maleness. Comparing them, she thought of a polished amethyst she'd once seen in a jeweler's display case. It had been set beside a rough geode containing raw amethyst quartz crystals in their natural state. Carlo was the polished gem.

Rafe O'Hara was all rough goods.

Or maybe *flint* was a better analogy, she amended, recalling his manner toward her from the very beginning. "Little nun" indeed! Between his mockery and his long silences, she never knew where she stood with the man. She was beginning to think he blamed her for their predicament. If so, maybe it was best to obey him and keep quiet. And to stay out of his way as much as possible.

Yet just when he'd had her believing him to be an insensitive, macho bully, here he'd gone and done all the work of making camp while allowing her the luxury of that bath and some rest! Sighing drowsily, Francesca returned her comb to the carryon. She yawned and stretched out on the parachutes' silky folds, her mind still on the enigma that was Rafe O'Hara.

She was sound asleep when Rafe found her there a half hour later. The fire had died down to red embers, but a half-moon was riding low in the sky, and he could make out her features by its light. They were soft and relaxed in sleep. And suddenly he saw that their delicate contours were an interesting counterpoint to the wild tumble of her hair, now that she'd freed it from that knot at the nape of her neck.

Thinking of the nape of her neck made him want to bend down and test it with his lips, just to see if it was as soft as he imagined. With a self-deprecating snort, he shoved the urge aside. *That way's trouble, old man, trouble like you don't even want to* think *about!*

Turning aside, he built up the fire, then used some green twigs he'd cut to make a spit for the mountain quail he'd killed and dressed—a good distance from camp to avoid attracting scavengers.

While the bird cooked, he went down to the stream to bathe, grinning when he saw she'd left her bottle of shampoo, and even one of those throwaway razors, on that flat rock for him to use.

Thoughtful little nun.

He shaved and bathed in a hurry. Although the breeze had died down, the temperature was dropping fast. If he hadn't needed to shock himself out of his tiredness, he'd have let the bath wait till morning.

He finished roasting the quail when he got back. He half expected the mouth-watering aroma to rouse Francesca, but she slept on. He finally had to wake her when it was ready to eat.

"Hey, little nun, wake up!"

Francesca stirred at the firm prod of a hand on her shoulder. She opened her eyes to see Rafe silhouetted against the fire.

"Chow's on, sleeping beauty. Better have some."

Francesca blinked, rubbing the heel of her hand across her eyes, then sat up quickly. "You shot something? Oh, Rafe, it smells wonderful! What is it?"

Rafe chuckled and handed her a leg joint. She reminded him of a little kid being offered a treat. All eyes and naked curiosity.

An inadvertent glance took in her jacket hanging open. He caught sight of peaked nipples thrusting against the green thing he'd seen on the plane, and it was too damn sheer by far. *This* was a nakedness he couldn't afford to notice, and he growled at her. "It's just a mountain quail. Shut up and eat it while it's hot."

Francesca took the joint and lowered her eyes, not wanting him to see how his words stung. He'd done the same thing a dozen times over, she reminded herself. A lightening up, a quick reversal, then he was all hard-bitten macho-tough again. *You'd think I'd have learned by now....*

As she nibbled at the fowl, she raised her eyes cautiously. He had turned away from her and was hunkered down by the fire, a piece of meat suspended between his fingers. He seemed to have forgotten the food and was staring at some point beyond the flames. She wondered what he was thinking, then decided it was better if she didn't know.

She contented herself with watching the broad, muscular spread of his shoulders and back while they finished eating. He was wearing the same clothes, of course, but she could tell he'd shaved—bathed, too; his hair curled over the collar of his jacket as if it had been wet when he dressed, and she'd caught the scent of her shampoo when he moved. She grinned, wondering if he appreciated the fragrance of night jasmine.

Finishing her meal, Francesca threw the bones into the fire. It was what Rafe had shown her to do with the turkey's remains. She shivered, realizing for the first time how cold it had gotten. She glanced down at the panels of her jacket, intending to belt them more securely—and sucked in her breath.

Dios! Was *that* what he'd seen? Heat pulsed furiously beneath the skin of her cheeks as she drew the jacket together and quickly turned her back to Rafe. Silently cursing her father for her lack of experience around men, she forced herself to stretch out again while the blood continued to riot through her veins. Mortified with embarrassment, she doubted she could sleep.

But the long day had taken its toll, and she soon found herself yawning and drifting off. Her last thoughts were to wonder if he'd ever call her "little nun" again.

Rafe waited until he heard her breathing in the even rhythms of sleep before moving. He banked the fire, then turned to look at the figure stretched out a few feet away from him.

Those long, supple limbs were a fluid line of silvered shadows in the moonlight.

Sweet Christ, did she have any idea how easy it would be to...

Mouthing an obscenity, he throttled the thought. Nothing about this situation was easy, least of all, Esteban Valera's virgin daughter.

Glancing around, he wondered if he'd be comfortable against some rocks he spied on the other side of the fire. Swearing softly, he set his jaw and made for the improvised bed. He'd be damned if he'd let Valera *or* his daughter keep him from another decent night's sleep!

He didn't worry about someone sneaking up on them. Years of conditioning had left him with the ability to sense danger even while he caught some shut-eye. All it took was the habit of light sleeping that was as much a part of him now as his name. Silent as stealth, Rafe eased himself down on the makeshift bedding.

It was long after midnight, judging from the position of the moon, when Rafe awoke suddenly. Instantly awake, he took only seconds to realize nothing threatened the camp. And then he knew what the problem was.

When he'd gone to sleep, Francesca was stretched out a couple of feet in front of him, there being plenty of room on the bedding for him to do the same. But sometime during the night she'd moved, and now she was curled against his body, spoon fashion. What's more, he must have responded to her warmth in his sleep. Because he had his arms wrapped around her, and one hand was cupping the fullness of an incredibly lush breast.

He felt himself go rock-hard with the awareness, and this only served to bring on a new realization that made him suck in his breath; her skirt had ridden up above her hips, and his erection was pressed against the cleft of her mostly bare bottom.

Shit!

Rafe ground his teeth against the surge of arousal that had sweat breaking out on his forehead, despite the chilly air. Cautiously, mouthing silent imprecations to forgotten saints, he tried to extricate himself without waking her. But he'd moved his hand barely an inch when she stirred in her sleep, snuggling her hips even closer. And her nipple grazed his callused palm, where he could feel it peak and harden with the friction.

Rafe let out his breath on a shudder, closing his eyes against a powerful wave of lust. He couldn't remember ever being this hard. Overhead, the stars were brilliant against an inky velvet sky, and the silk of her hair beneath his chin, the faint floral scent of it in his nostrils, sent his senses spinning.

But she was Francesca Valera, for chrissake! The daughter of a powerful, dangerous crime boss. And his bait. And he was dead meat if he gave in to the things his body was screaming for right now. He was nothing but stupid if he didn't find a way to break out of this and take a flying leap into that stream! *Stupid!*

Francesca came slowly awake, wondering at first where she was. Then she became increasingly aware of the most indescribable sensations running through her. Giddy sensations, full of sweet yearnings and delicious secrets. Her body began to glow and shimmer with the promise of even greater pleasure, and she struggled against the lassitude of sleep to find its cause. It was as if a dream had followed her out of sleep, into the waking world, and—

And then she knew. Rafe's big body enveloped her like a glove, his heat permeating every pore. She felt his breath warm on her neck, where her hair was swept aside. And then there were his lips pressed against the tender skin below her ear.

But the center of all sensation was a tingling at the juncture of her thighs. A tingling that became a throbbing when he moved his thumb over her—

Francesca caught her breath as realization penetrated. *Dios,* he was—

Rafe heard her moan and froze, then jackknifed away and rolled to the far edge of the bedding. He lay there for several seconds, breathing raggedly and expecting to hear... What? Recriminations? Tears?

But there was only silence. He thought he might have heard a sigh at one point, then chalked it up to his imagination.

Close, he told himself. *Damn close.* He heaved himself off the ground and headed for the icy stream.

CHAPTER TEN

"WE'LL BE STAYING HERE for a while," Rafe announced the next morning.

Francesca hadn't heard him arise, but apparently he'd been awake for some time. He was hunkered down beside the fire, sharpening a green twig with his knife. Beside him, on a bed of leaves, lay a large fish. When had he caught it? And how?

Rafe caught her glancing at it. "Mountain trout, little nun. Cagey rascals when you're angling for 'em, but they're suckers for a little tickling. If you're patient, that is."

"Tickling?" Francesca felt stupid. Or perhaps it was just that she felt mesmerized by Rafe's hands as he used the knife. Strong, sun-browned hands...hands that had—

"Yeah," said Rafe, wondering why she'd suddenly turned toward one of the parachutes. "You lull them into laziness with a little finger stroking, and then— *gotcha!* Trout for breakfast."

Finger stroking... Dios! "Um...why did you say we were staying here?" she asked as she rose to shake out the improvised bedding.

"Well, there's a good supply of fresh water, for one thing." Rafe carefully speared the trout with the sharpened twig. "And if it rains...see the ledge of rock over there?'' He pointed to a large slab of granite overhanging a relatively flat area beneath.

''*Sí.*''

''Shelter, in case it rains. But more than that, it's the food supply I'm worried about.''

''But surely the fish—''

''You up for a steady diet of 'em?''

Francesca had been watching his hands as he handled the trout. Now she glanced at him, flushed, then shook her head and looked away.

''If we stay in one place, I can try my luck with snares.'' *And this is as good a place to lure Tony Morano as any I've seen so far.*

''What—'' Francesca cleared her throat and began shaking out the parachutes ''—what will you use to make these snares?''

''Oh, maybe the chute cords. Even the right sort of vines'll do.'' He watched her finish shaking out the chutes and advance to some low bushes a few feet away. Her tousled hair hung down her back in a riot of coppery curls, and she moved like a— *Christ! Don't look at her, you idiot! You tired of living, or what?*

Rafe forced himself to concentrate on securing the speared trout across two forked stakes he'd cut earlier. He went back to his rationale for staying put for a while.

''Then, too, moving ahead won't make it any easier for search planes to spot us. Might even make it harder. Here, we're as visible from the air as we're likely to be.''

She seemed pleased by his explanation, although she hadn't asked him for one. Rafe eyed her surreptitiously as they continued with the morning activities. He could detect no hint that she was aware of what had happened during the night. Now he even heard her humming softly to herself while she finished shaking out the folds of the chutes and hung them over the low brush to air.

But his eyes were drawn to her again. Watching her move, with those long legs and that neat little butt all too evident as she bent to spread the chutes, he wished he could be less aware of it. *Valera's daughter. Christ!*

But Francesca was every bit as aware of the incident as Rafe. She'd been aware of it while studying the trout he'd caught with his bare hands and she'd had to turn suddenly, to hide her blush, remembering the exciting touch of those strong, tanned fingers.

She was aware of it again with the sexy flash of his grin after she shyly offered to share her toothbrush, which she'd found in her carryon.

"Don't know if I should, little nun. It might taste too good," he said.

And she was definitely aware of it later, when she bathed in the stream and the cold water made her nipples pucker, yet not with the same feeling caused by his touch. She tentatively ran her own hands over her breasts to test this phenomenon when Rafe was well out of sight. She realized now, more than ever, she knew next to nothing about her own body when it came to such things, and she found herself not only curious, but worried; she was to be married next month, and what if Carlo found her ignorance unappealing?

But it had been Rafe who came to mind, not Carlo, when the friction of her palms over the erect nipples under her wet teddy produced a shock of pleasure down below. Gasping, she'd been too stunned to move for a minute. Then she'd hurried out of the water, determined to put the whole business aside until she could examine it more carefully in a rational frame of mind.

But when Rafe returned a short while later, she could hardly look at him. If she met his eyes, she was sure she would somehow give herself away.

The day wore on in a desultory fashion, with no sign of rescue coptors or planes. Rafe seemed unconcerned about this, saying it was still early for them to have found the wreckage. But he built up the fire and frequently added dampened grasses to produce smoke that could be seen as a signal.

Meanwhile, the mild daytime temperatures and sunny skies were an added inducement to rest, which was something Rafe insisted Francesca needed, even if he didn't. He'd made and set his snares, using as bait fish entrails and the quail's head he'd saved and hidden.

But while they waited for the snares to work, he went upstream and "tickled" a few more trout to roast for an afternoon meal. They shared it unhurriedly in the shade of some gnarled scrub oak near the mouth of the ravine. With a faint shudder, Francesca forced herself to ignore the loaded gun she'd noticed was always within his reach.

"So, Rafael O'Hara, how is it you know so much about catching food in the wild? And building signal fires that will smoke when you want them to, hmm?" Francesca asked as they were finishing the meal. "Were you in the Boy Scouts or—"

A bark of laughter cut her off, and she immediately felt foolish. Of course. Not *him!* No more than the eagle she glimpsed soaring overhead had attended dancing school.

She hated the heat that rose in her cheeks and looked hurriedly away. Why did she always feel so gauche with him?

"I'm sorry, 'Cesca," he said when the laughter sub-sided. "It was an honest question, and I shouldn't have laughed. But if you'd been in my shoes—" He shook his head, chuckling.

"No, you shouldn't have," she agreed. But she was mollified somewhat by the apology and, oddly enough, by the easy familiarity of the "'Cesca." Silently, she sounded out the syllables in her head . . . *Chess-kah.* . . . No one had ever called her that, and she rather liked it.

"But you see," he went on, "where I came from, the only boys in groups were street gangs, and they didn't exactly go in for helping little old ladies across the street—unless it was to mug them."

He went on, then, to describe his boyhood on the streets of New York City. He detailed the few early, good memories he had of the big Irish cop who was his father, then glossed over the string of foster homes he said he'd rather forget. The story he told was eye-opening, if not entirely pleasant, and Francesca grew sober and quiet as she listened.

She was aware, without knowing how, that he wasn't a man inclined to talk about his past, and she felt oddly moved that he would share it with her. Moreover, she felt strangely drawn by these glimpses into his boy-hood, knowing they were bits and pieces that had shaped the man.

"And your mother, what of her?" she asked at one point. The loss of her mother when she was small had had a significant influence on her own life. She was al-ways curious about other people's mothers, wondering what it would have been like to have one.

"I don't remember her at all, really. The old man used to tell me things about her, and sometimes I'd get a glimmer—you know, like how she'd get these deep

dimples when she smiled, or the way her dark eyes'd
light up when he called her 'Peg.'"

The dimples she gave you, Francesca thought. *Ah,
Rafe, I know your pain. To have little more than the
secondhand memory of some dimples... Still, it is more
than I carry. I wonder if they made your father feel all
quivery inside, the way I do when you flash that grin.
Ah, but your blue, blue eyes—those, you must have
from your father....*

"Her name was Margarita, but the old man used the
nickname Peg. He told me nobody got away with calling her that but him."

"Margarita? She was Spanish, then?"

"Puerto Rican, baby. Or like they put it in good ol'-
fashioned street lingo—a *spic*. Of course, after a while,
they never said it anymore. Or not where I could hear
it."

"You ... fought them?"

He laughed, lightly this time. "Yeah, I guess you
could say that."

"Perhaps if your mother had lived, you would not
have grown up so..."

"Tough? Don't bet on it, kid. In that neighborhood,
you got tough real soon—to stay alive."

She nodded, then glanced at him speculatively. "But
someone must have taught you some gentleness, I think.
The way you handled those poor horses and got them
out of the plane when—"

He was shaking his head. "Animals and people are
two different things in my book, 'Cesca. Or animals and
little kids together, I guess I could say. They're the only
true innocents in the world...without guile, giving you
back honestly what you give them."

He looked at her sharply. "The only trouble is, little kids grow up. Then they become a different kind of animal—one you don't trust if you're smart."

Now it was she who was shaking her head. "There still must have been someone . . . some softening influence, I think. A—a human animal raised on the streets would not have been as kind and patient with an old woman like Tía Pilar, no?"

And you're a lot more perceptive than I figured, little nun. Where'd you learn to read people so well, locked up in that convent? Smart, too. But then, I figured that . . . saw it in those eyes. The eyes always tell you.

"No," Rafe agreed aloud. "There *was* somebody. . . ." He went on to tell her about Father Tomás, the Catholic priest who found him half-dead after a street war and got him to a hospital, where they saved his life. When he was only fourteen. Father Tomás, who became like a second father to him, getting him a job in the settlement house, coaching basketball and playing big brother to some of the younger kids. Father Tomás, who'd set him on a different path, where he might have stayed to this day—except that he got turned off it. Totally. Turned off it the morning he learned the good padre was dead—from a vicious mugging believed to have been at the hands of some of the same kids he'd been working with.

It grew very quiet after he finished. The only sounds to break the stillness were the furtive rustlings of some small creature in the scrub and a faint call of birds in the distance. Rafe looked deep in thought, as if he were back in time, with the people and things he'd talked about. Finally, his eyes shifted . . . met hers. There was an indecipherable look in them.

And then it was almost as if he regretted sharing those intimate details. He rose abruptly, barely glancing at Francesca.

"Hey, make yourself useful, huh, little nun? Throw those fish bones in the fire and see that it doesn't go out. I'm gonna go check the snares."

And then he left.

Francesca didn't see him again until it was dark. He was silent when he returned to camp, his face shuttered and unrevealing. Wordlessly, he spitted a small animal of some kind, which he'd skinned and brought with him, and he began to roast it.

Francesca felt intimidated by that taut silence. So much so, she refrained from asking him where he'd been. Or telling him that she'd worried. He'd been gone for hours. At first she'd used the time to mull over the things he'd told her. To ponder their implications and try to see how they might explain him. And then she'd fallen asleep, succumbing to a full stomach and the lazy droning of insects in the shade.

But a dream of Rafe and those grooves in his cheeks, those very male dimples, made her awake with a start, her body aching with some deep, nameless longing.

After a while, when he still hadn't appeared, she'd begun to fear something had happened to him. There were the wildcats she'd read about in mountains like these. Not to mention screed slopes with dangerous footing, where a man could fall and break a leg or hit his head on a rock.

She'd even considered taking Flama to search for him. But by then it was almost dark, and without a light to see where she was going, she knew it would be useless.

And now, here he was, as if nothing were wrong, roasting some meat for their supper.

The hunter home from the hills.

But with no word of explanation, no greeting. Only this—this *damned* silence! Furious that he could reduce her to such a blaspheming state—it had been a point of pride with her at school not to give in to what she'd regarded as the other girls' trivial rebelliousness—she ate her share of the meat in equal silence. Then she abruptly made up the bed and flung herself on it, with her back to him. Let *him* worry about the damned bones and the fire!

Rafe cleaned up the remains of the meal. Then, despite the chill in the air—or more aptly, because of it—he went down to the stream to bathe. He took a long time with it, shaving as well, and welcoming the icy water on his heated flesh.

Too bad it didn't cool his mind down, too. He could still see her sitting there that afternoon. Stretched out like a lazy cat, all sated and sensual after eating. Christ, could she possibly not know what she did to a man when she looked like that? Like she'd just had sex and was thinking about having more?

Yes. Yes, she could. Because she was that anomaly that shouldn't exist in today's world. Not in the nineties. An innocent who was no longer a little kid but who somehow hadn't been corrupted. Yet.

And then he'd gone and told her those things. He'd done it on impulse at first, and maybe because he'd wanted to get some reaction. To prick the bubble of that never-never land the little nun had been living in. And he'd gotten his reaction, all right. The changing expressions on her face, in her eyes, as he'd talked had made him feel as if she'd been right there with him all those years ago. He'd seen his own hunger for the mother he never knew, the father he missed so goddamned much, it hurt. Hunger he thought he'd hidden so well. Even from himself.

He'd seen in her eyes his own pain at the padre's betrayal. Not sympathy, but *empathy*. Like she'd *been there*. Damn! Where did she come off, having all that in her? She was just a *kid*, for chrissake!

A kid he wanted to make love to until they both couldn't see straight. He wanted to watch her face when he taught her sweet, unholy pleasure. He wanted to look into her eyes when he took her. He wanted to hear her moan when he carried her to those wide, mindless shores and made her a woman. *His* woman. And he wanted to keep her safe from the goddamned world forever.

And who's in never-never land now, hotshot?

Rafe's laugh rounded on a snarl as he left the stream. It was going to be a long night.

The fire had burned low, and he added wood to it, watching the flames lick and catch. It had gotten even colder, and they'd need the extra warmth. And then there was the outside chance they might send search planes out at night. It wasn't usual, but Valera was said to be a maniac when he went after something, and there was no doubt he'd be coming after his daughter. Of course, Tony Morano might come for her first.

The thought of Francesca made him sigh, and he turned to look at her. She was curled up with her back to him, and he figured she must be asleep. He knew she hadn't been too happy with him when he'd come back, but how the hell could he tell her what he didn't even understand himself? That being with her was threatening to tear him apart. *Valera's daughter.*

With another sigh, Rafe shucked his shoes and noiselessly lowered himself to the makeshift bed, well clear of Francesca's still body. He had just located the first constellation and was about to count its stars when he felt her shift on the chutes.

"Rafe?"

There was a brief hesitation before he answered. "Yeah?"

"I—I know you didn't mean to tell me all those things this afternoon. That—that you're a private person and...well, I just...I just wanted you to know that I'm sorry. I'd give them back to you if I could. But I can't, and...well, I just wanted you to know."

He didn't answer, and after a moment Francesca gathered her courage and went on. "I—I wanted to tell you, too, that—that I wasn't entirely asleep last night, Rafe. I mean, when you...when you held me. I was awake, and I...Rafe, would you hold me like that again?"

"'Cesca...."

"Because I don't think anything could make me feel more wonderful than that. It was—"

A quavering expulsion of breath interposed, and then she heard Rafe's husky whisper.

"Come here, 'Cesca."

She went, a bit uncertain, despite the boldness of moments before, and Rafe reached out and pulled her tightly against him. But he made no move to do more than that. For a moment he just held her, her head tucked into his shoulder, the light scent of jasmine from her hair drifting up to him like something out of a dream.

"You understand what you're asking, don't you?" he said finally. His voice still had that husky quality, and she thought she felt a certain tension in his muscles.

Hesitantly, she nodded, and the silk of her hair gliding along the underside of his chin, along his neck, made him clench his teeth against the surge of heat to his loins. He was hard as a rock, and the pressure at the crotch of his jeans was painful.

"I—I think so," she went on. "I think I want to know...that I want you to make love to me."

A tight sigh. "You've gotta know that's not possible, 'Cesca. Not at all wise and therefore...therefore not possible."

"But—"

"Shh..." He shifted and turned to look down at her.

The gibbous moon had cleared the mountaintops, and he could see her face clearly. What he saw made his breath catch.

She was watching him intently, cat-green eyes silvered by moonlight. Huge and translucent, they dominated her face, which had an almost elfin quality, superimposed on features already ethereal by the evanescent shimmer of the moon.

His breath escaped slowly while he raised a hand and lightly traced the contours of her face. "I want you to know," he murmured, and his fingers followed the winged curve of a brow, "that it's not because—" he touched a sculpted cheekbone with the backs of his fingers "—I don't find you desirable." He ran his thumb across her lower lip. "Because I do. Sweet, holy Mary, 'Cesca, you've got to *know* I do!"

"But then, why—"

His thumb pressed lightly against her lips, stilling her. "Because, dammit, you're who you are, and I'm—I'm not for you. *You're Esteban Valera's daughter, 'Cesca.* And I'm supposed to deliver you, virginally intact, if you'll forgive my bluntness, to the bridegroom he's handpicked for you. Does that say it plainly enough?''

Francesca swallowed and tried to nod, but found tears clogging her throat. ''But—but that's just the problem, Rafe. I'm supposed to be married—to a stranger—and I—*I don't know anything!* I'm twenty-three years old and I've never even been kissed by a man!''

Tears were shimmering in her eyes, and as she spoke, one traced its way down her face, catching in the indentation at the corner of her mouth. Without thinking, Rafe lowered his head and touched his lips to it.

Francesca released a watery sigh. Her warm breath mingled with his, and Rafe felt her shudder.

It was too much. With a low groan, he threaded his fingers through her hair and captured her head while his mouth closed over hers.

The kiss was as gentle as he could make it, given his hunger, but Rafe hadn't counted on hers. Francesca's lips trembled under his at their first joining, but a hint of increased pressure from him made them part eagerly to accept the first careful probing of his tongue.

Her response both astounded and scared him. He felt her arms twine around his neck while her tongue darted tentatively to meet his, then again. Her movements were hesitant, awkward enough to show her inexperience, but their effect on Rafe was cataclysmic.

With a harsh gasp, he tore his mouth from hers. His eyes were tightly shut, his breathing ragged, as he braced his forehead against hers, trying to gather his senses enough to think.

Francesca was equally overwhelmed. She had spent the long minutes waiting for him to come back from the stream with frustrated imaginings of what it would be like to kiss him. To have him kiss her back. But never had she imagined this! This intense, pleasureful longing that threaded its way through her body and curled and uncurled somewhere low and deep inside. The sense of being hot and cold all over. And above all, the certain knowledge that only Rafe O'Hara could make her feel this way. No one else. Never, if she lived a thousand years.

"Rafe . . ." It was a throaty whisper. "I don't want this from a stranger. *I want it with you.*"

Rafe took a deep breath, released it as he drew her close, her head tucked under his chin. She was right in a way. Why the hell should *any* woman—least of all, her—living in the last decade of the twentieth century, be expected to go as a virgin in marriage to a man she'd never met? It *stunk!*

And he'd had no idea she was twenty-three years old. Hell, she looked no more than seventeen or eighteen. A kid!

But she sure as hell doesn't feel like a kid, said a taunting voice in his head.

And then an idea began to form in his mind, and in seconds he knew what he would do—if he could only maintain the strength to pull it off. *Because if he didn't, Valera would likely kill him.*

"'Cesca . . ." he whispered as his hand lightly stroked her hair. "Baby? Look at me."

Francesca sighed, sensing a carefully articulated rejection, but she did as he asked.

Rafe gave her that lopsided half smile of his. "You win, sweetheart. I'm gonna give us what we both want, but—"

"*Oh, Rafe—*"

"To a point!"

"I . . . don't understand."

He chuckled, but even to Rafe, the sound had a sardonic edge to it. "No, but you will."

Then, seeing her frown, he cupped her chin to make sure he had her full attention and explained. "I'm going to make love to you, 'Cesca. I'll hold you, kiss you, touch you—including the way I did last night. I'll do any and everything to pleasure you. Anything that you want me to, that is—except one. When we're done, you'll still be a virgin. Understand?"

Slowly, tentatively, she nodded. "I . . . I think so."

Rafe laughed, drawing her back into his arms. "Uh-uh, kitten—you better *know* so!" And he nuzzled her ear, whispering in it exactly what he would—or would not—do.

Francesca groaned softly at the explicit images he summoned, and she felt heat surge to her cheeks.

But Rafe only laughed again, a soft, easy laughter that ruffled the tendrils of hair at her ear. Then he drew her beneath him and watched her hair spread out around her head like a thick cloud of undulating silk.

"Beautiful . . ." he whispered. "Christ, you're so damned beautiful, I can't believe you're real. . . ."

And then it began.

First with kisses, because she told him shyly of her imaginings as she'd lain there earlier. But these were kisses unlike anything she'd ever imagined, ever been capable of imagining. Some feather-light and soft as the warmth of his breath combining with hers; some quick and teasing, with subtle nibblings; some playful, as when he caught her lower lip lightly between his teeth, only to let it slip away and kiss the corner of her mouth, touch it with his tongue.

And then he was asking for more, covering her mouth entirely, moving his in languid, lazy circles while his hands captured her face to hold it for this gentle possession.

"Ah, 'Cesca," he breathed when they briefly broke apart, "I could kiss you all night and never get tired of it. I think—" he kissed her eyes "—I could kiss..." his lips moved to her ear "...you forever...." And then he found her mouth again.

She felt his tongue glide along the seam of her lips... teasing... skillful, and her heart began to thud in her chest. Her lips parted under the subtlest increase of pressure, and now his tongue was seeking entrance, now fencing with hers, now tasting the sweetness inside.

"Easy, kitten... don't rush it," he whispered when her arms wound around him to urge him closer. But his own heart was beginning to accelerate, to match the rhythm of hers; he could feel them beating in tandem, her breasts thrusting against his chest as she urged him closer, closer....

And now she clung to him while he tasted of her, exploring, bringing their mouths together in a seamless joining. These were drugging kisses, intoxicating, like a heady wine. Soon Francesca felt the world teeter and begin to spin, Rafe's warmth her only center as he held her; his big body against hers her only reality.

Rafe felt her begin to move and twist beneath him, asking for more, even if she didn't realize it. He broke away with a breathless laugh, burying his face in her hair.

"Shh, love," he murmured. "We've got all night. Slowly, now, hear? We'll just...slow it down...."

And then he began to remove her clothes, but ever so slowly, one piece at a time.

"You cold?" he whispered against her ear when her jacket landed beside them and he felt her shiver.

"Oh, no, Rafe! Just...all quivery inside. And—and a little like—like I did last night. You know...when I woke and you—and your—"

"And my hand was here?" he questioned, cupping her breast, testing its shape beneath the thin material of her blouse.

She gasped, then nodded quickly. But she turned her head and closed her eyes, unable to meet his.

Rafe felt a leap of fire sear his loins when her nipple hardened under his palm, but he fought it under control, keeping his eyes on her face.

"Uh-uh, baby. No fair closing your eyes. I want to see them. I want to see you looking at me. Come on, now, look at me—"

Her head turned, and her eyes fluttered open.

"—while I do this..." he breathed, and his thumb teased the puckered nipple and made it throb.

"Rafe," she groaned, feeling a sweet, piercing response at the juncture of her thighs.

"Tell me about it, 'Cesca," he urged. "Tell me how it makes you feel." And again his thumb worked its magic, and yet again, until she cried his name aloud. And he had to stop and hold her very close, stilling her with hushed words and soft, gentle kisses.

"Shh...It's okay, love. You're just so brand-new at this, that's all...."

"Oh, Rafe," she whispered, unaware that her blouse had joined her jacket on the ground. "It—you made me feel like—like every feeling I'd ever had was coming together all at once. Or—oh, I can't explain it! Rafe? Is this how—how it's supposed to be? Is it always this way?"

Rafe ran his eyes over the perfection of her breasts under the sheer fabric of the teddy, then swept her hair back from her temples and met her eyes. "Know it, 'Cesca. This is how it's supposed to be—but hardly ever is."

She looked at him with wonder. "Do—do you mean *you've* hardly ever—"

"I mean I've *never*."

"But haven't you—*ohh*..."

"You talk too much, 'Cesca," he teased as he pushed the cup of the teddy down below her breast and the friction of the lace excited an already-turgid nipple.

Then conversation ceased as his mouth captured the crest he'd bared and he gave it his full attention. Taking his time, he played with it like a master. Sucking, nibbling, he teased the puckered flesh with teeth and tongue. And Francesca could only writhe and moan beneath him, threading her fingers through the thick, dark curls of his hair, pressing him closer as she murmured his name, over and over again.

Rafe could scarcely believe how responsive she was. A slight touch here, and she was quivering beneath his hand; there, and she was moaning her pleasure. She was like a finely tuned instrument, and he was the master musician who knew how to make her sing. The memory passed briefly in his mind of how he'd called her "little nun," and he had a moment's urge to call himself a fool. Francesca...sweet 'Cesca...a thousand delights and endless surprises, and they'd hardly even begun....

But again, Rafe found his own responses careening dangerously, straining to break his control. Closing his eyes, he took a deep, shuddering breath, trying to focus on something besides the woman in his arms.

But it wasn't easy. Francesca had begun to take an active role. She had somehow parted his jacket and undone the buttons on the shirt underneath. And when he felt slender fingers slide inquisitively through the mat of hair on his chest and brush across his own, flat nipple, Rafe nearly lost it.

"What's wrong?" she asked, bewildered. "That's what you did to me, and I wanted to see if—"

Rafe let out his breath in a rush. "Nothing's wrong, kitten." *Not a goddamned thing, if I could only play this out the way my body's screaming to.* "In fact, it was all too damned right."

He shifted their positions until he was sitting and held her in his lap. In the process her skirt had ridden up around her hips, and he clenched his teeth and forced himself to look away when he caught a glimpse of the auburn thatch beneath the sheerness of the teddy's lace.

"I—I'm not sure I follow you," she said.

Rafe chuckled, his breath feathering wisps of hair below her ear. "Darlin', that's just the point. You *were* following me—doing something I'd done to you, remember?"

"Mmm..." It sounded like a purr, and Rafe ground his teeth to combat the effect it had on him. On an erection that was so in need of release, it was painful. He forced himself to recall what he'd been saying.

"Well, you *can't* follow me that way, 'Cesca."

"But—"

"Not because it's wrong. Because it's unbelievably effective. And we had an agreement, remember? You've gotta come away from here intact, and I can't let anything change that."

She wriggled around to bend over his ear and whisper shyly in it, and a stream of Spanish expletives exploded from him before he remembered it was her native language, and he shifted her from his lap. That little wriggling action, right on top of the bulge in his jeans, had almost done it. And now this. Hell, he was so hot, he was ready to explode.

Ruthlessly ignoring her bewildered protests, Rafe eased her down on the bedding and stretched out alongside her. Then he caught the back of her head with his hand and stilled her with a long, slow and achingly tender kiss. It went on and on, with endlessly subtle variations in pressure and movement.

When he finally eased them apart, Rafe grinned at her, the lopsided grin she was beginning to find could make her heart race faster than anything. "Back to basics for a while, kitten. Kissing. It's a lot safer."

"Is it?" she questioned, and he had a moment to wonder about the gleam in her eye before she curved her hand around the back of his neck and brought his head down to hers.

And then she kissed him. Mouth parted, wet, tongue seeking and probing, then darting and plundering, it was wild and bold and eager—and absolutely wanton. When she'd finished, Rafe was left wondering if any woman had ever really kissed him before.

"*Bruja,*" he accused. He was laughing, but with wonder, as her cat's eyes smiled triumphantly back at him.

"If I am a witch, then you are my familiar," she purred in sultry response.

Rafe growled low in his throat, then caught her to him. It was unreserved passion now as, for an unbridled moment, he kissed her fully, totally, as she'd shown him she'd learned how. Openmouthed, hot, greedy, they savored each other, tongue meeting tongue, mouths crisscrossing, reaching, yearning, straining. They clung together, their limbs intertwined, rolling on the ground until one was on top, then the other, and still they kissed. It was as if they couldn't get enough of each other, but they had to somehow try. Oh, they had to try!

Finally it was Rafe, barely recalling the limits he'd set, who broke them apart. Breathless, gasping for air and some semblance of sanity, he held her still beneath him, making her meet his eyes.

"'Cesca, this is crazy. If I'd known when I started— Ah, hell! I think maybe we'd better qui—"

"No!" Francesca's eyes pleaded more than her words. "No, please, Rafe. Don't say we've got to stop. I'll—I'll be good, I promise, only—"

A soft groan cut her off, and he buried his face in her hair. "God, sweetheart, you don't know what you're asking! I swear, I—" He took a deep, settling breath. "But... okay... only, do as I say, huh? Do *only* as I say?"

She smiled against his curls. "Oh, yes, Rafe... I *promise.*"

He released her and grinned, and again, it was that lopsided grin that made her heart leap. Then he kissed her lightly on the nose, the lips, the lips again. And then all at once his look grew serious. He traced the contours of her face with his thumb.

"Exquisite...beautiful...Francesca...so very, very... lovely...I could wish..."

The whispered words died away, and he was kissing her lightly everywhere. Eyes...nose...chin; brow and curve of neck; then the creamy expanse below, feeling the pulse that fluttered there. But while he kissed and caressed, she began to move under his touch, until he slid his lips to her ear and whispered, "Softly, baby...please...?"

And she went still, holding herself in check now, beginning to realize what it must be costing him to do the same.

"Good girl," he murmured, and kissed her ear while his hand strayed to her breasts. There, he fondled and teased, while his teeth nipped lightly at her lobe.

Her breath caught, and he murmured something low and inaudible but continued to stroke, teasing her nipples erect, nuzzling all the while the tender skin beneath her ear.

Then Francesca felt his hand move along the curve of her waist and hip, then lower still. She held her breath, released it, held it again as he stroked and caressed, moving to the soft inner flesh of her thighs.

She was trembling now, partly from the strain of holding herself back, but more in anticipation of Rafe's touch. This was unfamiliar ground—all new—and something deep inside was beginning to uncurl, sending a spear of longing to her very core.

Again he whispered something soft and low, but she never really heard it. All her senses were tuned to the butterfly touch of his fingers as they eased the teddy aside and found the slippery, moist heat of her.

"*Ra-a-afe...*" she moaned, but he captured her lips in a kiss so sweetly tender, she could only sigh into his mouth and kiss him back, her heart thudding wildly in her breast.

And Rafe was reeling. Hot and wet, she was more than ready for the joining he couldn't give her. His own flesh was throbbing, burning, hovering on the razor edge of his fragile control. But he'd said he'd show her, that he'd do what she wanted within the limits he'd set, and he was going to try. But, hell, she was so goddamned ready for him!

Slowly, he probed the tight, inner recesses of her virgin flesh with his finger. She was slick and hot past telling, and he could feel her tremble as he held her.

He trailed a path of kisses along her throat and neck, and then lower; he captured a nipple in his mouth and nibbled, teasing it with teeth and lips, while below, his thumb found the tiny, erect nub above the entrance to her pleasure. He stroked it . . . once . . . twice—

And heard her cry his name as she came, then came again, her hot, velvety shaft closing around his finger like a vise, her body quaking with the final surrender.

Rafe let her go on until she began to settle slowly back to earth, his own need savagely held in check.

And when she'd finished and was crying softly against him, he wrapped her fiercely in his arms and held her without words.

CHAPTER ELEVEN

RAFE AWOKE TO FIND himself in a condition that was becoming all too familiar; he was fully aroused, and he didn't need the softness of Francesca's unclothed body pressing against his to remind him why. It was enough to recall what that body had done to him when they were both awake. Hell, it was enough to recall the wet dreams that had jarred him awake during the night.

Mouthing a silent expletive, he called himself a fool ten times over. He hadn't endured this kind of prolonged discomfort since he was a boy. Finding women had never been a problem for him. But he'd always made sure they were mature, willing partners who knew what they were getting into from the start: a mutual pleasuring with no ties or commitments, implied or otherwise.

Yet here he was, holding the tantalizingly nubile, naked body of a virgin in his arms. An innocent who was no more capable of knowing what she was getting into than she was of sprouting wings and flying. Who was totally dependent on him—damn fool that he was—to keep her safe from the force of his own lust. And he had only himself to blame.

Rafe shifted slightly in an attempt to ease his discomfort, glancing down at Francesca's sleeping length as he moved. Then he wished he hadn't. The lush curve of a perfect breast slid into view, its coral peak already pebbling from the friction of rubbing against his chest. He swore softly and ground his teeth at the frustrated arousal thrusting painfully against his jeans. Francesca stirred in his arms at that moment, burrowing in closer to him. A smile tilted the corners of her mouth upward.

Hah! Easy for *her* to smile! He'd been unable to resist pleasuring her—satisfying her—several times during the night, despite the torture of his own unfulfillment. Well, he'd been trained to withstand certain forms of torture, hadn't he?

Yeah, a taunting inner voice mocked, *but you never suspected it would be put to* this *kind of test! Are you a masochist or what?*

But even as he mocked himself, Rafe knew self-punishment had nothing to do with it. It was Francesca and the dozen-and-one things he'd begun to see in her that had brought him to this untenable fix. Francesca...with her unsuspected strengths, her unwitting courage, her buoyant spirit and her untarnished soul.

But he knew it had been that last image of her that had been his undoing: Francesca as innocent pawn in Esteban Valera's game.

Yeah, and who else is using her as a pawn, smartass?

The unfamiliar stab of guilt hit him like a sledgehammer blow to the middle, effectively quelling his arousal. He was using Francesca as bait, using her as certainly as the don was using her in a different trap. He couldn't deny it, couldn't lie about it to himself, even if he were inclined to, which he wasn't. It was a nasty fact, and the plain truth was, even if he found it suddenly discomforting, he was stuck with it.

Damn.

Okay, so there was no going back now. But as he looked at Francesca's exquisite face with that smile that hinted at delicious dreams, Rafe made himself a promise. He would play this thing out the way his agent's code said he must, but with one difference—her safety must be paramount; he would protect Francesca at all costs.

This kid—no, scratch that—this woman had become important to him, somehow. She'd gotten under his skin.

He throttled a niggling voice that told him to examine his reasons for letting that happen when he hadn't allowed another human being to do that since Father Tomás died, not even Brad. Settling for the excuse that Francesca Valera was an innocent, he told himself that, like the kids and animals he'd always cared about, she simply deserved his best efforts at keeping her safe. Period.

A sleepy murmur purred against his chest, and he glanced down. Francesca was pushing her perfect, straight little nose into the crisp chest hair made accessible by his open shirt. He smiled as he saw the nose wrinkle, and then suddenly he was looking into a pair of blinking, cat-green eyes. They smiled back at him with heavy-lidded sensuality.

"You're . . . here," she murmured, wonder replacing the sated look as her eyes widened. "I—I didn't just dream you. You're really here, and we—"

Two bright flags of scarlet leapt to her cheeks, and she groaned, burying her face in his shoulder.

Rafe chuckled softly. He could feel the heat of her blush right through the denim of his shirt.

"Uh-uh, kitten," he said as he curled his fingers under her chin and gently tilted it upward. "No fair hiding and trying to pretend we didn't ... do what we did. Besides, I want to see it in your eyes ... see you remembering the things we did together. Call it my reward, if you like, and— Ah, darlin', don't be embarrassed.''

He lowered his head and captured her lips. Held as they were, for his gentle possession, Francesca had no choice but to kiss him back, though she still hadn't opened her eyes.

"Now, look at me, 'Cesca," Rafe murmured after releasing them. "Look at me, and delight in it with me, sweetheart.''

Francesca finally complied, and what she saw in the blue eyes gazing back at her made her breathing falter. There was tenderness there, echoed by the softness of his smile, and the undeniable memory of shared knowledge that made her blush ever more furiously. But more than that, she thought she saw something ... a longing, perhaps? She wasn't certain. It was something she couldn't put a name to, but which pulled at her in a way nothing ever had.

"Sweetheart," Rafe said, and his voice had assumed a sudden, familiar huskiness, "if you keep looking at me like that, I won't be responsible for the consequences.''

She gaped at him, wide-eyed. "But, Rafe, I thought you just told me to—''

"I *know*" he growled, "but that was *before* I realized what looking into your eyes, *and* remembering, would do to me." He glanced down at the erection that was threatening to split his jeans and the last of his control.

Francesca's laughter spilled over him like warm honey, until she followed the path of his gaze. The merriment abruptly ceased, and he watched her go beet red.

He met her eyes and nodded slowly. "That's what you do to me, 'Cesca. It was something you couldn't see, and probably felt only indirectly last night, in the dark. But now..." He captured her hand and trailed it across his abdomen and downward until it met the hard bulge swelling his jeans.

"Feel it...what you do to me, 'Cesca," he murmured thickly.

He saw her eyes widen in astonishment. And then, because everything she thought or felt was reflected in their green translucence, he saw her natural intelligence and curiosity take over. Her eyes shifted to where his hand covered hers and she gazed thoughtfully at the spot for a moment. Then, before he realized what she was up to, he felt her increase the pressure of her fingers and run them experimentally along his swollen prominence.

"Christ!" Rafe caught her hand and pulled it away with lightning speed.

"But Rafe—"

"No buts about it—*or* ands, *or* ifs *or* anything else!" he growled, quickly rising and pulling her to her feet. "Right now, I think a nice cold bath is in order, imp! But put some clothes on before we go down there, huh?"

Francesca had been about to ask him about the dampness she'd felt in the denim, where she'd stroked it, but decided it could wait until another time. Especially since the heat of his gaze as they stood facing each other suddenly made her acutely aware that she was standing fully unclothed before him in broad daylight! *Dios!* She must be blushing all over!

Rafe chuckled as he watched her go stock-still, then make a mad dive for her clothes, which were strewn around the bedding—exactly where he'd removed them last night.

He deliberately turned his back while she dressed, less in deference to her innocent blushes, which he relished, than to preserve his own dwindling control. The sight of her nude body standing at arm's length, bathed in sunlight, would have tempted a saint, and a saint he wasn't.

Francesca knew the Donna Karan suit would never survive a dunking, so she opted for the opaque slip and blouse she'd spread on a bush to dry the day before. Glancing downward after she'd tugged them on, she judged them adequately concealing and replied shyly in the affirmative when Rafe asked if she was "decent" yet.

Rafe used the interlude to shrug off his shirt—and regain control. So when he turned to find Francesca garbed in the virginal white, looking more the school-girl again, he decided it was okay to risk touching her.

"C'mere, darlin'." He smiled tenderly as he held out his arms to her.

With a soft cry, Francesca went into them, felt them wrap warmly around her like a benediction. She was a mixture of roiling emotions right now. They'd been unsettling her ever since she'd awakened naked in Rafe's arms. What did he think of her? Did he think her shamelessly brazen for instigating what had happened last night? Carnal and wanton? Immoral, even?

Yet even more disturbing were her own assessments in the aftermath of what they'd shared. Suddenly her every thought, each newly awakening feeling, was centered on him, filled with him. On Rafe O'Hara, a man she'd disdained as a creature of violence and death.

Ah, but *now!* Now, as he held her tenderly in the morning sunlight, the air around them filled with bird song and the clean, sweet scent of growing things, he wasn't *any* of that.

He might be powerful, yes, and dangerous, too, to the world at large; but to her he was so many other things first. Rafe O'Hara was a strong, intelligent man—a survivor, someone who'd endured a brutal childhood with deprivations she could only begin to imagine, yet he'd managed to grow into a sensitive, caring human being who'd put her needs ahead of his own, despite how difficult this must have been for him. Hardly characteristics of the brutal killer she'd made him out to be!

All these thoughts, and more, were spinning through Francesca's mind as Rafe gave her a swift kiss and caught her hand to run with her to the stream. But by the time they were splashing headlong into the icy water, she'd given up trying to sort them out.

Time enough for such things later. For now, there was just the joy of the moment: the sunshine; the clear, bracing water on their heated skin; his teasing laughter as he sprayed her mercilessly; and hers as she gave back worse than she got, sending him tumbling backward into the *ciénaga* hidden by ferns at the far edge of the stream.

"All right, brat," Rafe growled with unholy mischief in his eyes as he came up covered with oozing mud. He advanced slowly toward her. "You've had it!

An O'Hara's as tolerant of a little horseplay as the next guy. But as you can plainly observe—'' he held his mud-covered hands out in front of him like claws ''—this is no longer an O'Hara.... *This,*'' he added as he headed straight for her, ''is the Creature from the Gloppy La-goon!''

Francesca shrieked, mock fear and delight warring in her laughter as she backed away from him. ''N-now, Rafe,'' she managed to say between giggles, ''you w-wouldn't want t-to do something rash, would you? L-like accosting a poor w-woman who's practically a *nun!*''

Rafe's shout of laughter exploded hard on the heels of that last word, and he lunged for her, closing the gap between them. ''Nun, is it?'' he growled as he engulfed her in a muddy embrace.

Francesca's shrieks dissolved into helpless giggles as he proceeded to slather her with mud from her head to her knees, which was as high as the stream rose at that particular spot.

''Unfair, woman,'' he accused as he ran a slimy fin-ger down the curve of her neck while Francesca wrig-gled against the arm that held her tautly to his side. ''We goopy creatures have ways of dealing with such tac-tics!'' And he proceeded to capture her laughing face with both mud-laden hands and bestow a smacking kiss on her mouth with even muddier lips.

Francesca made a face at the boggy taste this left on her tongue. But in the next instant the corners of her mouth twitched, and she burst out laughing.

''Y-you...'' she said, pointing at Rafe in helpless merriment, ''look...aw-awful!''

"Oh yeah?" Rafe tried to assume a scowl but found it impossible when he was grinning from ear to ear. "Well, you're not looking so hot yourself, lady!"

Francesca glanced down at the garments whose pristine cotton whiteness had covered her so modestly. Not only were they no longer white, but their mud-painted fabric had been rendered semitransparent in the process of getting wet; despite the smears of mud, she could see every detail of the body they clung to, including the pink nipples that had reacted to the cold water by puckering and thrusting against the wet cotton that was molded to her skin.

Rafe had noticed, too, and now his voice went husky as he rephrased his initial comment. "On second thought, lady, *you*—" he took a ragged breath and went on "—are suddenly too hot for comfort."

Francesca swallowed hard, ignoring the heat she felt rising to her face. She was responding instead to the heat in Rafe's gaze. By now, when he looked at her like that, she knew exactly what he was thinking... feeling...because she felt it, too. In the aftermath of last night, she realized, this would always be between them...this elemental knowledge of each other and the intimacies they'd shared.

"Definitely too hot for comfort," Rafe repeated thickly, recognizing the response in her eyes. But he made no move to break away. Like her, he stood there in the knee-deep water, wrapped in shade-dappled sun and the gentle murmur of the stream, as if mezmerized, unable to move.

His eyes left her face and slowly traveled the length of her. They lingered momentarily at the juncture of her slender thighs, where an auburn triangle nestled. Moving upward, they paused again on her breasts, whose weight and shape he knew so well now, watching their tips harden and peak even further under his perusal.

Then he raised his eyes and they locked with hers.

Francesca was the first to speak, though what she said did little to break the spell that bound them. "Rafe," she whispered, "why is it—" she had to clear her throat, start again "—what makes me go all slippery... you know... d-down below, whenever you even l-look at me or..."

A helpless groan tore from Rafe's throat, and he closed the distance between them. "*Inocente... mi hermosa... inocente...* 'Cesca," he rasped as he caught her in his arms and began planting hot, adoring kisses over her mud-streaked face. "So innocent... so impossibly beautiful..."

And then he was lifting her in his arms and carrying her to the deeper part of the stream. There, in waist-high water, he set her down, but not before whispering in her ear the answer to the question she'd asked.

The explanation should have made her blush, she later realized, but Francesca was beyond inhibitions now. Her breathing accelerated as Rafe began removing her muddy garments, placing hot, unnerving kisses on every inch of skin he bared.

Her limbs went limp, and a heaviness settled in her breasts and lower, in her belly and thighs, as he cupped handfuls of water and cleansed her heated flesh, lingering lovingly, expertly, on nipples already aching for his touch, and on the slippery source of the question she'd asked.

She moaned and mewled like a cat when he teased the bud of pleasure above this source, and when he whispered in her ear what it was and why he rubbed it the way he did, she convulsed against him in a paroxysm that made her splinter into a thousand tiny fragments of pleasure.

"Easy, sweetheart," Rafe cautioned thickly as Francesca bucked against him, pressing the swollen, needful flesh of her sex against his hand, which she squeezed between her thighs in a viselike grip.

He took her gently by the shoulders and set her apart from him. "I think maybe we'd better—"

He sucked in his breath as Francesca's hands went to the fly of his jeans and deftly undid the snap and zipper. A groan escaped him as he felt those hands move to the wet denim at his hips and tug downward. He felt his sex spring free, and his immediate inclination was to put a safe distance between them, but a glance at Francesca stopped him.

She was gazing at what she'd revealed, a look of wonder on her expressive face. Hell, it wasn't just wonder, it was almost...reverence. No woman had ever looked at him like that. Rafe wasn't able to decipher entirely his own reaction, how this was making him feel, but he knew that no matter how much it strained his control, he wouldn't move.

He let her look her fill, forcing his ragged breathing to go shallow with the effort it was costing him. He locked his muscles and made himself as still as a statue, even when she bent and pushed at the sodden fabric of his jeans until they lay submerged around his feet. But it was when she straightened and lifted her face to meet his eyes, her own shimmering with wonder and longing, that he nearly lost it.

"'Cesca..." he breathed, the sound of her name wavering on an outrush of air as a shudder seized him. "Kitten, I...don't think I can—"

A harsh cry tore from his lips when he saw her gaze lower and felt her fingers touch the tip of his sex.

She snatched her hand away, her eyes flying to his face. "Oh, *Dios,* I'm sorry! Does it hurt when—"

"God, no!" His eyes, bluer than the bright dome of sky overhead, burned into hers. "It feels like pure heaven and makes me want to bury myself in you! What's painful is knowing I can't and..." Sweat beaded Rafe's brow as he clenched his teeth and ran a hand haphazardly through his hair, trying to make himself focus on the simple act of kicking off his jeans underwater.

"Rafael..."

The throaty timbre of Francesca's voice as she gave his name the Spanish inflection made him eye her sharply, even as its sexy cords vibrated through his body. They were standing about a foot apart, both completely nude for the first time, and he was keenly aware of the danger.

The auburn thatch at the apex of her thighs beckoned through the crystal-clear water, and her full, perfect breasts, tip-tilted and proud, were beaded with tiny droplets that caught the sunshine and sparkled with prisms of light.

But he closed his eyes and bit down hard on his desire, forced himself to listen as she told him, in her native tongue because she said it was somehow easier for her to be so bold, what she meant to do: to pleasure him in the same way he'd pleasured her, if only he'd show her how.

Reasons for refusing flickered through his mind; they were playing with fire, and anyone with an ounce of brains would stop before they both got scorched. But he rejected them, one by one, drawn by her plea, by the anticipation shining in her lovely eyes.

Slowly, he nodded, and watched her eyes slant upward, never more catlike as she smiled at him. Planting his feet apart in the water, he reached for her slowly. His hands cupped her face, and he threaded his fingers through the damp hair at the sides of her head, tilting her face up toward his. Then, his every muscle taut with control, he lowered his head and claimed her mouth.

The kiss was languid and sensual, belying the tension in Rafe's body as he clamped down on the desire pounding through his loins. He knew his full erection was grazing her belly, despite the space he'd tried to keep between them, but he made himself concentrate on the sweetness of her mouth as he explored it lazily with his tongue.

Then his lips slid to her ear and, in husky Spanish, he began telling her what she might do to please him.

Francesca listened in wondering delight to Rafe's softly murmured words. They matched the movements of the hands that took hers and placed them on his flesh, guiding her trembling fingers...encouraging... coaxing...urging—

Until a harsh, animal groan of pleasure wrenched his lips apart and he pulled her hard against him. Held tightly in his embrace, her hand wedged between them, fingers still curled around his throbbing sex, she felt the hot spewing of his seed against her belly.

And Francesca, giddy with wonder and a strange sense of power, knew for her there'd never be a greater joy than she felt right then—at the pleasure she'd been able to give him. It was the first thing she told him, standing on tiptoe and shyly whispering in his ear, when his arms finally relaxed around her.

Rafe touched his knuckles to the underside of her chin and tipped it up until she was looking at him. His eyes, heavy-lashed and sensual, were as blue as the gentians she'd seen in Madre Dolorosa's garden as he smiled at her.

"No greater joy? Maybe..." he said as his thumb found her lower lip and traced its fullness. "But I suspect there's still a thing or two waiting in the wings to give you joy, 'Cesca...joy you have no way of imagining yet. But your time will come, darlin'. For a woman like you, there probably can't be a complete fulfillment without marriage, and... Well, let's just say I envy your Carlo Pag—

"'Cesca? What's wrong? Hey, don't go tearing off in a huff!"

Francesca had wrenched herself out of his arms and was pushing through the waist-deep water in a thrashing fury. How *could* he bring up her fiancé at a time like this? After—after what they'd just shared! Didn't he realize—she felt the sting of tears and swiped at them angrily with the back of her hand—didn't he realize she didn't *want* such things with Carlo Pagnani? Didn't want them with *anyone* else?

She heard Rafe call after her before muttering some choice Anglo Saxon curses only half under his breath, but she didn't turn or slow down. The tears were falling faster now than she could wipe them away, and the last thing she wanted was for him to see what a fool she was being, crying over him!

Yet she was not only in tears, but shuddering with sobs when Rafe found her, catching up to her near the spot where they'd shared lunch the day before.

"'Cesca...? Ah, sweetheart, *don't!*" Rafe dropped to the ground where she was huddled and pulled her into his arms. "Kitten, listen to me," he murmured. "I know I'm an insensitive clod who says things—"

"You *are* not!" Francesca pulled away enough to look at him, green eyes fierce, despite the tears spilling onto her cheeks. "You are the most sensitive, caring man I know, and I won't listen to you denigrating yourself that way!"

Rafe couldn't help the grin that tugged the corners of his mouth upward. "You couldn't know too many... men, that is."

But while he teased, his mind was busily sorting out the things he'd said that could have hurt her enough to make her act this way. *Christ, to make her cry!* And when he recalled that it was his mention of Pagnani, of her future marriage, he figured he had a pretty good idea of what the problem was. What was it she'd said to him last night? *I don't want this with anyone else. I want it with you.*

So that was it, she'd begun to bond to him in a way that was more dangerous than she knew. He'd become more to her than a surrogate lover... a stand-in for the husband she'd worried about not knowing enough to please. And if he knew what was good for him—for both of them—he'd better begin to disabuse her of that, pronto!

Well, he knew a surefire cure for virginal infatuation, at least where *he* was the object. All he had to do was let her really get to know him... learn some of the heavy stuff about him, stuff that would disillusion her wide-eyed attachment quicker than she could say, "Rafe, you're a bastard!"

Ignoring a flicker of something that felt dangerously close to regret, Rafe turned his full attention to the woman looking at him with green fire in her eyes.

"And don't make jokes," she was saying. "I know you by now, Rafe O'Hara, and you could never be the clod you just called yourself!"

Do you, 'Cesca? Let's see if you still think so in a little while. "C'mon," Rafe said after wiping away her tears with his fingers and giving her a light kiss on the forehead. "Let's get some clothes on, and then, maybe... Feel like taking a walk with me? Stretch our legs a little?" Francesca gave him a dazzling smile that went straight to his gut. It was almost painful and nearly made him reconsider. But Rafe reminded himself of the consequences if he did, and stuck to his plan.

Leaving Francesca to dress, he fished his jeans out of the stream and tugged them on soaking wet. Then, deliberately shunning his shirt, he converted his holster back into the shoulder variety and strapped it over his bare chest. The last thing he did before they set off was to check the clip in the semi, in full view of Francesca, before carefully inserting it in the holster.

They walked until his jeans were nearly dry. Talking at length about things Rafe skillfully steered into the conversation, they strolled hand in hand, never straying far from camp, their voices low and desultory, blending with the sounds of nature all around them.

But as he maintained this casual air of unhurried exchange, Rafe proceeded to tell Francesca things he hadn't told anyone in years—not since Father Tomás—things that, in the years since then, he'd revealed to no one. He told her about his years on the streets, but in detail this time... the gang wars... the stiletto he'd wielded with consummate skill, including the incident in which he'd sliced open and rendered permanently useless the arm of a foster parent.

"But what happened between you to cause such a violent reaction?" Francesca questioned sharply at that point.

"Nothing happened," Rafe said evasively. He should have figured she'd want to know details, causes. But he wasn't about to tell her the bastard had been beating him with a belt buckle; his objective didn't include having her sympathize with him, or worse, making him out to be some kind of a hero. "He was drunk, that's all."

But what Rafe hadn't figured on was Francesca's passing acquaintance with something similar. One of the children at the convent, a twelve-year-old named Consuela, was there on a scholarship provided by the diocese; she'd been rescued from a foster home by the bishop himself—a home in which she'd been brutally beaten by a foster father who was drunk.

"I see" was all she said to Rafe.

But she averted her gaze, not wanting to let him see the light of understanding she felt he might notice in her eyes. Rafe seemed to know everything she was thinking or feeling, and she was certain it was her eyes that gave her away. Besides, if he wanted to hide the things that had made him vulnerable in the past, she wouldn't let on that she knew or suspected his vulnerability; she'd learned enough from sharing things with Ramón over the years to recognize macho pride when she saw it!

The talk shifted to his years at the settlement house. Not that Rafe had planned to dwell on what he regarded as one of the few positive periods of his wayward youth, but Francesca had a way of asking questions....

"You...loved him very much, Padre Tomás, didn't you?" she asked at one point.

Rafe hesitated, then nodded. "Enough so that when he was killed by those punks, I made up my mind never to let myself get that close to someone again." Here he paused, turning to look at her. "Nothing's worth that kind of loss to me, 'Cesca," he added pointedly.

"You mean if you don't allow yourself to—to feel for someone, you can't be hurt if they're taken away?"

She was watching him carefully, those green eyes probing his with all the intelligence and insight he already knew she possessed, and Rafe knew he had to be careful about how much he revealed, and about what.

"Something like that," he answered as he caught her hand again and resumed walking. "Although I know I didn't think it all out consciously at the time, the fact is, the day after the padre's funeral, I walked out of that kind of life and never looked back."

"'That kind of life,' she repeated softly. "You are speaking of a life in which you...cared for others, no?" *A life in which you dared to love, my darling?*

"Look, it wasn't the way it was for most people with me, 'Cesca." He stopped walking again and looked at her. "I was a loner, you see...someone with no family, no other...attachments besides...the padre. It's like putting all your eggs in one basket, y'know? And then one day, somebody comes along and—" He snapped his fingers. "The basket's gone, and so are all your goddamned eggs!"

The look in Francesca's eyes was nearly his undoing, and he quickly glanced away, resumed walking without recapturing her hand. There it was again, that look of empathy, of complete understanding for the way it had been for him. God, what was wrong with him? He was supposed to be disillusioning her, not baring his soul!

"You know," she said thoughtfully as he paused to hold some branches out of the way for her, "the same thing might have happened to me, I think. If I'd been older when my mother died. And if I hadn't had Papa and Ramón...but Papa, especially."

Something in her voice made Rafe stop and look at her. It was the first time she'd brought up the subject of her father in more than a casual way. But what had him carefully scrutinizing her face was the fact that she wouldn't meet his eyes—and the hint of pain he thought he'd caught in her voice.

"Wanna tell me about it, 'Cesca?" he asked softly. The question in no way fit into his plan to distance her from him, but at that moment Rafe didn't give a damn. She was hiding something, *hurting*. And if he could help—give her some relief by talking about it—he'd damn well do it!

She shook her head and tried to look away, but Rafe stopped her. Catching her chin gently but firmly with his fingers, he forced her to meet his eyes. And when he saw the shadow in hers, he wanted to yell, punch something, shout his rage to the heavens.

But he did none of those things. Instead, he ran the backs of his fingers lightly over the contours of her cheek and temple, paused to tuck an errant strand of hair behind her ear then caught her hand and pressed a kiss to it, his eyes closing for the briefest of moments as his lips met the sun-warmed skin. But his eyes were immediately back on her face, his own solemn when he said, "Tell me about it, *querida*. You need— Baby...? Can you...?"

Francesca read the deep concern in his eyes, heard in his voice the sensitivity he couldn't disguise with macho pride, felt his strength in the hand that continued to hold hers after he'd kissed it—and she knew she could trust this man as she'd never trusted anyone before.

A smile trembled on her lips as she nodded, and then the floodgates opened. She told him all of it—the early years when Papa had been the sun and the moon to her, the day she'd learned the truth about him, and the aching sense of betrayal she still couldn't wipe away; her futile attempts to reconcile all this in her mind, knowing she never could. And finally, she told him the thing she'd never before admitted, not even to herself: that her efforts to please him, especially after learning what he was, were driven by something that felt suspiciously like guilt. Perhaps, if she'd been a better daughter, been a more dutiful child, he wouldn't have—wouldn't have—

She broke down and wept then, her sobs coming in deep, convulsive gasps as Rafe wrapped her in his arms and held her protectively against his chest.

"I kn-know it's crazy," she stammered finally, when she was able to speak coherently again. "I mean, I've read enough psychology in m-my course work to know—to know children often b-blame themselves for..."

Her words trailed off, as if, thought Rafe, she'd been trying to make them count, to internalize them—and couldn't. Holding her slightly apart from him so that she could see his face, he said them for her. "For the sins of their fathers."

All the blood seemed to drain from her face, and she began to shake her head in denial, but Rafe would have none of it.

"Say it, 'Cesca," he said as he reached out and took her by the shoulders, letting her feel his strength, willing her to draw from it. "Say it."

The eyes that met hers through the shimmer of her tears were resolute, but gentle, too. *Trust me,* they said. *Take from my strength and lean on me when you must, but, above all, trust me.*

Swallowing past a lump in her throat that felt as if it would suffocate her, her eyes never leaving his, Francesca made herself speak: "For—for the sins of their fathers."

"'Atta girl," Rafe whispered hoarsely. "Now again. Say it again."

She took a deep breath. "For the sins of their fa-fathers."

He was smiling at her. "Again, *querida.*"

Francesca smiled tremulously back at him. "For the sins of their fathers."

"Again."

"For the sins of my father!" she shouted, laughing and weeping at the same time, feeling lighter than air as Rafe swept her into his arms, lifting her and whirling her round and round, his own laughter echoing hers.

And when he finally set her on her feet again, Francesca met his gaze with shining eyes before throwing her arms around his neck in a fierce embrace. "Oh, Rafe," she cried. "I love you!"

Rafe's arms weren't entirely steady as he held her to him. *God in heaven, what have I done?*

CHAPTER TWELVE

"'Cesca..." Rafe disengaged Francesca's arms from his neck, but was careful to keep hold of her hands as he met her eyes. "I think we'd better talk."

Francesca nodded happily, too ecstatic over the emotional catharsis he'd just helped her achieve to notice the cautioning tone in his voice.

Rafe led her back to the campsite in silence. But his mind was busy trying to sort out what he knew needed saying. Trying to find the right words...words that would make her understand without hurting. It had been a long time since he'd been in such a position; people didn't agonize over other people's sensitivities in the world he traveled in.

He waited until they were both comfortably settled in the shade of a large oak near where the horses grazed before speaking.

"'Cesca..." The words, carefully phrased in his mind seconds before, seemed to stick in his throat. *Dammit, you knew this was going to be hard!*

"Rafe...what is it?" Francesca shifted from where she'd been sitting beside him, leaning against the oak; facing Rafe, she sat on her heels and met his gaze. "You...you suddenly look so *serious.* What's wrong?"

Rafe caught her hands again, running the pad of his thumb in a circular pattern over her knuckles as he went on.

"'Cesca, a few minutes ago, you said something to me...something pretty major—or it could be, if you weren't just mouthing the words, which I somehow can't see you doing. Do you recall what it was?"

Francesca appeared to ruminate for a moment, but she lowered her eyes, and from the high wash of color on her cheeks, he could tell she was stalling. "You mean," she finally said, "when I told you—told you I love you."

She hadn't meant to, of course. It had just come bursting out in the ecstasy of the moment—that shared moment of triumph. A personal triumph for her, but Rafe had been a quintessential part of it.

Well, it was true. She hadn't realized it until then, but she suspected it had been sneaking up on her for days. She loved Rafe O'Hara, loved him with a full and happy heart, with a mind that suddenly couldn't imagine life without him. And now he knew it, too. *Bueno.* She was saved the awkwardness of trying to decide how to tell him. If, in fact, she would ever have mustered the courage to do so.

She raised her eyes and met his without wavering. "*Sí,* it is true. I love you."

Rafe heaved a sigh, and his smile was sad as he released one of her hands and lightly touched his fingertips to her cheek. "No, *mi querida.* You don't. You merely think you do."

The green eyes grew stormy as she snapped back at him. "So now you are an expert on the workings of my heart? How can you— "

"Maybe not an expert, but trust me on this, 'Cesca. I *have* lived a little...been around a bit more than you. I'm thirty—"

"Oh, so now it's our age difference, is it?" Angry tears were welling in her eyes, and she snatched away the hand he held, using it to dash at one that began to trickle down her cheek. "You n-needn't invent reasons to reject my f-feelings, Rafe. I'm a big girl, despite what you seem to think! I can take—"

"'Cesca, 'Cesca...." Rafe shifted, reaching out to pull her into his arms. She gave what seemed a token resistance, then went into them with a hicuppy little sigh.

"Sweetheart, listen to me," Rafe went on. "First of all, I want you to know I'm *not* rejecting your feelings. It's just that we disagree on what those feelings amount to."

He was holding her close against his chest, the words of assurance spoken into her hair. Now he released her with one arm, using the free hand to smooth her hair away from her face before touching his knuckles beneath her chin to raise her face toward his.

It was something he'd done on other occasions, and by its very familiarity, it made Francesca want to cry her love anew. This was Rafe, whose actions and gestures were becoming as familiar to her as her own, yet each one so uniquely a part of him and no other! Dear God, if what she felt wasn't love, then perhaps, like him, she should wall herself away from that emotion. The one she felt was enough to tear her apart!

"And," Rafe was saying, looking deeply into her eyes, "I also want you to know that I feel nothing less than...honored to have received such a declaration—even if it is...mistaken."

"But I—"

"Shh." He pressed his thumb lightly against her lips, stilling her. "Just listen to me, darlin', okay?"

She nodded, her eyes, huge and troubled, never leaving his face.

"But you see, 'Cesca, there are good reasons why you should mistake the thing you feel for love. And they have mainly to do with—with the fact that I'm the first man to...know and touch you intimately. Passion is a powerful thing, sweetheart, and it stands to reason—"

"You're saying it's just that? *Lust?*"

The way she said the last word nearly made Rafe wince. He could well imagine what her acquaintance with the Church—with nuns—had led her to associate with *that* word. Hell, he could remember enough from his own upbringing! Wanting at all costs to spare her that, and especially its attendant guilt, he rushed in to disabuse her of it.

"No, 'Cesca, I said *passion*. A very special passion, that came from two people who respect each other, *care* for each other! And I do care about you, 'Cesca. I care very much."

Francesca's eyes searched his face. "Then how do you know it's not...?"

"Love?" An odd smile quirked his lips upward. "Have you ever thought yourself in love before, 'Cesca?"

"You know I haven't."

"Then how do you tell? How do you count this as genuine when you have nothing to compare it to?"

"And how do *you?*"

"Touché," said Rafe, smiling at her whiplash comeback.

"Never mind the fencing, Rafe! Just answer me. You said yourself, you'd never allow— Just what makes *you* such an expert on love, hmm?"

Rafe couldn't help himself. He'd told himself he'd keep his hands off her while he explained. To avoid confusing the issue with the very thing that had brought them to this pass in the first place! But she was so adorably fierce, looking up at him like that, like a spitting kitten—a highly intelligent kitten, he reminded himself, who wasn't about to let this thing go without some cogent arguments!

He cupped her face in his hands and kissed her. It was a long, utterly sensual and nerve-shattering kiss—Rafe used all of the skill at his command to make it exactly that.

"No..." he breathed when at last he released her mouth, "but I *am*, I think you'll agree, an expert on the other." And as if to drive home his point, he threaded his fingers through the hair at the sides of her head and kissed her again. Slowly. Thoroughly.

Francesca shuddered, weak with need. His fingers were still laced through her hair. He hadn't touched another part of her body, yet every part of that body yearned for those expert caresses he'd taught her to know and long for. Was that it, then? Was she merely responding to the passion he'd spoken of?

But what about the other things she'd learned about him that made her yearn for him in her life? What about the Rafe O'Hara who was both strong and vulnerable...sensitive where it counted? Who was no stranger to compassion? Who loved the innocents of the world, despite the brutal forces that had shaped his childhood and ought to have made him hard and impervious to such things?

"You're awfully quiet, *querida*," Rafe murmured. He'd taken her gently in his arms, and now he held her against his chest, smoothing the long tangle of hair along her back with his hand, stilling the tremors of passion he'd known his kiss had engendered. "Thinking it over?"

Francesca nodded, and he smiled against the hair at the crown of her head before kissing it. He'd known she would, of course. Trust that incisive mind of hers to mull over any new information, sort it out until she could get a handle on it.

"And?" he asked, the smile in his voice now.

Heaving a sigh, she pulled away to look at him. "You are right about one thing at least, Rafe. There is respect between us. And because I respect you, I am willing to concede..."

"Well, don't stop now," Rafe urged. He was resisting the temptation to smile, knowing it was important to her that he take this seriously. But hell, that was just the trouble! She looked so damned serious sitting there, her eyes reflecting every nuance of thought in that furiously working mind! Like a precocious child weighing all the evidence of a newly discovered adult problem. He loved seeing that intelligence in action, loved her when she—

Loved? Whoa, hotshot! Ice that word, or before you know it, you'll be falling into the same—

"What I shall concede," Francesca responded, saving him from further ruminations along discomforting lines, "is this. You have a point about the...passion, and that I must—must weigh that against these feelings I have...before drawing any further conclusions. *Bueno,* Rafe. I...we shall wait and see, yes?" *But I know what I feel is love, my stubborn darling. Now it simply remains for me to get* you *to know it, too!*

A sudden smile lit up her whole face. It had the astounding effect of making Rafe feel as if somebody had knocked the wind out of him. God, that she could do that to him with a simple smile! If he didn't know better—

But he *did* know better, and if her answer wasn't exactly the one he'd wanted, he'd take it for now and work on it until it was.

"Okay," he offered cautiously. "We wait and see. Got anything particular in mind while we do that?" he added with a roguish grin.

Punching him playfully on his bicep, she told him sternly to pay serious attention, because she most definitely had! Then she told him she wanted to continue talking as they had been, sharing pieces of the past with each other, learning from each other, who they were.

"Only this time, Rafael," she added with a playfully wagging finger, "there will be no more deliberate attempts to make yourself the brute in my eyes. An honest accounting—nothing less—or, I swear, I shall go around here carving Francesca Loves Rafael on every tree in sight!"

"Good enough!" Rafe agreed with a grin. *Might have known I couldn't fool her. Too damned perceptive, and that's no lie!*

They began to talk, then, their conversation flowing easily as it was exchanged within the established spirit of openness and honesty between them. Each told the other about the past in intimate detail, often dwelling on hopes and dreams long forgotten or set aside.

Rafe was surprised to learn she'd been a teacher at the convent, with a degree in languages—he made a mental note to let the guys at Langley know they were getting sloppy in their data collection. But his surprise was nothing to Francesca's amazement at learning of his degree in engineering. And when he told her he'd always admired good teachers himself, her surprise became an enthusiasm that was contagious; they quickly found themselves discussing children and their readiness to learn, if only they were motivated by the right teachers.

"Yeah," said Rafe. "Trouble is, there are too many teachers out there who do just the opposite. Who kill enthusiasm for learning instead of encouraging it. Hell, all you've gotta do is take a look at a brand new group of little kids at the beginning of school. Ever see that?"

Francesca nodded, smiling. She remembered the shining faces, the eagerness.

"I did, once," he went on. "When I was an adult, I mean. I happened to be passing a schoolyard during some sorta nature walk or something in early September. They hadda be kindergarten age, y'know? Five-year-olds, I'd bet on it. And there they all were, gathered around this teacher as she held up a leaf, letting the sun shine through it as she talked about the veins in it and all. I tell you, 'Cesca, the looks on those little faces... It was all pure wonder, y'know? Wonder... and *joy!*"

Francesca nodded again, well remembering the looks on certain students' faces as they'd discovered the beauty within a new word or phrase, in a language she was helping them to understand.

"Yeah," said Rafe, his face suddenly darkening. "But take a look at those same kids several years down the line. The kids I saw that day were mostly Latinos in a poor neighborhood outside of L.A. Wanna bet on how many of their faces still retained that look of wonder when they got to...fifth, sixth grade, maybe? That is, if they even *went* to school anymore."

"Sí, but it isn't just poverty and poor schools that destroy the joy in learning, Rafe. The education offered by El Convento de los Santos is considered the finest money can buy." Francesca laughed ruefully. "I should know. My father researched the matter thoroughly before sending me there!

"But do you know," she went on, "there are teachers there who actually believe learning must be *painful* to be effective?"

Rafe snorted, remembering being smacked with a ruler at age nine in a lower east side Catholic school where he'd been sent as a charity case when he was newly orphaned. "The way I see it, the nuns in the teaching orders accept that premise when they make their vows!"

Francesca shook her head sadly, easily guessing what his own experience must have been to make him think that. *Ah, Rafe, how I long to comfort the child you were, who had to suffer such callousness! And how I love you for not being callous in return!*

"Not true," she said to Rafe. "Some of the gentlest, most gifted teachers I had at the convent were nuns. And I once had a lay teacher whom we nicknamed 'La Sadisma,'" she added with a wicked grin.

Rafe didn't return the grin. Just thinking of Francesca at the mercy of some sadistic bitch who called herself a teacher made him want to strangle somebody. Instead, he changed the subject, and they moved on to a discussion of music and other things that allowed him to associate her with pleasant thoughts.

He was beginning to become all too aware of the passage of time here, in this isolated, unreal little world they'd found themselves in. Any day now they'd be rescued or whatever, and they'd be forced to leave that world behind. When that day came, he knew he'd never see Francesca again, and he suddenly wanted his memories of her to be upbeat... positive, with nothing sad or cruel to spoil the beauty of it... of *her*. Hell, it was hard enough to think of her going to the bed of that rich Italian stud Valera had picked out for her!

They continued to talk, their conversation frequently peppered with laughter and occasionally spiked with sharp rejoinders, as when they disagreed over the proper way to cook *steak au poivre*.

They spoke, too, of the subject that had brought them to this point: her father. And for the first time, Francesca was able to discuss her ambivalent feelings at length, free of the former guilt. Rafe had done that for her, she knew, and while she might not yet have resolved all those ambivalences, she told him she now felt empowered to begin working on them. It was a start.

The afternoon wore on, and still they talked. That they ranged over such a breadth of topics surprised Rafe; given their disparate ages and backgrounds, he wouldn't have believed they could exchange such a variety of ideas so easily. Francesca, on the other hand, was less surprised; she had once read a novel about a pair of lovers who were soul mates, and while she'd regarded it as fanciful fiction at the time, she was now embracing the concept as valid. She felt as if she'd known Rafe O'Hara all her life, and perhaps in another life, as well.

It was late afternoon when hunger finally prompted Rafe to suggest it was time for him to check his snares. "I don't know about you, kid," he said, "but I'm starving. How about it? You hungry?"

Francesca wrinkled her nose in distaste at his calling her "kid." It reminded her all too much of their relationship before they'd grown so close, become lovers, and she decided it was appropriate to remind him of the latter.

"Oh, I don't know, *querido*," she said lazily, running her forefinger slowly along his lower lip. "I may be... hungry, *sí*, but not for food...."

Rafe sucked in his breath, all thoughts of the snares forgotten. He grabbed the finger that was playing havoc with his senses and lightly bit the tip, then pulled her into his arms.

"*Bruja*," he growled, finding himself instantly hard for her. "Already I suspect I've taught you too many things!"

Francesca's sultry laughter flowed over him like a warm summer rain as he proceeded to teach her some more.

CHAPTER THIRTEEN

DURING THE DAYS that followed, under Rafe's strict, circumscribed rules, Francesca and he became lovers in every way but the ultimate one. They bathed together, slept together, awoke together. They talked intimately, often far into the night. She told him of her hunger for details about the mother she barely remembered; he told her about the pain of missing a father he remembered only too well.

They grew more at ease with each other, especially Francesca, who had begun to sunbathe nude, learning to enjoy Rafe's pleasure in her body as he watched. And each new intimacy made their passion blaze hotter, with only Rafe's iron control standing between desire and the final act.

But within this deepening intimacy, Rafe's conscience began to gnaw at him over his covert assignment—over the fact that Francesca was his bait to lure Morano. He wished, at times desperately, that he were free to confess it to her. But aside from how this would violate his agent's code he realized that telling her the truth could make her so jumpy, she'd only make things more difficult for him. And more dangerous for her.

So with this latter thought especially in mind he held his tongue. The situation was precarious enough for her, despite his resolve to protect her at all costs, and he'd rather die than put her at greater risk, he realized.

And for Francesca there was a growing certainty of her love for Rafe. There came the inevitable moment one night, as he awakened her from sleep with unimaginably arousing yet tender kisses, that she tried to tell him so again. But Rafe wouldn't even let her say the words, insisting, as before, that what she felt was only a "crush," because he had been the first.

Upset, having hoped he might at last accept it, even daring to hope that he might tell her he loved her, too, Francesca withdrew from him. But this estrangement lasted only until the morning. Until Rafe's teasing and cajoling had her relenting and throwing herself madly into his arms, laughter vying with tears in her cry of his name.

But what she didn't know, what Rafe couldn't tell her, was how close he'd come the night before to telling her what she'd wanted to hear. Because Rafe O'Hara had begun to fight his own private war inside his head. And heart. Constantly aware now that their idyllic interlude soon had to come to an end, he found he could hardly bear to think what that would mean.

He tried to tell himself his foremost concern was to protect Francesca, not only from the danger posed by Morano, but from the pain their separation was already bound to bring. But somewhere along the line— he didn't know when, exactly, but somewhere in their long hours together—he began to realize that the kind of emotional attachment Francesca was talking about would, if he let it, bring *him* more than pain. He was afraid it could destroy him.

And he could barely think about what it might do to her if she continued to believe she was in love with him, if she began to suspect how deeply he cared about what happened to her. With all this firmly in mind, Rafe swore to himself not to let them become any more emotionally tied to each other.

And then, a few days later, came a moment that changed everything for Rafe. It was late morning, and he'd just come back from checking the snares. But they'd been empty, and he was in the process of resigning himself to another meal of trout when he heard Francesca calling.

"Rafe! Oh, Rafe, *look!*"

There was laughter in her voice, and he turned and saw her coming toward him along the stream. And he knew, if he lived to be a hundred, he'd never forget the way she looked at that moment.

Wearing her flared skirt over nothing more than the sheer, lacy teddy, she walked barefoot and bare limbed, her heavy, unbound hair running riotously over sun-browned arms and shoulders. Every fluid movement was imbued with that unconscious, innate grace that was as much a part of her as breathing.

Her hands were holding the hem of the skirt up in front of her, revealing long, nut-brown legs that seemed to go on forever, and in the pouch formed by her skirt, she had gathered something and was trying to show him what it was.

"Look!" she called again, and then he saw her shift the burden to one hand and reach in, withdrawing—

"Cherries, Rafe! Wild cherries!"

She slipped one between her teeth as he watched. Then she was drawing nearer, smiling around the succulent morsel in her mouth, her green eyes shining with light and laughter and a simple delight in what she'd discovered.

"See, darling?" She closed the distance between them and spread the folds of her skirt so he could see her find. "They were on a tree beyond the far bank . . . wild cherries, Rafe. Look at them!"

But Rafe could only look at *her.*

His breath stilled as he reached deep into those vibrant, laughing eyes, green as leaves in the shade, and he lost himself in the elemental joy shimmering there. She was all things rare and fine in that moment. Young and free and oh, so lovely, she was the eternal, quintessential spirit that is woman. Woman in all her thousand and one mysterious delights.

And he loved her as he'd never before loved anything in his life—and would never love anything again.

Rafe's throat closed around the emotion that clogged it, stunning him with the simple truth that had been chasing him for days. He loved her. God and all his lost saints forgive him, Valera's daughter, and he loved her—loved her more than his own life.

"What is it, Rafe? Darling, what's wrong?"

"You haven't fed me one of those pretty cherries yet, *bruja,*" he lied, praying she couldn't guess at the pain he ruthlessly shoved aside. "And I'm damned jealous of that juicy little tidbit that's filling your mouth right now."

"Oh, here, silly!" She laughed, reaching for one of the small, ripe globes in her skirt.

"Uh-uh," he answered with a devilish grin, pulling her up against him. "I want—" his mouth descended slowly, until his lips brushed hers, then hovered, so close, he could smell the faint, tangy sweetness of the fruit "—yours."

And then his lips covered hers, unhurried, lazy in their taking; then they opened, parting hers with them, allowing him access to the cherry-stained succulence inside. This, he tasted and savored until Francesca's limbs grew weak with need. Her breathing became shallow and her knees threatened to buckle under her as the now familiar tendrils of passion curled and unraveled along the edges of her spine. And lower, deeper, at her very center.

Without conscious thought, she raised her arms to circle his neck, freeing her skirt and showering cherries onto the ground around their feet. But neither noticed. Rafe had gathered her close, pulling her against the lean, hard length of him. She could feel his arousal jutting against her belly. Knowing she had this effect on him made her shiver with wanting him, creating instant moisture up high, between her thighs.

It was always this way now. He had only to touch her, and often not even that, but simply to let her see the desire in his eyes, and she would ache, wanting only to be in his arms. To come to him, ready and open, longing for the heaven he made with his touch. To love him, despite his refusal to see; for it *was* love she felt—of that she had not a single doubt. Rafael O'Hara was the center of her existence now; she had only to imagine life without him to see it suddenly bleak and bare.

Rafe released her slightly, keeping her loosely within the circle his arms made around her waist. "Know what, *bruja?*" he asked thickly. "I have a problem.... I haven't made love to you in hours."

Francesca's face went pink under her tan—he still had the power to affect her that way—and she lowered her lashes, glancing downward. "Oh, Rafe...the cherries—"

"Stuff the cherries!" he growled, then swung her effortlessly into his arms. "We'll get them later and I'll feed them to you, one—" he caught her lower lip lightly between his teeth, released it "—by one—" he kissed

one corner of her mouth, then the other "—by one."
He claimed her mouth, savoring the taste of her, still
faintly tart and sweet and redolent of cherries.

He carried her to the shade under the ledge where
they'd left the bedding, laying her gently down on the
parachutes' folds. And for a moment he just looked at
her as he knelt beside her.

She was more beautiful than dreams, he thought. A
woman now, in every way except one. And the knowledge that he held the power over that small difference
nearly made him cry off.

It had been the hardest thing he'd ever made himself
do, these days and nights of loving her within the limits
he'd set. Exquisite torture of the highest order, and it
drove him, each time, to the brink of going out of his
mind.

And yet, to give it up, he knew, was not within his
power. Not now. Not yet. When the time came, and he
knew it would come soon enough, he would do what
had to be done. For her much more than for himself.
For 'Cesca and the bittersweet love he carried in his
heart.

But knowing he loved her now was a further test.
Could he still handle it? Keep control when the ultimate emotion was tied up in the lovemaking? As he
looked at her now, talons of need were raking his loins,
threatening to shatter his control. And then Francesca
smiled at him, and the inner argument faded like mist
on the wind.

He made love to her slowly, then, his own need held
fiercely in check from the start. Unhurriedly, lan-
guidly, he bared and worshiped each part of her sun-
kissed flesh, loving her with his hands, his lips, his eyes.
And with his heart and mind.

"You'll be brown as a monkey soon, *bruja*," he teased as the teddy slid from breasts tinted golden by the sun. "Your skin here—" he pressed his lips to the heavy, rounded underside of one satiny mound "—will soon be as dark as here." His lips moved to the peaked coral crest at the center, and he drew it into his mouth, sucking gently while his teeth worried the sensitive flesh.

Francesca made an inarticulate sound deep in her throat and lightly scored his shoulders with her nails. She'd been wet and ready for him even before he'd carried her here, and now her hunger was raging beyond her ability to wait.

"Uh-uh, love," he murmured, forcing the words past a throat threatening to close with the impact of the endearment, fully realized for the first time. "We've got miles to go and all kinds of time to get there. No way we're gonna rush it."

"Then—" she sucked in her breath as his hands undid the snaps of the teddy between her thighs "—at least let me undress you again, the way I did when . . ."

His mouth closed over hers, effectively stilling speech. "No way, love," he murmured thickly against her mouth, remembering how her hands on him in the water had nearly made him lose it. Nearly made him thrust inside her instead of spilling himself against her belly. "I can't trust myself that way again."

"But it would give me something to do!" she pleaded.

His smile was slow and lazy, his eyes knowing as they met hers. "Oh, there'll be lots for you to do, 'Cesca. Lots and lots..." And he took her again in his arms and began to show her, but slowly...thoroughly and slowly....

Even when she finally lay naked beneath him, uttering breathless cries that were his name, her hands beating a tattoo on his back, he refused to hurry the pace. Caressing, stroking, teasing, until she thought she would die from it, he praised her quavering flesh as a paean to his love. The love he couldn't tell her with words. But he could show her in a hundred different ways, and he did.

Then, when at last his lips had followed his eyes and hands to the smooth inner skin of her thighs, when he cupped her wriggling buttocks with his hands to raise her to his mouth, until she could feel his breath on the creamy, wet recesses of her woman's flesh, then she knew what he meant to do.

"*Rafe!* I don't think— You can't mean to— Oh, God, *Rafe!*"

Her cry became a moan as his mouth descended, tasting her fully. She was sweeter than anything he'd ever known, hot and slippery with the nectar of her own longing. His tongue penetrated the pulsing slit at her center, delved and dipped, then traced its way back, finding the small, hard bud above. She was writhing and arcing against him now, but he held her still, his hands firmly on her hips as he readied her for the final pleasure.

And then he kissed the throbbing nub, teasing it with his tongue, and on the first pass, she dug her nails into his shoulders. On the second, she sobbed his name. On the third, she screamed it into the sky, and then she came, and came, and came again, her hips trembling violently with her release.

And Rafe, his body drenched with sweat, his own need shuddering through him like a drum, wrapped her tenderly in his arms, savoring her pleasure for his own.

FRANCESCA OPENED her eyes to see Rafe leaning above her, propped on one elbow. The crescendo that was her heartbeat had slowed at last to a level where she could speak, and she said the thing that filled her mind.

"I love you."

Rafe shut his eyes, afraid she would read the echoing response in them. He took a deep breath, mastering emotions never so near to breaking. "'Cesca..."

"No, Rafe. Don't say it... please? I know I've never been in love before, that I've never even kissed a man, much less—never kissed anyone before you. But I also think I'm old enough to know my own mind. And my heart, Rafe. My heart."

"'Cesca—"

She stilled his lips with her fingers, shaking her head, denying his denial. "And my heart, as well as my mind, tells me I love you, Rafe. They tell me so that I know it, deep in my soul, that without you in it, my life would be something barren and dry. Shriveled, like those wild cherries had they tried to grow without the sun and the rain.

"Oh, no, Rafe," she went on, her heart in her eyes, "whatever you try to tell me, I *know* I love you. With all my heart, with all that I am."

Rafe kissed the fingers she'd raised to his lips, then held her hand to his cheek. "You shame me, 'Cesca." *And I'll die remembering the way you are right now.* "I'm not worth—"

Francesca shook her head slowly, sadly. "I don't want you shamed, *mi amor.* I only want—I only wish for you to accept that I love you." *It might even be enough... for now.*

Blue eyes met green, and he knew he had to give her this much. Knew in his agony that it was even, miraculously, true.

"*Sí, mi querida,*" he told her in a raw whisper. "I believe it."

With an iron will, Rafe blinked back the sting of tears as Francesca flung herself into his arms.

CHAPTER FOURTEEN

RAMÓN VALERA'S FACE was grim as he stared at the wreckage of the 727. Francesca's plane. The site swarmed with Mexican officials. They'd been called in as soon as the wreck was spotted from the air by one of the search plans Barbero had hired. Scurrying over the burnt, blackened area, they reminded him of bees converging on a charred hive.

The sighting had occurred last night, just before dark. By the time Ramón had arrived on the scene, just minutes ago, they'd been at it for hours, measuring the extent of the scorched area...sifting through the remains. Like him, they'd probably set out as soon as it was light, but he'd been caught in a snarl of Mexico City traffic on the way to the heliport where Barbero had engaged a private copter, and now it was nearly 10:00 a.m.

Probably just as well he'd gotten here this late, Ramón told himself. There was nothing to do but wait, anyway, and his patience had been stretched to zero during the three days the planes had gone out and returned with zilch. It could still be hours before they arrived at any conclusions regarding "body identification and the possibility of survivors," the Mexican police investigator had just told him.

As if there could be any survivors from an inferno that size, Ramón thought darkly. *Francesca...little sister...God, I can't believe you're gone!*

But he had to begin to believe it, the voice of reality told him. They'd already turned up a fragment that positively identified the plane as his father's jet, and the fat little Mexican Barbero had pointed out as the local coroner had thus far established there were the remains of three bodies on the site, one of which was female.

Three bodies: the pilot, of course; the other male would be the bodyguard Papa had told him would be doing double duty as copilot; and...

Ramón tried to throttle the spark of hope that flared when he considered the fact that only one female body had been located. There'd been two women aboard: Francesca and the old aunt, her duenna. Maybe...

He shook his head, telling himself not to be a fool. A fourth body could be anywhere, flung from the fuselage by the force of the explosion that had shattered and twisted all that metal like it was nothing... or shattered to bits, itself, by the blast....

Still...

"Ramón!"

Valera pivoted as he heard his name shouted. Seizing on the eagerness in Barbero's voice, he couldn't quell the thread of hope spun by his optimistic musings of seconds before.

"Yeah, Barbero—what?" Ramón felt the spark of optimism fan to life as he watched his man approach at a run, accompanied by a tall, thin Mexican in a policeman's uniform; Barbero was *smiling*.

"They just found..." said Barbero, pausing to catch his breath, "found some footprints...and *hoof* marks, down...down there—" he gestured over his shoulder with his thumb "—and it looks like two people made it outta here! A man and a woman, Ramón! On some nags your father must've—"

"Is this true?" Ramón cut in, addressing the Mexican in Spanish. He wasn't aware that any horses had been on the plane. But it did have those specially padded stalls, and he could easily envision his sister refusing to leave her horses behind.... "A man and a woman on horseback?"

"*Sí, señor,*" the police captain confirmed, going on to explain that while it was too soon to be absolutely certain, it appeared as though two people—one, a large man, and the other, a woman wearing espadrilles—had ridden away from the site. The muddy ground left by the recent storm had captured many clear prints.

A woman wearing espadrilles.

Ramón steeled himself against the tears that fought to accompany the grin emerging on his face. The duenna, whom he couldn't even *picture* climbing on a horse at her age, had worn only what could be called "sensible" shoes the few times he'd seen her.

But *Francesca*...Francesca, who rode horses like she was born on one, wore *espadrilles!* She had a whole collection of the damn things, in every color of the goddamned rainbow!

"Take me down there," he said to the Mexican in Spanish, unable to hide a quaver in his voice. And to Barbero he shouted over his shoulder as he set off behind the police captain, "Round up some of these other bozos and tell 'em to join us down there. I'll want some input on where they were headed. It looks like my sister left here alive, Barbero, and I want her found!"

FRANCESCA STRETCHED lazily in the sun, her nude body coated with suntan lotion, her thoughts filled with Rafe. Rafe...who'd smoothed the lotion over nearly every inch of her in the process of making delicious, nerve-shattering love to her this morning. Rafe...who seemed not to be able to get enough of her, nor she of him.

And incredibly, finally, that stubborn Anglo had accepted the fact that she loved him! She still couldn't quite believe she'd gotten through to him, but she was beginning to.

For one thing, his lovemaking was somehow... different. Inordinately tender, yet at moments almost fierce. It was almost as if—

A faint, unfamiliar sound intruded, and Francesca abandoned her reverie to listen more attentively. Rafe had gone to check the snares, and she was in charge of the campsite, which included the horses. A glance at the Thoroughbreds told her they'd heard something, too. Their heads were raised, and the stallion's ears were pricked, as if he was listening for something.

At first she identified only the routine noises she'd come to associate with the camp...bird song, the steady susurration of the stream, a furtive scurrying of some hidden creature in the underbrush. But now they were competing with a newer sound, the rushing of wind through the trees, and she noticed clouds building in the east.

There! It was coming through more clearly now, a steady, penetrating hum, and—that choppy sound! It was—

Dios! It was a *helicopter.* A helicopter was flying somewhere nearby!

She craned her neck back and scanned the sky overhead, shielding her eyes from the sun's glare with her hand. There was nothing visible at the moment, but with those clouds—

Suddenly she dropped her gaze, fastening on the carry-on bag near the fire whose glowing embers were being fanned by the rising wind. Her clothing! If rescuers were at hand, she'd better—

She made a mad dash for the carryon, darting a quick glance overhead as she ran. Nothing in sight yet, but the choppy sound of the blades was definitely growing louder.

She made short work of clothing herself in the Donna Karan suit and the white blouse, but didn't bother with underwear, to save time. Her mind raced ahead of her hands as she dressed, skimming over the things Rafe had—

Oh, *Dios*— Rafe! Where was *Rafe?* Had he—

Giving her head a shake as if to clear it, she finished slipping on her espadrilles and told herself not to be silly. Rafe knew what he was doing and was probably heading back to camp this very minute. Because if she'd heard the helicopter, he was bound to have heard it, too.

But meanwhile, *she* was in charge, and that meant building up a signal fire! Glancing up, she saw the clouds were moving in faster now, and there was the smell of rain on the wind. Still no visible sign of the helicopter.

She hurried toward the pile of kindling and larger pieces of wood Rafe had stacked near the fire site. But as she reached for one of the dead branches, her hand froze.

Rescue was nearly at hand. But what did that really mean? The answer, which she'd been ignoring for days, was swift in coming, a haunting voice inside her head. *It means the end of all this. Your time with Rafe.*

Your life...

And yet, what else could she do? What other path was open to her? Unlike her, Rafe had not lost sight of what must happen eventually. From the very beginning, he'd laid careful plans for their rescue. This very campsite.

Her throat clogged on a spasm of raw emotion as she gazed around the place where they'd shared so much together. Over there was the stream where they'd laughed and played and made love...there, the spot where she'd shown him her find of wild cherries...there, the ledge where he'd carried her after—

She stifled a sob with her fist, remembering Rafe's acceptance of her gift of love. But she remembered, too, that *he* had made no such commitment of the heart. No commitment of any kind.

The chopper blades were very loud now, and Francesca forced herself to swallow past the lump that had formed in her throat as she scanned the sky. A glint of something metallic shone through a break in the cloud cover, high above the treetops.

With arms that felt as if they had leaden weights attached, she reached for a piece of firewood.

RAFE FINISHED DRESSING the small peccary he'd snared, washing his hands in the small rivulet that, farther down, fed into the larger stream at the campsite. He dried his hands on his jeans and began to reset the snare, vaguely aware the sun had disappeared and it was building toward rain. He was working automatically, his mind not really on the business at hand.

His mind was on Francesca. As it had been all through the night and now the day as well, every waking minute of it. 'Cesca. His 'Cesca, who was not his at all. Who would be delivered by him, into the arms of another man...

He had an urge to howl his rage into the sky, and he would have, if it weren't for the thought she might hear him. Or if he thought it might do any good.

Ah, God, he loved her so damned much, he ached with it! He, who'd never given a damn about any woman, who'd guarded his heart for years against just this kind of an assault.

Well, you've really gone and done it this time, hotshot. What good did it do you—all those years of tending your soul? Insulating it from pain. The pain's here, and it's bigger than you ever—

A vivid oath erupted from Rafe's throat as he accidentally cut himself with his knife while sharpening a stake. Par for the course, he told himself, when your mind isn't on your work. When you let distractions—

As if to underscore just how distracted he'd been, a sound suddenly came to him above the rush of the rising wind—a sound he belatedly realized had been somewhere in the background of his consciousness for some minutes now. He froze as realization hit.

A chopper! A goddam chopper, with 'Cesca alone at the camp.

Cursing himself with a violent oath, Rafe pivoted and broke into a dead run, peccary and snares forgotten. As he ran, he pocketed the Swiss army knife and withdrew his semiautomatic pistol from its holster. He was as far away from the campsite as he'd allowed himself to travel without Francesca along; it had seemed a reasonable distance at the time he'd located peccary tracks among the acorn-studded ground and decided to try his luck with the larger size game. But now, with Francesca there, and him here, it felt as if she were a continent away, and Rafe cursed himself again for a witless fool.

Birds squawked and scolded him from their perches amid the foliage as he crashed through the brush beneath them, but Rafe's ears were tuned to the *chop-chop-chop* that sounded ominously close to the place where he was headed. He tried to tell himself the chopper didn't necessarily mean danger. That it could belong to Valera or the Mexican authorities. But a sick feeling in his gut reminded him that the odds were just as likely that it was Morano. *And he'd had no business gambling on* any *kind of odds when Francesca's safety was at stake.*

Then, just as he was telling himself to slow down and move quietly, because he was drawing near enough to the camp to be heard, the sick feeling in his gut became a wrenching spear of agony. The chopper sounds had disappeared, and in the lull that ensued, he heard a woman's scream.

"WHO—WHO *ARE* YOU?" Francesca stammered as the last of three men emerged from the helicopter, each bearing an ominous-looking weapon trained directly on her.

"Scream one more time and you might never find out," said the one in front. He was a short but muscular, balding man with a beard. *"¿Comprende?"* he added in an ugly voice.

Swallowing convulsively, Francesca nodded. She felt stupefied by the sudden shift of events. One minute she'd been waving the helicopter down, resigned but trying to put a good face on things for the benefit of her rescuers; the next, she'd felt terror rising in her throat, building into a scream, as she'd seen the hard looks on these men's faces—and the weapons.

But *why?* Why would someone come here meaning her harm?

The next words, spoken by one of the other gunmen—a thin, wiry sort, wearing dark glasses—suggested an answer. "She ain't alone here, Morano. Botha them nags got bridles."

Morano. She'd come across that name several times while researching her father! He was a rival gangster of some kind...powerful, just like—

Suddenly the words of Ramón, issued so glibly long ago, came to mind. *Our father is an international businessman with many jealous rivals. Some are unscrupulous enough to try to use his innocent family to force him to capitulate....*

Dear God, she thought as Morano ordered the other two to have a look around, *he must mean to use me, somehow, to—*

"Now...Miss Valera," Morano said to her with a nasty smile, and his use of her name convinced her as nothing else had that she was in danger. "Into the chopper, and be quick about it!"

Francesca hesitated, watching his accomplices begin to circle behind the helicopter, one to either side; they held their weapons in front of them, looking for—Rafe! Where was *Rafe?*

"I said, *move,* little girl!" Morano's eyes, which held more than a hint of cruelty, narrowed on her. "You might be smart enough to guess you're no good to us dead, but you might wanna think about what it would feel like to have some ammo drilled into your knees. It won't be pleasant, believe me."

His cruel parody of a smile made her stomach clench. And as his gaze dropped deliberately to her knees, the third man, who hadn't made it out of sight around the helicopter yet, added his own warning.

"I'd do it if I were you, lady. Tony likes to...hurt people."

Francesca felt her knees threaten to buckle, but she stiffened her spine and forced her shoulders back as she prepared to comply. But she hadn't taken the first step when, suddenly, gunfire erupted from somewhere beyond the helicopter. A rapid staccato not quite loud enough to override a man's agonized scream.

Dear God, Rafe— Francesca pressed a fist to her mouth, stifling terror and a twist of nausea that surged in her throat.

Morano whirled toward the sound of the gunfire, whipping his machine gun around in an arc ahead of him. "Bruno!" he shouted. "Vito?"

Only silence answered him, and Morano took an uneasy step backward. He glanced over his shoulder at Francesca, who stood, frozen, about two yards behind him. She caught a look of indecision on his face.

Then, just as he lunged toward her, Francesca spied a fist-size projectile of some sort, maybe a rock, arc past the right side of the helicopter and crash into some waist-high shrubbery. Morano heard it and spun toward the sound, machine gun blazing.

Francesca's head echoed with the sound, and her heart felt as if it was about to leap out of her chest. Then, out of the corner of her eye, she caught a flicker of movement to her left. She turned and gasped. Rafe stood there, hair whipped by the wind, feet braced wide apart, his arms straight out in front of him as he used both hands to steady the pistol he aimed at Morano.

But Morano, who'd quit firing, had caught her startled gasp. He whirled toward her.

"'Cesca, *down!*"

Francesca dropped to the ground, her body obedient to the command in Rafe's voice before he finished getting the words out. As she hit the spongy turf, her ears rang with the report of rapid gunfire overhead.

She wasn't entirely sure what happened next. She only knew she was huddled on the ground, convulsive sobs racking her body. The sound of Rafe's voice seemed to mingle with the wind and come at her from a great distance.

"'Cesca...sweetheart, it's okay. They're all dead and can't hurt you. God, baby, I was so scared I'd—'Cesca, it's all right. It's *over.*"

Francesca blinked as if in a daze and looked around them. Bodies on the ground...blood...so much blood....

And suddenly she couldn't bear it. Tearing away from Rafe, she began to run, blindly, wildly. *Oh Dios, the blood!*

"'Cesca, wait!" Rafe pounded after her. He'd seen the wild look in her eyes, recognized it from other battlefields whose memory he could never erase.

He caught up to her a good distance from the carnage. Pulling her into his arms again, he held her close while murmuring her name and soothing words over and over.

Francesca felt the familiar warmth, the strength of his arms as he carefully lifted her and cradled her against him. The words he murmured began to penetrate, and she clutched his shirtfront, shaking with a violence she couldn't seem to control.

He's alive! We're both *alive!* she kept telling herself, but when she couldn't stop sobbing, Rafe only held her tighter and continued to soothe her with soft words.

"'Cesca...shh, love, it's okay now. It's over, and I love you. You're all right. Thank God you're all right!"

"Oh, God, Rafe! They—they were g-going to—" As awareness suddenly took hold, Francesca swallowed a sob and held her breath, afraid she hadn't heard right. Slowly, she released her convulsive grip on Rafe's shirt and raised her face to his.

"Wh-what did you...?" She was suddenly trembling, trembling so hard she could barely get the words out. "Rafe? Did...d-did you just tell me you—" She couldn't say it, afraid to believe, afraid a miracle would disappear in a wisp of smoke.

Rafe smiled that beloved crooked smile at her, closed his eyes for a moment as if to contain some emotion, then said the words. "I love you, 'Cesca."

She blinked through her tears, searching for truth in his face—and found it in his eyes. They were a deep, clear blue now, and though his face was shadowed with remnants of the terror they'd just lived through, there was a message of love in their depths she couldn't deny.

"Oh, Rafe." She choked on a sob. "I never thought I'd hear you say it!"

"I never thought to hear myself say it, *mi amor,*" he told her in a rough whisper. He was wiping the tears from her face with gentle fingers. "But all I could think of back there was that one of us could die...we *both* could die, and I'd never told you.

"I love you, 'Cesca of my heart," he repeated as he pulled her against him again, murmuring it into her hair. "I love you more than anyone, or anything, I've ever held dear. More than my life. No matter what happens, remember that. It'll never change. *Te amo.*"

"*Te amo, mi corazón!*" she cried, wrapping her arms tightly around his waist, as if afraid he would disappear. In a calmer moment she would reflect that adrenaline was still coursing through her system, but for now, all she could think, feel, was that once again she and Rafe had missed death by inches. They were here—*alive!* Alive, and Rafe *loved* her!

And in the wake of this, something new began to throb through her body. Raw passion—wild, fierce, greater than she'd ever known.

"Ra-a-afe," she moaned, hardly recognizing the sound of her own voice as she clutched at him with a desperate strength.

"Easy, baby...." Rafe cautioned, recognizing the violence of her passion for what it was—the affirmation of life in the face of death—yet he felt ignited by it, too, and by the heat he felt in her.

But Francesca was having none of his caution. Her breathing grew ragged and she could feel a surge of liquid heat as she shifted and began to tear at Rafe's shirt with clumsy fingers. The rain had finally begun to fall, great, pelting drops of it, but she paid it no heed.

"Rafe!" she cried. "Rafe, *please...*"

Rafe wanted to tell her, no. Not here. Not now. Not so near this battleground of death... But one look at her—her face fierce in its elemental beauty, framed by cinnamon hair whipped by the wind, eyes kindled with a green fire that seemed to take energy from the building storm—and he was lost.

With a harsh groan, he brought his mouth down on hers. Francesca's was open, eager—hungry for his claim. Her arms sought his neck, wound tightly around it with a primitive need as he crushed her to him. Tongues met, fencing wildly, mating. They fell to the ground, rapacious, greedy for each other, oblivious to the rain that had already soaked their clothes and was plastering their hair to their heads.

When they finally broke for air, gasping, their mutual need pounding through their veins, Francesca lay beneath him, and she could feel his arousal against her thighs. Again, her hands went to his shirt. She tore at the buttons, her task made more difficult by the sodden fabric, while Rafe pressed fevered kisses along her hairline, murmuring incoherent words that were snatched by the wind.

He heard her utter a small, triumphant cry as the last of the closures gave way, but his mind was intent on her trembling body, his hands filled with the lush ripeness of her breasts. Kneading them, teasing their hardened peaks through the thin, sodden fabric of her blouse, he was unprepared for the added surge of heat to his loins when her nails suddenly raked his own flat nipples.

"'Cesca!" His hoarse cry rose over the moaning wind, but Francesca ignored its implications. With a fierce strength, she pushed at his chest until she felt him move, and then she rolled on top, reversing their positions.

Rafe tried to speak, to warn her that he was dangerously close to losing it, but her lips took away his words, and he blindly groped for whatever control he could seize as he surrendered to her hunger.

Above them, all around them, the rain came down in driving sheets. It soaked the grassy turf beneath their straining bodies. It ran and poured in runnels, down cheek and neck and limb. Neither noticed. They were consumed with each other, tasting wildly, glorying in the pulse that reaffirmed life with each kiss, each stroke, each harshly whispered urging.

Rafe felt her hands go to the fastening of his jeans, and then the zipper, but at the moment when he strained for some semblance of sanity and would have stopped her, he felt her mouth on one of his nipples, and a harsh cry escaped, instead. He bucked wildly under her hands and tried to pull them away, clenching his teeth against the need for release as he felt his member spring free.

The cool rain on the heat of his erection helped him resume the control he so desperately sought. But now Francesca was all over him, peeling the rain-drenched clothes from his body, and he knew it couldn't last. She was like a wild thing, driven. There were emotions here, he knew, greater than she'd ever experienced, driving her beyond control, beyond any wish to control...

"'Cesca ... for God's sake— Ah, *God!*"

He felt her mouth close over him in a wildly disbelieving moment of renewed arousal and pure joy. In all their hours of sensual sharing, he'd never shown her this, never asked it of her, or even hinted that it existed as a means for a woman to pleasure a man. He was always the teacher, she, his virgin pupil. That was how he'd intended it, and that was how—

"'Cesca, *don't!* Stop! Stop now, dammit, or I'll—"

He caught her under the arms and dragged her up the length of him, stilling her protests with his mouth and rolling until she was pinned beneath him. But stripped of his clothes, he had a heightened awareness of every inch of her that lay pressed against him—the texture of wet fabric, of rain-slicked skin, of undulating curves as she writhed against him and whimpered her need.

It was his undoing. Telling himself there was still safety in the barriers of her own clothing, Rafe pressed into her. He thrust his sensitized flesh against the cradle formed by her pelvis and the sodden skirt that had ridden to the tops of her thighs.

"Sí!" she cried, opening her thighs and arching against him. *"Ah, mi Rafael, sí!"*

Driven by the need in her voice, dimly aware he was relying on the safety provided by the thin barrier of her clothing, Rafe arched and thrust again, finding—

The woman-slick heat of her! She was *completely open* to him! How—

But his question became moot as Francesca arched against him again. A roaring filled his ears as he felt himself drive into the tight, slippery warmth that encased him like a glove, past the frail barrier he was helpless to avoid, down, down into the pulsing, throbbing heart of the woman he loved.

Francesca cried out in pain as he tore through the virginal membrane. She felt him stiffen and at once go motionless.

"Shh, darling...lie still." Rafe's hoarse whisper came to her on the heels of a rumble of thunder. "It's done, love, and I'm only sorry I hurt ... God, baby, does it—does it hurt real—"

A second peal of thunder cut him off. Francesca's tear-filled eyes opened, and she took in Rafe's face. There were lines of tension around his mouth, and she could feel him trembling. Yet she could also see desire etched across his chiseled features. She realized how much this restraint must be costing him at the same instant she became aware that the sharp pain of seconds ago was disappearing. And in its place—!

"Love me, Rafe," she urged in a rusty whisper. "Just love me!"

Rafe reached deep into her eyes and felt a shudder run through him. All evidence of the pain he'd seen in them seconds ago was gone. In its place was desire, pure and sweet, sweet as the siren's call in that throaty voice he would hear until he died.

He began to move on her then, but with infinite care, straining mightily against the desire that thundered through his body. She was his now . . . for now, at least, she was his, and he loved her with a force as elemental as the storm that crashed around them.

The cessation of pain left desire trembling in its wake. Giving in to the cadence of its claim, Francesca soon found herself caught in the rhythm of a dance as old as time. Rafe's weight upon her, the hot, turgid power of him filling her, drove her to height upon dizzying height. Responding to his whispered urgings . . . encouraging her . . . guiding her . . . she moved with him, yearned with him, reached for the long-awaited rapture.

And rapture beckoned with each stroke, each pleasuring thrust, while, overhead, the thunder rolled, and lightning split the sky with arc upon arc of blue-white fire. The storm was reaching its peak, and the tidal wave of passion on the ground below rose with it, building to a fever pitch.

"Rafe!" Francesca's cry rose over the keening wind, an impassioned plea. "Ah, Rafe, I want— I need—"

"I know, love, I know. . . ." he rasped against her ear. Then, before she could answer him, he reached between them and found the hard, tight bud above their joining and caressed it lightly . . . then again—

And heard her scream his name as she splintered beneath him.

And as she came, and came, and came, her slippery sheath tightening around him with each shattering throb, Rafe closed his eyes and let the first hot spasm claim him.

"Te amo!" he cried before another rocked him to the core, and then another. Reveling in it, at one with the woman in his arms, he uttered a final harsh cry and let the life force thundering through his body take them to the stars.

CHAPTER FIFTEEN

HEAVING THE LAST ROCK atop the makeshift cairn, Rafe grimaced and flexed the muscles in his back and shoulders. Wanting to keep them away from scavengers, he'd covered the corpses of Morano and his henchmen with rocks. After he alerted McLean and the authorities, he wanted them to see the bodies just as they'd been left after the shootings. It would corroborate his explanation of what had happened.

Not that McLean and his people would appreciate the fact that they were *only* bodies to be found, he reminded himself. They'd wanted Morano taken alive, and he'd sabotaged his mission.

For 'Cesca.

Briefly he sifted through events in his mind, wondering if there might have been a way to do it differently, but in the next instant he gave it up. 'Cesca had been at risk, and that was the bottom line. He knew there hadn't even been a question of trying to capture Morano alive. Not after he'd heard her scream.

He glanced toward the rock ledge, satisfying himself that Francesca was still sleeping soundly beneath it. It had stopped raining and the sun was out; in fact, it had been out since they'd regained their sense after that cataclysmic joining. He'd carried her to the ledge afterward, tenderly removing her wet clothing as they'd exchanged murmured words of love, as he supposed lovers usually did in the aftermath of making love. Really making love.

Not that he would know from past experience. This had been as much of a first for him in some ways as it had been for her. Not just having sex, but making love.

He smiled as he remembered how she'd fallen into an exhausted slumber by the time he'd tossed the last piece of her clothing onto a bush to dry. Small wonder. She'd been wrung out, and he wasn't far behind.

Suddenly Rafe closed his eyes against a wave of emotion that threatened to break him apart. For the longest time after she'd fallen asleep, he'd simply held her in his arms, overcome with a flood of protective tenderness. Of love. Love, the way he'd never even suspected it could be. But soon the knowledge of what must happen next had penetrated, and the pain—

"Dammit!" The word exploded from him, and he made a gesture of angry futility. There was no way out. He'd been over it so many times in his head, he was getting stupid from it. Stupid, as in senseless and dim-witted, like those rats they trained to go through a maze and then drove nuts by sending them through it again after it was blocked.

She had to go back. She was Valera's daughter, and as he'd known from the beginning, he had to surrender her to her father, no matter what. Even if that *what* included the fact that she was no longer a virgin and was in love with the man who'd—

"Sweet God in heaven..." Pain, merciless and raw, sliced through him like a blade, and he almost staggered under the force of it. He hadn't felt this helpless since he was a kid, and there was no comfort in remembering how it had come close to destroying him then.

He made himself take a deep breath, and then another, willing away the weakness, the power of feeling to hurt and dismember the soul. Slowly, by inches, and only by keeping his mind a complete blank, he felt a semblance of strength return.

This was how it would be, he told himself when at last he could think clearly again. For all the long years of his life that he could see stretching out ahead of him like a highway of the damned. But he was a pro. He had merely to keep sight of that fact, to use all the little tricks and gimmicks he'd developed over the years to keep him on track, and he'd be okay. He'd survive, goddammit, he had to, at least until he squared things away for 'Cesca. Yeah . . . he'd survive, he told himself.

He moved on legs that felt like deadwood, toward the ledge where she slept, ignoring the fear that lay coiled in his gut. He'd survive. . . .

But would she?

"You can't mean it!" Francesca's eyes were wild with disbelief, her face bloodless beneath the golden tan. "Rafe, I beg of you, don't *do* this!"

Armored with the shroud of numbness he'd borrowed from the man he'd been before he knew her, Rafe met her brimming eyes with a dispassionate gaze. "It's like I told you, 'Cesca. We both knew this day would come."

"But—but not *now!* Now that we love each other, and we've—and I'm no longer an *inocente!*"

Ah, but you are *an innocent yet, my love,* Rafe answered silently, ignoring a forbidden voice that taunted, despite his iron resolve. *But for how long, now that she's going back to the don and his world, hotshot? How long?*

He made himself address her in an even voice. "Well, I'll admit that little accidental deflowering complicates things, but—"

"Little! Accidental!" There was outrage in her eyes now, Rafe noted with a satisfaction bitter as gall. Good. She would need every bit of anger he could summon as a buttress against the pain.

"Well, it sure was accidental on my part," he told her. "I mean, how the hell was I to know you weren't wearing any underw—"

"That is not what I am talking about here!" she retorted with angry tears this time. "Planned or not, that moment when we—when we consummated our love was the most important of my life. It was—it was earth-shattering! Earth-shattering and beautiful, Rafe, and I cannot believe you would reduce it to—" she gestured helplessly "—to a m-mere *accident!*"

Don't look at her eyes, Rafe told himself as the monster inside threatened to claw through his guts. *Look anywhere but in her eyes. Just focus on something else and you'll be fine....*

"Well, sure," he said to her. "I mean, it was your first time and all. That's bound to make it important to a woman. But what I figure we need to concentrate on now is some way to convince your Italian bridegroom—"

"Don't." Francesca's voice was little more than a broken whisper, but the undiluted pain in it was enough to stop him. "Don't tell me these things."

She could bear almost anything else, she told herself, but not this casually detached Rafe who was like a stranger to her. Even the man who'd awakened her and helped her dress with gentle hands, all the while explaining that he'd be flying the helicopter out of here shortly to deliver her to her father as planned.

That Rafe, at least, had countered her arguments with feeling...with more than a little indication that he still loved her. When she protested that she'd go to her father and reason with him, she'd glimpsed a world of agony in his eyes as he held her and explained what they both knew deep down: Esteban Valera would never release her to marry someone who wasn't of his choosing; they both understood him well enough to know that.

Then she'd tried to convince him to marry her, anyway, even if it meant a complete break with her father.

"You mean a life on the run?" Rafe had questioned sadly. "Yes, even that," she'd answered, knowing it was true. She would rather chance a life on the run with Rafe than face a lifetime without him. The alternative was too ugly and bleak to contemplate, and she'd told him so. How could she endure it? Married to a stranger, a lifetime with a man she would never love...not now...not after...

But Rafe had sketched a bleak picture of his own for her. Of what such a life would do to them, to their love. He'd spoken of the tension upon tension that would come of constantly running and looking over their shoulders, and how it would eventually destroy them.

"There's no way I'd condemn you to such a fugitive existence," he'd said. "I want something better for you, 'Cesca."

"And this is *better?*" she'd exclaimed hotly. "Condemning me to a life—to a life without love? Without *you!*"

She'd broken down completely then, sobbing her heart out and clinging to him like a helpless infant.

A thought struck her then. Was that what had brought about this change in him? This Rafe she didn't know anymore? He'd told her more than once during those long, intimate talks how courageous he thought she was. Had she permanently alienated him by proving to be just the opposite?

Swallowing hard to combat the sudden dryness in her throat, she touched him lightly on the arm, wondering briefly why he wasn't looking at her. "Rafe...I—I know how it must seem to you...that I'm being such a baby about this, so—so I just wanted to tell you I'm sorry. I—I'll try to be brave, truly I will, if only—"

Rafe jumped to his feet, cutting her off with an odd animal sound. *Like some wild creature in pain,* she thought for a split second, then dismissed the notion when she saw his face. It was devoid of any emotion whatsoever.

"Being brave has nothing to do with it, 'Cesca. But maybe being less naive and somewhat better informed *does.*"

"Informed? Informed of what?"

This is it, then. You were afraid you'd have to do it this way, and you were goddamned right! "Of a thing or two about this trip I never told you," Rafe said tightly.

"Such as...?" *He's not even looking at me. Why won't he look at me? Am I suddenly so repulsive to him?*

"Such as the fact that I've been acting as an agent for the CIA, for one thing."

"The—the CIA? Why...how would that—"

"How would that have anything to do with you? Think. We both know what your father is. And although we haven't discussed it, I know you recognized the name Morano." Rafe gestured toward the Bell Jet Ranger and the odd-looking piles of rock flanking it. "You spoke it twice in your sleep a little while ago."

Francesca nodded uncertainly. "I know he is... *was* my father's enemy. A rival in the—the international underworld."

"The *capo* son of the rival, actually," Rafe went on. "And a man I've wanted to kill for some time."

Her eyes went wide with shock. Rafe noticed and looked quickly away.

"W-wanted—" she swallowed convulsively "—*wanted to kill?*"

"Tony Morano killed—tortured to death—my best friend, a guy I knew from the days we worked together for the agency."

Francesca was still reeling. "You *belong to the CIA?*"

"Not on a full-time basis anymore. My days of belonging to someone or something are over. But the agency wanted Tony Morano, too." *Not dead, of course, but it's no good letting you know I messed up, sweetheart—or more to the point, why.* "So when they heard I'd hired on with your father for this little escort assignment, they recruited me for some undercover work on a one-shot basis."

Francesca was trying to digest it all, but it was almost too much to take in. She was preoccupied with one thing in particular... *My days of belonging to someone or something are over.... * Had that been for her benefit? Was it his way of saying he'd never commit to her? That he'd never intended to commit?

"That undercover job involved certain intelligence the agency had, that there would be a kidnap attempt on you when you left the convent for Miami."

The monster was drawing blood, and Rafe reached for some inner strength and forced himself to look at her as he drove the message home. "And they were certain it was Tony Morano who'd be doing the kidnapping."

Francesca went very still, and he could almost hear the wheels turning in that brain of hers. "Then that would mean..." she began, then shook her head. "No. I don't believe it. Morano had no way of knowing our plane would crash. I can't imagine—"

"He *planned* a crash, 'Cesca. When I went back for the horses, I saw the evidence." And he went on to tell her about the phony groom and the M16, the suspicious loss of fuel, all of it.

"The only thing they didn't figure on was the storm— the fact that nature might beat them to the punch, and with a little help from Fuego, sabotage the saboteurs."

Francesca nodded very slowly. "And I suppose it was possible the kidnappers heard enough of that distress signal to—to—"

"Trace the site of the crash and follow us here," Rafe finished for her, then took a slow, steady breath and wrapped it up. "I couldn't be sure, of course, but I was hoping, if not exactly counting on it."

There was a deathly silence between them as Francesca digested what he'd said. In the distance birds fluttered and chirped, while nearby a honeybee droned inquisitively over the last of the wild cherries she'd gathered. Francesca's eyes fell on the forgotten fruit, and her face became a mirror of unspeakable anguish. She had to force herself past the roiling agony before she could speak.

"You were using me to lure them."

The monster snarled and sank in its fangs, but Rafe was ready for it. *Just keep focusing on that point above her shoulder... don't look in her eyes, don't watch her face, and you'll be okay. It's almost over, and you'll... survive.*

"That's all I was to you," Francesca went on as she dragged herself up from the ground. "All this time... a—a decoy."

"'Cesca, I—'" Rafe's voice nearly broke as the monster snapped its jaws. "Yeah," he finally managed to say as she turned to pick up her carryon, "I guess you were."

It was better this way, he told himself as he watched her move brokenly toward the copter. Better the smaller hurt now than the one she'd have to live with if she went to this arranged marriage while still in love with him. While still believing he loved her.

Rafe fell in behind her, and the monster closed in for the kill.

CHAPTER SIXTEEN

FRANCESCA SAT NUMBLY beside Rafe in the helicopter, not wanting to think. Not wanting to feel.

Dear God, especially let me not feel.

But the thoughts kept coming, whirling around in her brain like a shrieking maelstrom, and with them, the pain. *It's over, and you are nothing to him . . . you were never anything to him . . . he merely used you, poor, silly fool that you are, and you had better get used to—*

She pressed her fist to her mouth, strangling the cry that would have emerged. Beside her at the controls, she thought she saw Rafe jerk his head her way, but then she saw he was adjusting his headphones and realized she must have imagined it.

She heard him use the radio again, maintaining contact with the small airport at Tampico, where they would arrive in less than half an hour. He had already alerted them as to who he was and who was with him. Now it sounded like they were telling him about a plane that would be ready to take them to Miami. She heard him mention Papa's name, and then Ramón's, before she willed herself to shut out the sound of his voice.

What did the details matter, anyway? She already knew the important ones: he was taking her to Miami, where Papa waited. Ramón was somewhere in the Sierra Madre with a search party, but someone was contacting him. Arrangements were even being made to send someone for the horses; Rafe had thought of everything.

Her lips twisted into a bitter smile as she recalled the only thing he'd said to her since taking off. "There might be speculation about us, about your being alone with me in the mountains for so long, but you don't have to tell them anything. Your bridegroom is another matter, but if you play it right, he should accept the fact that a ruptured hymen can result from riding bareback over rough terrain. And even if there should be a child, the timing will be too close for him to decide it's not his. He may wonder, but there's no way he'll ever prove otherwise. Stick to your story and you'll be okay."

Yes . . . he'd thought of everything.

Everything but how I am dying inside . . . It was the first trace of the bitterness to break through. The bitterness that had been leaking, like deadly bile, into the place where she supposed her heart used to be.

Suddenly disgusted with herself for giving in to it, she turned her head and looked down, concentrating on the view below. The mountains looked smaller now, less threatening than the jagged peaks between which he'd threaded their way after first taking off.

They were heading toward the eastern coast of the country, toward the sea. She'd always loved the seashore, preferring it to the mountains as a place to get away the few times they'd done so when she was a child. But that had been a lifetime ago. Now, when she thought of mountains, she would always—

Santa Maria, when would it cease? For how long would every thought, every careless musing, lead her back to . . . *Ah, Rafe! I loved you so! No, worse than that, God forgive me, I still love you!*

There it was, the thing she'd been trying to run from in her mind since he'd told her the brutal truth: she still loved him, and probably always would. No matter what he'd done, no matter what he was, Rafael O'Hara was tangled up somewhere deep inside her... in her soul.

One didn't just erase such things. Maybe there were people who could, but she wasn't one of them. She suspected it was something she'd been born with, this unfortunate tendency to love one person until you died. It was in her genes. Ramón had once spoken briefly about Papa's loving her mother that way, and it must be true; he'd never remarried, hadn't even taken a permanent mistress again, as far as she knew.

She stifled a self-deprecating snort. *As far as she knew*—hah! She didn't know anything! For all her proudly owned education, even her dubious satisfaction at having found a way to learn the truth about her father, she was a virtual babe in the woods. Else, how would a smooth-talking liar like Rafe O'Hara—

Oh, God, Rafe... always it came back to him. When would she begin to let it go? *Dios, mi Dios, por favor*...

Silently she picked up the thread and began to pray....

AIDED BY THE RITUAL of prayer she'd been taught by the nuns, and by a stoicism she didn't know she possessed, Francesca kept herself together until Miami. It didn't matter, she told herself, that inside she had shattered into tiny fragments like that character in the nursery rhyme. She'd been schooled by the best in a catechism of duty and obedience—hard taskmasters. Hard enough to teach her how to put Humpty Dumpty together again—if only for a face the old fraud needed to present to the world.

The small plane circled Miami International for the third time before the Mexican pilot received permission to land. The officials in Mexico had wanted to detain them for questioning regarding the crash, but her father must have pulled some strings, because after only a small delay at Tampico, they'd let her and Rafe board and take off for Miami.

The aircraft landed with a soft thump of its wheels on the tarmac, and then they were decelerating rapidly along the runway. Francesca heard the high-pitched whine of the brakes as if from a great distance. Rafe was sitting across the small aisle from her, but she didn't look at him. She didn't need to look at him to see what was there: a face that gave nothing away—the face of a stranger.

The plane finally coasted to a stop, and she undid her seat belt. She rose automatically from her seat, vaguely aware of her crumpled clothes, of the mane of hair that hung loosely down her back because she hadn't bothered to search her carryon for pins. Remembering the carryon, she turned to reach for it and found a strong, sun-browned hand holding it out to her by its handles.

She found her gaze gliding involuntarily to Rafe's face as she took the bag. For a second their eyes met, and she had the impression of a collision before Rafe's eyes shuttered and he turned away.

Quickly she shut her own, trying to recapture what she had seen in that split second. She must have been imagining it—she must have! But the sense of—of torment, of a glint of unspeakable agony in the blue depths of those eyes wouldn't leave her alone, and she chanced another glance at him, wanting to know.

But there was nothing there. Not a hint of anything but the impassive, emotionless face he'd presented to her since leaving the mountains. Her imagination, then. Feeling a fool all over again for even daring to hope there might still be something there, something of the Rafe she knew and had fallen in love with, she straightened her shoulders and made herself walk past him to the exit.

Papa was waiting, and he smiled the familiar smile and opened his arms to her as she hurried down the ramp. He reminded her so much of the Papa of her childhood, of her lost innocence, that she had to blink back tears as he folded her into his arms.

"Mi niña . . . mi querida . . . ah, mi Francesca!"

Esteban Valera's voice held tears as he hugged his daughter to him. It was an outpouring of genuine emotion, Rafe realized. He had no trouble believing the man cared for Francesca, cared deeply for her, and he breathed a small sigh of relief. Letting her go was the worst kind of hell, but he didn't think he'd have been able to go through with it if there hadn't been every indication that he was surrendering her to a man who loved her, despite what he was.

His gaze moved to the small group of men that stood behind the embracing pair. The two on the outside he dismissed immediately as bodyguards, their cool, shifting eyes and alert stances giving them away to anyone with a practiced eye. The pair in the middle, with their expertly cut, hand-tailored suits, looked so much alike, except for the difference in ages, they were obviously related. It had to be the Pagnanis—father and son.

The fiancé was slightly taller than Rudolfo, the father, who was a little above average in height, his salt-

and-pepper hair shaped by a two-hundred-dollar hair-cut. Carlo Pagnani's smooth Roman handsomeness was marred by a clearly disapproving look as he ran his eyes over Francesca's suntanned dishevelment. Rafe felt a momentary urge to slam his fist into the young Italian's pretty face.

But he shoved the urge aside with a ruthless determination. She belonged to the sucker now, or would in a few weeks, while he had no claim on her at all. *None but this hopeless love that's eating you alive...*

He reached for the old habit of turning off all emotion. It was simple...a *click,* and the mind went blank. Easy. It took a little longer this time, but he succeeded as the introductions were made.

Valera shook his hand, thanking him for a job well done, but Rafe thought he detected a certain restraint, although he could have been imagining it. The Pagnanis thanked him, too, in heavily accented English, and there was no mistaking the reserve there. Rafe was sure the slight flaring of the nostrils on the part of the son signaled the age-old challenge of a healthy, virile male to a possible rival—even if Carlo wasn't aware he'd issued it. *Well, what the hell did you expect, Romeo—the tooth fairy?*

A limo waited to take them to the Hilton in Miami Beach. It was, Valera explained, the only place he ever stayed when he was in town. He and the Pagnanis had been waiting there since flying to the States after Ramón's news about the 727's disappearance. They'd booked a suite for Francesca, and Valera told her he'd taken the precaution of engaging a physician to examine her there when they arrived.

"But, Papa, there is no need," Francesca protested as the limousine took off. "As you can see, I am fine, for all I've been—for all that's happened, really I am."

It was the first time she'd spoken at any length since landing. Rafe kept his face turned toward the window, his eyes on the passing scenery as he fought an almost visceral reaction to the sound of that throaty timbre. That he could react that way to the simple sound of her voice! *Christ! I've got to get away from her—fast. She's killing me, and she doesn't even know she's doing it! Ah, baby, I'll hear your voice in my dreams forever. I'll hear it in my grave!*

But it seemed he wasn't going to be able to get away that easily. Valera had booked a room for him, too. Of course, if he'd been thinking more clearly, he'd have known as much. Valera obviously wasn't letting him out of his sight until he came up with his version of all that had happened. He was asked politely to make himself available for "a little talk," but he knew it wasn't really a request.

There was a veiled reference to Rafe's "remuneration," which he supposed was the sly old bastard's ways of saying, "You'll stay around until I get all the answers or you'll never see your fat fee." Fee, hell, if that was all that was involved, Rafe would have taken great pleasure in telling him to stuff it where the sun don't shine. But there was a greater threat behind the don's implied words. There always was when you did business with the mob. *Do it on our terms,* it said, *or you won't live to do it on anybody's.*

Not that he could blame the don for wanting some answers. Morano's involvement alone would dictate that. Well, fine. He'd already put in a call to the agency, using one of the Mexican officials' phones when they were at Tampico; the phone at the secret number he had reached was bug-proof and untraceable, and he'd left enough of a coded message to let McLean know he and 'Cesca were alive, but that his chief mission had gone south. He'd also told them they were bound for Miami. Okay, so now it was Miami Beach. Tough. If the agency wanted to see him that soon, they could damn well hunt him up!

Sullen-faced and inwardly snarling at the whole world, Rafe kept his eyes on the scenery outside the window and willed the limousine to speed him through the blackest day of his life.

ESTEBAN VALERA WATCHED his daughter's serenely smiling profile as she sat beside him in the limousine, listening to an entertaining anecdote Rudolfo Pagnani was relating. Despite her dishabille from the ordeal in the mountains, she displayed the outward serenity for which he was aware she'd been known at the convent. The smiling serenity she'd gotten from Rosa.

But, as with her mother, he knew it was something she could don like an actor's costume; it did not necessarily reveal the emotions that were bubbling underneath. And something was very definitely bubbling underneath his daughter's calm exterior. The problem was, what?

His eyes strayed to the far-too-handsome and virile man sitting across from them, looking out the window. A mistake, perhaps. But he hadn't selected O'Hara for his looks; his credentials had been the best for the job. And if what Ramón had suggested to him was true—that Morano was mixed up in this somehow—the American had earned every cent he was paying him, and then some. Francesca looked healthy and unhurt, for all she'd endured.

Still, there was something new about her...something he couldn't exactly place, but—

Suddenly his mind had a fleeting image of his dead wife as she'd appeared in her last film—a tragicomic role, and rare for an Oscar nomination in those days. Rosa had just lost her parents in a hotel fire before that picture was made, yet she'd insisted on doing it, anyway. Some speculated that the real-life emotions she'd had to suppress had been responsible for the greater depth of her acting performance in *Lonely Laughter*. It had certainly been her best.

But what Esteban remembered, what Francesca recalled to him so vividly now, was how Rosa had been half-dead inside as she'd made the audiences laugh. And how finally she'd made them cry.

Later she'd told him she'd only been able to pull it off by retaining her grief for her parents while drawing on her love for him. "If I hadn't been in love with you, I couldn't have done it, Esteban," she'd told him. "Grief made the tears flow—love, the smiles and laughter."

Valera's eyes strayed again to his daughter, then grew hard with speculation as they wandered over the handsome, blue-eyed American.

CHAPTER SEVENTEEN

TRAVIS MCLEAN RAN A HAND through his dark blond hair in agitation. The switchboard operator at the hotel had put him on an interminable hold while she checked to see if they had a Rafael O'Hara on the guest register. Bad enough, but the elevator music some idiot was piping in his ear was about the last straw.

His irritation had begun when Rafe's semicryptic message had come while he was away from Langley. So the operation had gone south. Okay—bad news, but considering the fact that they hadn't even known if he was dead or alive until then— *Dammit, Rafe, where the hell are you?*

He hadn't been able to locate O'Hara in any of the myriad hotels in Miami. Even though the control tower at the airport had informed them the plane carrying Rafe and the girl from Tampico had landed there a couple of hours ago. And if that wasn't enough, Jason Cord had put Travis *personally* in charge of tracking O'Hara down!

Cord, you son of a bitch, I'll get you for this! Think you can lord it over all of us just because of a goddamned promotion, huh? Well, think again, Jason, ol' buddy. I didn't sign on with this outfit to do secretarial duty, not even for a bad-ass ol' dude like you, and if you don't—

"Yeah?" McLean's voice was none too gentle with the switchboard operator at the other end. But in the next second he was apologizing to the woman for his rudeness; he'd been raised as a gentleman in the time-worn tradition of genteel Tidewater society—not dead yet, despite what outsiders might think had happened to southern manhood in the decades since the Civil War.

The switchboard operator sounded as if she couldn't care less as she proceeded to inform him that an R. O'Hara had registered a half hour earlier.

"Kindly ring his room for me, ma'am," McLean said, barely keeping the growl out of his voice. God knew, the poor woman didn't deserve his rancor, and neither did Cord if he was honest about it. O'Hara, on the other hand—

"Rafe? McLean, you ol' reprobate! What d'y'all mean by makin' us let our fingers do the walkin', huntin' all over creation for—"

Travis reeled in as Rafe cut him off. It was a terse recitation—in one of their carefully predevised codes—of why he was ensconced in a fancy suite at the Miami Beach Hilton. But there was something in O'Hara's voice that warned him to tread softly, no matter what his justification to do otherwise.

He'd known Rafe O'Hara for nearly fifteen years, worked with him in the worst of some impossibly delicate situations—life-and-death situations—and he'd never heard him sound like this. Rafe sounded . . . dead inside. What the hell had happened to him in those mountains?

But whatever had happened, O'Hara wasn't about to enlighten him. McLean could tell that right off, and he knew better than to press him on it. For all his unemotional account of how he'd screwed up in their objective of taking Tony Morano alive—and he took full blame for the screwup—Rafe somehow gave Travis the impression of a man sitting on a powder keg. A man daring someone to come along and light the fuse.

McLean hung up after saying he'd be in touch later. He heaved a sigh, running a hand haphazardly through his already tousled hair.

The Rafe he'd spoken to was a stranger. Even his lame apology at the end was uncharacteristic: "Sorry I don't have a trophy to show you." The word *trophy* was part of the code they'd devised that centered around a hunting trip O'Hara was supposed to have taken the month before Valera hired him. Rafe O'Hara never apologized for his shortcomings. He never had to, because as a professional, he didn't seem to have any.

He'd been one of the best damned agents Travis had ever known... intelligent, coolheaded under pressure, sure of himself. And while he gave the impression of not believing much in anything—not in any idealistic sense, like a lot of the men—he'd always believed in giving one hundred percent to the job.

So why, McLean asked himself, did his old friend sound like a man who no longer gave a damn about *anything?*

RAFE HUNG UP THE PHONE without giving McLean and the agency another thought. He gazed absently at the damp towel in his hand as if wondering how it had got there. A second towel wrapped around his lower torso reminded him he'd just finished a long, hot shower when the phone rang.

He used the towel in his hand to give his hair a final swipe and had just slung it over his shoulder when he heard a knock at the door.

"Room service, sir," said the voice outside.

Rafe grunted and let the man in. He went into the bathroom and fished a fiver out of his jeans while the uniformed hotel employee made a fuss of setting up a glass on the cart and giving the unopened bottle of tequila an extra spin in the ice.

"'Pears pretty chilled, sir, like you ordered it," said the man as Rafe approached. "There's salt and lemon, too, in case you want 'em. Can I open it for you?"

Rafe shook his head, then ignored the man's thanks as he accepted the five and left.

The tequila beckoned, but the air-conditioning in the room was going full blast, and he was growing chilled after standing around in nothing but a damp towel. Giving a weary mental shrug, he headed for the bathroom and climbed back into the jeans that hadn't seen any laundering since he'd scrubbed them with 'Cesca's shampoo in the mountains.

Ignoring the stab of pain that came all too regularly now with any memories of 'Cesca, he headed for the bottle of liquor on the cart. He'd never been a hard-drinking man, although he'd done his share of social boozing on occasion. He wondered idly if it had anything to do with the pride he'd taken as a kid in his Irish half. There'd always been those who'd ragged him about his Irish surname, jokes about his father's people and their legendary drinking. "God invented liquor to keep the Irish from ruling the world," he recalled a bumper sticker proclaiming in one of New York's Irish neighborhoods.

Well, that phony pride that had made him set out to prove them all wrong no longer mattered, he thought as he filled the glass the guy had left. What mattered was the oblivion he sought, and he only hoped the tequila was strong enough to do the job. He'd demolish the whole goddamned bottle if he had to.

He'd just downed the first swallow, wincing at the raw taste of the stuff, when there came an unexpected pounding on the door.

He wasn't expecting anybody, unless it was one of Valera's lackeys, and right now he didn't have the stomach to deal with any of that. Telling himself the bastards could go to hell and take their stinking fee with them, he had every intention of ignoring the furious summons.

He'd just raised the glass to his lips again when a familiar voice cut through the banging, instantly changing his mind.

"Rafe! Rafe, for God's sake, let me in!" 'Cesca's voice—and she was sobbing!

He was at the door in an instant, adrenaline coursing through his body in waves. Something had happened to her, something— Christ, he'd kill anybody who—

The door swung wide, and Rafe felt the blood drain from his face at the look of her as she tumbled into him. He swore a violent oath, and automatically, before he could give it thought, closed his arms around her.

She collapsed against him in a storm of helpless weeping, and Rafe knew a moment of blind, unthinking rage at whoever had caused her this kind of pain. Swearing softly under his breath, he swung her up in his arms, kicking the door shut behind them as he moved with her toward a settee across the room.

"'Cesca...." he murmured against her hair as he lowered himself on the cushions, cradling her in his lap. He heard his voice break on her name and tried to collect his spinning emotions, reaching for the calm he needed to soothe her.

Holding her, speaking her name, was something he'd thought he'd never do again, and he had to struggle to get past its power to tear him apart. But she was hurting, hurting bad, and that took precedence over his own wounds. He found the control he sought and began to quiet her with soft, wordless murmurings while she clung to him like a hurt child.

Rafe held her like that for a long time. He stroked her hair and pressed kisses along her brow and temple while her choking sobs threatened to break his heart. Eventually the sobbing subsided, dwindling to a stream of silent tears broken by an occasional hiccup. Finally she heaved a long, gut-wrenching shudder and was silent.

"Talk about it, baby," Rafe said hoarsely into the silence. He was rubbing his chin along the well-remembered silk of her hair, and it was all he could do to get the words out. "You need to talk about it, and I need to know."

Francesca's first impulse was not to tell him. Her mind was filled with the aching sweetness of Rafe's presence, and all she wanted was to surrender herself to it, forgetting what had brought her here. The very feel of his arms around her again was like a benediction, and she wanted to lose herself in it forever. Close her eyes and melt into his warm, familiar strength and never leave.

When he held her so gently, as if afraid she would break, she could almost believe he loved her again. Pretend she had never seen that shuttered face and the eyes that wouldn't meet hers in that last agonized moment of parting. *Vaya con Dios, Señorita Valera*, he'd said in the lobby downstairs before her father had led her away... *Señorita Valera*... like a stranger he'd just met.

"'Cesca?" Rafe's voice was a husky whisper against her ear, but there was an insistence in it that brought her back to the present. Taking a deep breath, she pulled herself together and drew back to look up at his face.

She wasn't sure what she'd expected, but the face she saw now belonged to the Rafe she remembered. Loved. His look was open . . . vulnerable, his eyes hiding nothing and full of anguish as they searched her face. It was enough to let her shed her uncertainty. Though stumbling with each recollected detail, she launched headlong into a recitation of the unspeakable things they'd done to her.

"You were mistaken about my being able to—to brazen it out, Rafe. About what happened between us, I mean." She uttered a bitter, mirthless laugh that chilled Rafe to the bone. "We should have remembered that a man like my— God help me, *my father*— would be far more thorough than we supposed."

Rafe felt a chill of stark premonition, but he said nothing, only running a hand soothingly over her back and shoulders.

"As promised, they—they had a physician waiting for me. . . ." She had begun to tremble, and Rafe cursed silently, pulling her closer as he let her continue. "But what my—my *sire* neglected to t-tell me—neglected to tell either of us on the way here—"

She had lapsed back into broken sobs, and Rafe was torn between the need to soothe her so she could go on and the screaming in his head that said he didn't want to know, that whatever had happened to her was all his fault because—

Oh, God! The anguished plea was silent, a wail inside his head, but it was enough to restore him to his senses. His own feelings, his guilt were unimportant now. 'Cesca was here because she trusted him...needed him, and he wasn't about to let her down again. Not ever again!

His voice was hoarse and thick with emotion as he spoke. "Shhh, love...it's okay now. I'm here and—"

An anguished cry cut him off, and then she was screaming the words. "The table had *stirrups*, Rafe! And—and leather *restraining straps!* They didn't care that I didn't even *know* about such things! They forced me to lie down, and they *b-bound* me! They spread my legs for— Oh, God! My bare feet in those cold stirrups! One doctor, and then another—the Pagnanis brought their own— They—they examined me, but even that's not all of it! Rafe, they—"

"Don't!" Rafe's voice was a raw, bleeding whisper as he cut her off. An internal exam. Perfectly routine for millions of women, but not routine in this instance, not routine at all...not for an innocent raised in a convent where he supposed they didn't even mention there were such things. "It's okay, 'Cesca," he went on. "You don't have to—"

"But I do!" she cried. "I do have to go on—because I haven't told—haven't told you the final hu— Oh, God, the *humiliation!*"

Rafe was shaking his head, urging her to stop, but she'd gone too far now; she had to tell—tell it all. Pulling away to look at him through tears that streamed down her face and blurred her vision, she delivered the final blow.

"Rafe, you don't understand! My father and Señor Pagnani *remained in the room while they did this thing!* Both of them! They nodded to the doctors to proceed. They ignored my pleas—I was *begging* them—and they positioned themselves behind those stirrups, and they *watched!*"

Rafe snarled an obscenity that was drowned out by a high, keening wail from Francesca as she buried her face in his shoulder. He tightened his arms around her slender frame as she clung to him while fresh sobs racked her body.

Those bastards... those unfeeling, self-serving bastards! A murderous rage seized him. He was engulfed by its searing force, a terrible, white-hot fury that pivoted in his gut and raked its talons along every inch of muscle and sinew until he shook with it.

They'll pay, he told himself, making a superhuman effort to put his intent into words, into something coherent that would defuse the anger enough for him to think, to act.... *The scum will pay for what they've done. I swear it!*

But with the lessening of the choking rage came a full-blown realization of the earlier notion he'd sought to throttle, and it wasn't pleasant. Like it or not, he'd had a hand in this. By sending 'Cesca back to those pigs, he'd enabled them to do this thing to her.

It didn't matter that he'd salved his conscience by convincing himself that Valera loved her. He'd known what Valera was. Men like him didn't love—they owned. To them a so-called loved one was a possession, an object to be manipulated toward their own ends. And when that object ceased to function in a manner that was aligned with theirs, its welfare, its very happiness, was expendable. How the hell had he lost track of that? Why hadn't he re—

Francesca stirred in his arms, bringing him back to his present imperative: he had to get her away from her father—out of here, and fast. Even now, those bastards could be—

"'Cesca. . . .'" He spoke her name softly, noting with some satisfaction that she'd quieted, even though she still clung to him like she'd never let go. "Sweetheart, listen to me because it's important. Where are they now? Can you tell me that? Where were they when you left?"

There was no need for him to explain who *they* were, and in the aftermath of the emotional storm that had wrung her dry, Francesca was left strangely lucid. Lucid and well able to detect the sensitivity of the old Rafe in his words; their names were anathema to her now, and he wouldn't pollute her ears with them.

She was fleetingly aware this notion might seem fanciful, yet somehow she knew it was not: Rafe—the familiar Rafe she knew and loved—would protect her, even from a hurt so slight as the utterance of a name she abhorred.

The realization gave her strength, and she released her stranglehold on him. Then, meeting his eyes, she told him—calmly this time—the rest of what had happened.

"When the doctors verified that my...membrane had been broken, I told them what you—what we had prepared. That I had ridden bareback for days, and so forth. The doctors confirmed that a ruptured hymen could have been the result, and they adjourned to their own suites to...'ponder'—I believe that was the word that was used—my story. But not before locking me in!"

Rafe heard the anger return with the last statement and almost smiled. *'Atta girl!* he wanted to say. *Get good and mad, and stay that way if it helps. Even those*

bastards would have to go a long way to break you!
Only they'll never get the chance now. Not now. Not
ever again!

But Rafe kept quiet, aware that every second counted
now, while Francesca wound up her story. "I am here
only because I was able to bribe a passing chamber-
maid to ignore the Do Not Disturb sign they'd hung on
the door and unlock it. I...had a very valuable piece of
jewelry tucked in my carryon."

A note of satisfaction entered Francesca's voice as she
thought of the use to which she'd put the Pagnani engagement ring, but she hurried to finish. "I slid it under the door, told her it was hers with no questions
asked, and prayed. But she must have believed me because she opened it. And as far as I know, they are all
still in their own suites, believing that I am in mine."

"Smart thinking," said Rafe, smiling as he hugged
her. Francesca wanted to ask him to do it again, it felt
so wonderful. But Rafe was in motion now, rising and
setting her on her feet, reaching for the rest of his
clothes while he told her what he had in mind.

"I was wrong to send you back to those wolves,
'Cesca," he began, and when she looked as if she would
interrupt, he stopped her with an abrupt gesture. "No,
it's true, and I only hope that someday, after you've had
time to think about it, you'll be able to forgive me for
that stupidity." *Even if I can't forgive myself.*

Francesca opened her mouth to protest, to tell him it
didn't matter now that they were together again, but
Rafe continued, intent on what he was saying.

"It won't be easy, getting you away from them, but
you won't be safe otherwise, and that's the bottom
line." He shoved a foot into one of his battered Reeboks. "So it might have to be a life on the run for you,

after all, but I have another idea before we resort to that...."

He went on to tell her there might be a way he could arrange protection for her through his CIA contacts. He wasn't at all certain of any help from that quarter after he'd sacrificed their objective for 'Cesca's benefit, but he didn't tell her that.

The protection he sought would involve giving her a brand-new identity, with full documentation to support it—"a new life," he told her as he finished dressing.

Loving him more deeply than ever, even daring to hope this new life he spoke of would be possible for them, Francesca watched him pick up the phone and begin to make the necessary calls to his friends at the agency. But as she listened to him, a chill began to settle in the pit of her stomach. Nothing in his words gave any indication that the protection he sought was for himself as well as for her. It was always "*She'll* need..." and "I want *her* to have..."

Not "*we,*" nothing of "*us.*" He wasn't planning on a future where the two of them would be together. This "new life" for her didn't include Rafe at all!

The burgeoning euphoria she'd begun to feel evaporated, replaced by a hollow void. Even tears were beyond her now. She'd shed them all when she'd huddled in his arms in this very room, hurting but still alive with the hope that he might love her after all.

Now she knew it had been a foolish illusion... an illusion called love. And she was the fool to think it could ever be hers.

CHAPTER EIGHTEEN

AFTER PRESENTING his case to both Travis McLean and
Jason Cord, Rafe had what he wanted: covert trans-
portation out of Florida for 'Cesca and himself and a
promise to provide her with a new identity and move her
to a safe haven.

"You've got it," McLean had finally told him after
conferring with Cord. "The girl gets the Witness Protection Program treatment, but what about you,
O'Hara? Once y'all do this, Valera's gonna want your
ass awful bad."

Rafe had told him he'd worry about himself later,
when there was more time. Francesca had priority now.
'Cesca, and a promise I made, he added to himself.

He'd glanced at her when he said this, but noticed she
didn't appear to be listening. She'd grown strangely
quiet and withdrawn during the time he'd been on the
phone, but he'd chalked this up to emotional exhaustion.

The recollection was another stab to the aching
wound in his gut. He'd been a party to her humiliation. Him and his stupid, goddamned shortsighted-
ness. Now she'd have to live the rest of her life with
memories of that abuse. And she'd have to live it in
hiding—as another person.

Guilt, vicious and unrelenting, gnawed at him, but
he'd held it at bay as he hung up the phone. For now.

He'd sworn to himself that he'd make the pigs pay for what they'd done to her, and that helped to keep him functioning.

Before losing her—and the guilt—ate him alive.

Rafe set about getting them out of the hotel, and Francesca found the experience hair-raising. Even in her drained state, she felt excruciating tension as they made their way toward a service entrance where Rafe had been told a car would be waiting. Her pulse accelerated to a rapid staccato, and perspiration dampened the thin silk sheath she'd had sent up from the hotel's boutique when she'd first arrived in her suite.

Using a service elevator, they reached a back stairway leading to the exit, Rafe darting quick glances over his shoulder. They moved with urgent stealth, knowing that any second some men in dark suits could appear with guns and it would all be over. At last they made it outside, hurling themselves into the back seat of a gray Buick that pulled away even before Rafe slammed the door shut.

The driver was the first to speak, and Francesca detected a southern accent as she watched the man maneuver the sedan into the early evening traffic on the strip. "Mighty pretty lady you have in tow there, buddy. Gonna introduce us, or are your manners as bad as they ever were?"

Rafe, who'd had his eyes trained on the view out the rear window, swung front. "McLean? What the hell are *you* doing here? I thought you were in Virginia!"

McLean chuckled. "The convenience of modern transport and communications maketh all things possible, O'Hara. Even you shouldn't be surprised at that—or did that li'l ol' excursion in the mountains lead you to forget there are such things as car phones and high-speed copters?''

Rafe grunted something unintelligible, and McLean went on in that same easy drawl. ''Truth is, I happened t' be in my car outside of Jacksonville when they beeped me, and it wasn't far t' the secure phone where I called you back. Cord was at Langley when y'all spoke t' him, but I was already on my way down here.''

''Even before Cord agreed to this?'' Rafe's tone was nearly flat, barely betraying a weary skepticism. Travis noted how it was in keeping with the hollowness he'd picked up on earlier, but ignored this for the moment. Time for questions later, when he could demand some answers.

''Ol' Jason may be a son of a—uh, son of a gun, these days, but there was no way I was gonna let him give y'all no for an answer. He owes you a few, Rafe...we all do, notwithstandin' the botched—''

''Ah, guess it's high time I repaired those manners you spoke of, McLean,'' Rafe interrupted hastily. ''Señorita Valera...'' He turned toward 'Cesca for the first time since they'd been picked up. ''Meet Travis McLean. McLean, this is Francesca.''

As Travis turned his head slightly, telling her he was pleased to meet her, Francesca noted his tanned, perfectly chiseled profile and squared-off jaw that looked even more stubborn than Rafe's. He was a blond version of Maria's standing expression for the epitome of masculine good looks: ''movie-star handsome.''

Replying to Travis with a polite murmur, she wondered absently whether devastating good looks were some kind of standard requirement for CIA agents. Then she recalled that Rafe had told her he didn't actually belong to the CIA anymore... *My days of be-*

longing to someone or something are over.... Ah, God,
Rafe...

Francesca knew she had to keep herself from dwelling on the source of the dull ache that claimed her mind
and body. To keep it from flaring up into something she
knew would be unbearable. Groping desperately for a
distraction, she began questioning Travis about where
they were headed and what she could expect when they
got there.

McLean deftly avoided any details about their destination, although she could see they were heading north
now, on a highway called I-95. As for the rest, he explained how it was often necessary for security agen-
cies like the FBI and the CIA to provide protection for
innocents—usually witnesses and those related to
them—who were involved in the government's fight
against crime and other threats to the national security.

"When it happens that those innocents are deemed
unsafe despite more routine security precautions," he
told her, "the law of the land says they are entitled to
the ultimate form of protection: a brand-new identity... a new start, in a new place, with all the legal papers required to make that possible.

"As the daughter of... uh, someone like your father," he added, "you don't exactly qualify in the
standard sense, Miss Valera. But on the other hand,
Rafe has explained enough to convince us you'd be in
danger if you didn't receive that protection, and since
this endangerment did come about while we were, uh,
involved in your situation..."

Francesca nodded as he let the words trail off, but
her mind was reaching for more questions to keep the
conversation going. *Questions, comments, observa-*

tions... Dear God, anything to keep from thinking about—to keep from thinking ... feeling.

She brought up the specifics of her personal situation, saying she feared it might not be that easy. After all, she'd just emerged from twelve years spent in a convent in another country and had no formal job experience outside of her teaching duties there. In fact, because of her family's wealth, she hadn't even taken any pay for those duties. How would she find work under the new identity? How would she live?

McLean chuckled, a deep, rich sound that, oddly enough, made her think of the warm honey one of the housekeepers used to pour on her farina when she was a child. "You'd be surprised, how much 'work experience' can suddenly turn up—on paper, that is—under a new name. Just you leave that to us, okay? And as for the *type* of work, the way you'd earn a livin'—"

"She is more than qualified as a teacher." It was the first time Rafe had entered the conversation. Without thinking, Francesca swung toward him, then wished she hadn't.

Slouched casually against the rear seat's opposite corner, the black curls of his longish hair brushing his forehead and collar, his sun-bronzed skin playing delicious counterpoint to lazy blue eyes, Rafe oozed sexuality.

A dangerous animal sexuality to any observer taking in the harsh planes of the strong jaw beneath the high cheekbones, the arrogance implicit in the set of the mouth and the flare of the nostrils, the devil-be-damned way he held himself. But Francesca wasn't just any observer. She was the girl who'd become a woman in the arms of that utterly male animal. And she knew down to the last pore just how unthreatening and sensitive he could be when he employed that sexuality with all the consummate skill of a master.

"And by qualified, I'm not just talkin' her university degree or her skill at languages," Rafe was saying. "She's the kind of person who can keep the wonder of learning alive when she teaches." *Because she never lost the wonder herself,* he added silently, unable to erase the image of a sun-browned nymph exclaiming over the wild cherries she'd found.

As if suddenly aware he'd said too much, Rafe pulled one of the forgotten toothpicks out of his shirt pocket and jammed it between his teeth, then focused his gaze on the scenery outside the window.

So that's the lay of the land, Travis mused silently. *Looks like big, bad, hard-as-nails Rafe O'Hara has fallen. Got it bad, too, if I'm reading it right. And the course of true love isn't exactly running too smooth right now, either. Whoo-ee, good buddy—wouldn't want to be in your shoes for all the cotton in Dixie!*

He'd had a slight inkling, of course, as soon as he'd seen Francesca Valera. Convent girl, hell! She was the most gorgeous creature this side of a *Vogue* cover—with a healthy touch of a Botticelli Venus and maybe a Raphael madonna tossed in....

It was that touch of the pagan mixed with the angelic that had thrown him at first; he'd seen Rafe O'Hara with a lot of beautiful, sexy women over the years, and none of them even remotely resembled Francesca. Valera's daughter was an unlikely blend of the sensual and the serene, all wrapped up in a package marked "class." Who'd have thought—

Suddenly prompted by a more than idle curiosity about what had happened in those mountains—beyond the obvious, he wanted to add, but he didn't think

O'Hara liked to live *that* dangerously—Travis registered the Fuel This Exit sign and swung off the highway. *Time for some answers, good buddy.*

Rafe's mind was on the exchange that had just taken place, so he didn't focus on McLean's maneuver right away. He was thinking about 'Cesca's concern over how she'd live in the new life. He wasn't sure exactly how much cash the government might provide, and he'd made up his mind to make certain she didn't lack for any. He had some respectable savings set aside, even without the addition of Valera's filthy lucre, and he'd see that 'Cesca got it. It shouldn't be too hard to send it through agency channels, and she'd never need to know where it—

Rafe's head jerked up as the Buick pulled into the service station. "What in hell are we stopping here for, McLean? I saw the gauge registering full when we left, and it's too soon to be safe."

"Pit stop for the driver, ol' buddy," Travis lied. "You know we've both been checkin' the road behind us, and there's nothin' on our tail so far. Besides," he added as he climbed out and motioned with a jerk of his head for Rafe to join him, "the lady might appreciate the time t' powder her nose. It'll only take a minute, and could be I have somethin' I want t' show you."

This last was thrown at Rafe with a pointed look. Noting that 'Cesca was exiting through the door McLean was holding open for her in that disgustingly southern-gallant manner of his, Rafe yanked the toothpick out of his mouth and got out of the car.

As Francesca passed on her way to the ladies' room, Travis had his first opportunity to see her face at close range, and what he glimpsed surprised him. Those sensual green eyes not only belied the composure she otherwise exuded, they mirrored some deeply felt pain. The lady was hurting, and unless he missed his guess, Rafe O'Hara was at the root of it. *They're both miserable, and I want to know why!*

Travis picked up the key to the men's room and motioned for Rafe to join him inside. When the door had shut behind them, he took a second to assess his old friend. O'Hara looked suntanned and fit. Handsome as ever, too, in that wiseass way that drove the women crazy.

But there were little things that told another story... tired lines around his mouth and eyes that McLean suspected had less to do with a lack of rest than with some emotional burden he was carrying.

Travis saw himself blink in the washroom mirror. Rafe O'Hara troubled by emotion? The enormity of this apparent contradiction stunned him.

"You wanted to show me something." Rafe's reminder was delivered in that flat monotone that was becoming all too familiar.

Travis nodded, eyeing the crumpled denim shirt. "You're packin' a piece. The same ol' semi?"

Rafe's smile was mirthless. "The same, but minus any ammo. Emptied the last clip on some garbage in the mountains."

Travis nodded. "I'd like to hear about that. But in the meantime—here." He removed a clip of ammo from the inside pocket of his suit jacket and handed it to Rafe. "It's the right fit."

Rafe accepted the clip, withdrew the semi from its shoulder harness under his shirt, and inserted it.

"Thanks" was all he said as he returned the semi to the holster, leaving his shirt open when he'd finished.

Travis nodded approval, knowing they weren't out of the woods yet, and easy access to their weapons might prove crucial in any confrontation with Valera and company. He carried a similar handgun under his jacket, and there was a pair of M16s on the floor of the Buick's front passenger seat.

"Now, about what happened in those mountains, O'Hara..."

Rafe went on, then, to relate what had occurred in the Sierra Madre. Succinctly and quickly, he recounted everything, from the details of the plane crash to the moment he'd buried Morano and his gorillas under piles of rock. Of 'Cesca, he said very little, and to Travis, the omission spoke volumes.

"So you see how it was," Rafe concluded. "It was her life or theirs. *Nullo contendre,* as the legal eagles say...no contest."

McLean had startlingly light blue eyes, as different from Rafe's as blue-white diamonds from sapphires. He fixed them on Rafe's in the mirror.

"It was no contest because you didn't even consider a playin' field. You sacrificed the mission for her."

Rafe merely stared at him for a long moment. Then he said, "I told you I take full responsibility for the screwup."

"Right. And you told Cord, too. But what you neglected to tell anybody was that you're in love with her, and—"

"That's nobody's business but mine, and even if I were—"

"If, hell! It's written all over you, buddy! Take what little I just saw—when we were gettin' out of the car. You couldn't take your eyes off her!"

Rafe turned from the mirror and faced him directly. "Yeah?" There was a disparaging undertone to the word. A sneer.

"Yeah," McLean echoed "except for the times when you thought she might notice. Then you were mighty careful to avoid lookin' at the lady, weren't you? Now, what ol' Travis wants t' know is, *why?*"

Rafe turned his back on him and reached for the door handle, but McLean was having none of it. He had two inches on Rafe, and perhaps fifteen or twenty pounds, and he used the advantage by blocking his path.

"Rafe..." he said softly. "It's me, Travis, remember? I know you...know you well enough t' see you're... Well, let's just say you're not yourself, okay? And that woman out there's one little ball of misery in case you haven't noticed."

He saw Rafe wince and waited.

Several seconds passed, but finally Rafe ran a hand through his hair and sighed tiredly, then told him what he hadn't yet revealed.

He explained that 'Cesca knew nothing of their objective of taking Tony Morano alive. That he'd deliberately left it that way, purposely alienating her so she'd suffer less in the long run. He didn't want her in love with him when she had to go back to Valera, he said.

Travis was incredulous. "But now she's *not* going back! And she's still in love with you, I'd swear it! So why in hell haven't you disabused her of that lie by omission and told her you still love her? *Why?*"

Rafe was shaking his head. "She'll be safer this way, Travis. Without me. Have you forgotten that Valera will be hunting me, too? With a vengeance...your classic mafioso vendetta! No, it's better this way...safer for her."

McLean was incensed by his disregard for the other ways she was hurting, and he told him so—lacing his words with the choicest set of expletives Rafe had heard since leaving the marines.

Rafe let him finish, silently refusing to budge an inch. He hadn't told him about the guilt that was consuming him, and he didn't intend to. The guilt that he intended to expiate by going after Valera and Rudolfo Pagnani personally. No, that little detail was something McLean and his boys didn't need to know.

Travis saw the adamant look in his eyes. "You intend to go through with this, don't you? You're bent on lettin' her walk out of your life never knowin' what you did for her, that you love her, not any of it?"

Rafe gave him a grim nod. "And you're not gonna tell her anything different, McLean. Hear me? I want your word on it right now."

Travis looked as if he might refuse. But after several tense seconds he heaved a sigh and nodded. "You win, O'Hara, but I want t' go on record lettin' you know what a horse's ass I think you are!"

"I've been called worse," said Rafe as he turned toward the door.

CHAPTER NINETEEN

TRAVIS SWUNG THE BUICK back onto I-95 and tried not to think about the pair in the back seat. But it wasn't easy. The yearning hunger on Rafe O'Hara's face when he'd looked at Valera's daughter wouldn't leave him alone. Nor could he forget the pain that bruised Francesca's green eyes.

They weren't his problem, he kept telling himself. But he'd always been sensitive to the people around him, and it would take a clod not to see that these two needed help from someone who could be objective. To save them from themselves, if nothing else.

O'Hara was a funny guy. While with the agency, he was known throughout the organization as a cool customer. "Need somebody smart, untroubled by a bleeding heart?" they used to quip. "Get O'Hara—he doesn't have one."

But Travis remembered a night the two of them were pinned down in a slum on the outskirts of San Salvador, waiting to be picked up by an agency copter after accomplishing a covert mission. The job had taken days longer than it was supposed to, and they were not only bone weary, but half-starved; out of food except for a hunk of stale Indian bread they'd been carefully rationing between them until help came.

Then a pair of filthy, malnourished urchins—they couldn't have been older than five or six—blundered onto the rooftop where they were hiding; they were scavenging among the garbage that lay strewn there, looking for food. And without a second's hesitation, Rafe gave them his half of the stale bread, shaming Travis into doing the same.

Rafe never said a word about what he'd done. Not even during the three extra days they'd had to wait to be rescued—without food, catching rainwater in their borrowed army helmets to stay alive.

Travis often wondered if Rafe had been poor enough as a child to know what it was like to go hungry. It might account for the heart—bleeding, or otherwise— he'd shown he had that night. But O'Hara never talked about his past much. Travis only knew it hadn't been privileged like his own...burdened with the habit of plenty that had blinded him to the urchins' need before Rafe's selfless actions made him see.

But if O'Hara's carefully guarded heart lacked immunity only when it brushed up against that kind of poverty, how did that account for his losing it to Francesca Valera? The don's daughter had been raised in the lap of luxury, hadn't she? Of course, a convent education, no matter how fancy the school—

Rafe's voice broke into his thoughts. "Big Mercedes, way back—been on our tail for the last five miles or so. See it?"

"Been seein' it," said Travis, not adding that he ought to have registered its possible significance sooner, would have if he hadn't been so damned consumed by the plight of the two poor fools in the back seat. "She's beginnin' t' catch up."

"Yeah," said Rafe tersely. "I've noticed."

Travis glanced at the pair of M16s on the floor as if to reassure himself they were still there. A check in the rearview mirror told him the Mercedes was gaining. He stepped on the accelerator.

"No good, General Lee, and you know it," said Rafe, using the nickname he'd given Travis during some forgotten mission. "That sucker has a much bigger engine. If they're after us, it's only a matter of time till they catch us."

"I don't have to make it easy for them," said Travis, reaching for the microphone on the car's radio. "And headquarters might have some help it can spare if we can outlast—" The radio crackled to life. "Hello, Mama Bird . . . this is Baby Bird Three. . . ."

Francesca finally gathered the courage to turn and look at the large black sedan following them. She hadn't wanted to. It was as if, by actually seeing it, she would have to accept the fact that it was real.

But it was there, all right. Closing in on them like a sleek black predator out of nightmare. If it was her father—

"'Cesca, get down on the floor and stay there." Rafe's voice was all authority, the voice of command. It carried her instantly back to the hours and days of their early acquaintance, when he'd taken control of things—of her life—as if he were born to it.

A small smile quirked her lips as she lowered herself to the floor. How she'd fumed against that control, that overbearing arrogance of male command! Only to learn it had its gentler counterpart . . . an achingly tender side that had nothing to do with dominance. That had made her eager to follow wherever Rafe might wish to lead. Now it seemed he still was controlling her life, but hardly in a way she could welcome. What did his protection matter when she didn't have his love?

Travis McLean's voice intruded on her thoughts. "That you, Cord? Listen . . ."

Francesca huddled on the floor of the Buick only half listening, trying to avoid thinking about the big black sedan she could no longer see, but which crowded her mind like a dark, winged nemesis. Only a few seconds later she gave a gasp, then sat frozen in shock.

The voice Travis had identified as belonging to someone named Cord was clear, despite some long-distance static: "I'm telling you, it can't be Valera. Valera's dead. He and his entire entourage were killed when his car exploded outside the Hilton in Miami Beach—a hidden bomb, probably planted by Mor—"

"Well then, who the hell is tailing us?" Rafe was leaning over the seat, yelling into the mike. But Francesca was more aware of the warmth of his hand as it held hers, squeezing it with a firm, reassuring pressure that helped counteract the trembling that had started throughout her body.

"We think it's Morano," said the statical voice. "He's the most likely candidate for the car bomb, and he may be after the girl—to use her against Ramón Valera, now that Esteban's dead. We'll do what we can to get you some help, but—"

"Look out!" The microphone thumped to the floor as McLean's warning split the air. Francesca was aware of a roar of engine noise as Rafe threw himself on top of her and the Buick swerved sharply to the right.

"The bastards are tryin' t' run us off the road!" McLean was yelling. "Stay down, both of you! There's a pile of rocks off the road up ahead, and I'm headin' for it. They may not want t' shoot because of Fran—"

A spray of machine-gun bullets raked the rear side window, just where Rafe's head had been seconds earlier. McLean swore furiously, and the Buick swung sharply to the right, then rocked and bumped over uneven ground.

"Hold on!" McLean yelled. "They didn't expect this maneuver and overshot us, but— Oh, hell! Here they come!"

Francesca thought surely the car would overturn. It careened on two wheels in an impossible arc, spinning them into a position that was more than ninety degrees askew of where they'd been heading. McLean hit the brakes and flung something onto the rear seat behind Rafe, shouting, "Here!"

"Stay down, baby...hear?" Francesca barely had time to register the naked entreaty in Rafe's voice before a staccato of close-range automatic fire filled her ears. It was from McLean, who'd somehow exited on the front passenger's side and was firing from a position somewhere near the right front tire.

Then she noticed the machine gun in Rafe's hands. She wanted to cry out, tell him it was too deadly, too terrible to use, but the cry froze in her throat as a barrage of gunfire shattered the windshield.

"'Cesca, stay where you are and don't move!" She felt the weight of Rafe's jacket settle over her head and shoulders, and then he was opening the door and gone.

More glass splintered and broke, and it seemed the air was alive with bullets and flying glass. Dimly she realized the jacket he'd thrown over her was to protect her from the flying shards, but it was only a fleeting awareness. Her mind was an incoherent riot of skittering thoughts and jumbled emotions held together by an undercurrent of fear more potent than any she'd known.

She was also vaguely aware it didn't come from the prospect of dying; she'd faced death before. But not even when the jet had gone down, or during those awful seconds when she'd tumbled down that escarpment in the mountains—no, not even in those moments when those men came for her in the camp—had she felt this mindless, clawing terror. It came, she realized in an instant of utter clarity, from being forced to wait like this—helpless—while death erupted all around.

And then suddenly it was over. An alien quiet, almost as terrible as what had gone before, hovered in the fractured air. Francesca remained where she was, huddled on the floor with Rafe's jacket over her, the familiar, living smell of him faint in her nostrils. She couldn't move. What if they were all . . . what if Rafe—

"'Cesca . . . no, God, please . . .'" Rafe's voice broke, and the agony in the sound released her; she pushed the jacket aside and heard her name break again from his throat, this time in an explosion of relief. And then he was pulling her into his arms with no words at all, hauling her out of the battered car and running his hands over her body in urgent inquiry.

"You're all right? No cuts from the glass? No . . . Ah, God, 'Cesca, I thought—"

He crushed her to him. Fiercely, in an embrace so tight not a whisper of air lay between them. When he'd first looked in the car and seen her lying there so awfully still, he'd thought she was dead. It had been a moment of nightmare, blacker than he could ever have imagined. For that one, terrible instant he'd known what it was like to be without hope.

And then she'd moved, and he was alive again. 'Cesca . . . sweet God in heaven, 'Cesca—who *was* his life. . . .

"We took 'em all out."

McLean's voice seemed to jar Rafe back into the moment; Francesca felt the bone-crushing grip loosen. Although she was able to breathe easier, she felt a brief stab of regret. Her only thought as he'd held her was that she wanted it to go on forever. He was alive—they both were, and the emotion she'd heard in his voice when he found her...

She lifted her face to his—and saw his own wet with tears. Slowly...disbelieving, even as her eyes told her, she raised her hand and touched the wetness with her fingers.

"You love me." She said it softly, but with the kind of certainty that can only come from a woman who knows she is loved, knows it in the marrow of her bones.

Rafe heard the words, saw the aching wonder in her eyes, and offered her a shaky smile. "I love you," he acknowledged, and his eyes reached into her soul. "I never stopped."

"Damn right. Any fool could see he never—uh, beg pardon, Francesca. I didn't mean you, of course." Travis's voice had an odd sound to it, and both of them pulled apart to look at him.

"You're *hurt!*" Francesca's eyes widened in horror as they took in the blood on his shoulder and sleeve. "Rafe, he needs a doctor! Can we call—"

"Just a flesh wound," Travis insisted as Rafe began to inspect the damage. "And no one's callin' for any-one until I hear O'Hara say certain words to you, pretty lady."

They both looked at him. "What words?" Rafe asked curtly.

Travis winced as Rafe gently probed his wound, but he managed to look him in the eye. "They go like this, ol' buddy—*Francesca, will you marry me?*"

Rafe stiffened. "Shut up, McLean."

"Why? Because according to your ingeniously foolish reasoning, it's still not in the cards?" McLean's tone was light, but the intensity in the light blue eyes was unmistakable as they moved from Francesca's suddenly tense frame to Rafe's angry face.

"Something like that," Rafe growled, thinking of the guilt he could never assuage now that Esteban Valera and Pagnani were dead. Then, seeing 'Cesca's stricken face, he added, "I...I'm not good enough for her, McLean. She can do better."

"Not good enough, hell!" Travis's handsome face bore a look of disgust. There was pain and uncertainty in Francesca's eyes again; she reminded him of a hurt child, and he didn't like it one bit! Promise or no promise, someone had to put a stop to Rafe's bullheaded stupidity!

"Do you know what this self-proclaimed unworthy did for you in those mountains, Francesca?" McLean asked as he shot Rafe a menacing glare.

"McLean, I'm warning you...."

Travis ignored the famous O'Hara look, the one that had had lesser mortals trembling in their boots over the years.

In no uncertain terms Travis told Francesca the real objective of Rafe's mission in the mountains and how he'd deliberately sabotaged it to protect her. He ignored the furious invectives Rafe muttered between clenched teeth, preferring to focus on the slow smile of dawning comprehension that lit up Francesca's exquisite face.

"Now, that's the first time I ever betrayed a confidence," Travis finished as he finally met Rafe's eyes. "I'm not exactly proud of it, but I'm glad," he added with a smile for Francesca. "Yessir, I did it and I'm glad."

Rafe looked at the pair of them smiling at each other, but mostly he was seeing the joy on 'Cesca's face. *She* obviously had no trouble forgiving him, loving him, in the light of all that had gone down, but could he forgive himself?

And suddenly he was astounded to realize he could. The guilt that had been hounding him since she'd come to his room all of a sudden paled in comparison to what he was seeing in her eyes right now. Had been seeing, in a gathering abundance as McLean—the damned traitor—revealed the truth to her.

His head was beginning to spin with the rapid shift of events. There was one more factor they hadn't considered—and it could be a big one. McLean wasn't going to like this, and 'Cesca—oh, God, he didn't want to think about how she was going to take it!

Still, he had to try. Looking McLean straight in the eye and avoiding 'Cesca entirely, he said, "I still might not be able to...to be with her. Ramón Valera's known to be every bit as dangerous and vengeful as his father, and Ramón's still alive. Because of him, she could still be in danger if we—"

Clear, ringing laughter cut him off as Francesca flung herself into his arms. "*No peligro, mi amor!* No danger at all!" she cried, hugging him around the neck so fiercely her feet lifted off the ground. "Ramón adores me, and he always gives me what I want! When he learns how we love each other, he will only rush to give us his blessing!"

Rafe let out a long sigh and buried his face in her hair. He wasn't entirely certain she was right; there was heavy stuff out on Ramón Valera—Esteban hadn't made him his right arm for nothing. But he was tired of fighting this . . . tired of fighting against his own glimpse of true happiness—the only glimpse he'd ever had since those dark days of his childhood—and most of all, tired of fighting her when he only wanted to love her and spend his life making her happy.

"You win, *querida*," he murmured as he set her gently on her feet and held her face between his hands. "Will you marry me?"

Tears choked Francesca's throat, and she could only manage a joyous nod before he kissed her, long and lingeringly.

Travis watched them for a moment, feeling a deep satisfaction. Love wasn't something he'd had any personal experience with, figuring it was something best left to poets and fools. Look at the way those two had acted, especially O'Hara.

Still, he mused as he considered using the car radio to call headquarters and maybe get himself a local ambulance, it was high time O'Hara got himself hitched. Put out of commission, so to speak. They'd frequently been attracted to the same women, causing not a little competition over the years. This left the field open for him . . . as long as that sucker Cord didn't crowd it, he added as an afterthought.

Whistling to himself, with only a passing wince at the pain in his shoulder, McLean headed for the car.

CHAPTER TWENTY

RAFE STOOD UNDER the pulsing hot spray of the shower in his suite at the Miami Beach Hilton. Damn, but it felt good to work some of the tension out of his muscles. It had been the longest day of his life, and his body was telling him to ease up, even if his mind wasn't ready to do that just yet.

For the third time since entering the shower stall, he ducked his head out and glanced through the open door to the adjacent bedroom. The dresser mirror he'd angled to catch the king-size bed still reflected 'Cesca lying curled up in the middle of the big mattress. Not that he expected anything different, but after what they'd been through, he wasn't letting her out of his sight.

He smiled as she stirred in her sleep and snuggled more deeply into the pillows. She was still sleeping soundly. Good. She'd been near exhaustion when the agency helicopter brought them back. When she'd slumped against him in the elevator, he'd carried her into the suite and put her straight to bed.

That was why Rafe had refused to let Cord and his boys question her as they had him. Cord hadn't liked it one bit, but Rafe had told him to stuff it. They could question her only when she was feeling up to it, he'd told Jason, and the same went for the local authorities.

Besides, Cord knew he could get all of the essentials from Rafe and Travis. Rafe grinned as he ducked his head back under the spray and thought about McLean. Ol' General Lee had sworn a blue streak when the medics pronounced his wound more serious than they'd thought and a second copter had rushed him off to Bethesda for treatment. Travis had insisted that he had enough medical training to know a simple flesh wound when he saw one. But nobody paid any attention to him, and off he went. Served the sucker right. Let him see what it was like with someone else calling the shots for a change.

The phone rang just as he was turning off the shower. Rafe grabbed a towel and hurried into the bedroom, afraid it would wake 'Cesca before he could pick it up. Who the hell was calling here, anyway? He'd left strict orders with the desk—

"Yeah?" he growled into the receiver, making no effort to conceal his irritation. Beside him, 'Cesca shifted restlessly on the bed.

The voice on the other end was unfamiliar, yet Rafe had no trouble identifying the note of steel underlying the softness of the man's Spanish-accented speech. Ramón Valera addressed him by name and inquired politely as to the welfare of his sister.

Rafe knew better than to ask him how he'd known who it was and how he'd gotten past the desk to speak to him. Or why he assumed Rafe was in a position to answer the politely phrased inquiry, for that matter. Men in Ramón's position knew how to get information, and get it fast.

Rafe answered carefully, telling him 'Cesca was unharmed and resting quietly at the moment, giving nothing more away. Valera seemed satisfied—for the moment, at least—and proceeded to inform him he was held up at the airport but that they could expect him in

an hour or so. All depended on the annoying intransi-
gence of a customs official, and traffic, of course.

Rafe hung up the phone and walked to the windows
that looked down on the strip, drying himself with the
towel he'd grabbed. It was after nine, and the lights
along the strip mingled with the myriad reds and whites
of what seemed like a zillion head- and taillights moving along the thoroughfare. Barely moving. There was
some kind of rock concert in town tonight and the traffic resembled a log jam.

Rafe smiled. Ramón would be lucky to get here by
midnight. There'd be time...

FRANCESCA DREAMED she was floating in an aquama-
rine sea. She was a child again, and they were on holiday at a wonderful Acapulco resort called La Brisas. A
thick pink stone wall enclosed part of the ocean for
swimming and snorkeling, with apertures fitted with
safety netting to let fresh ocean water in but keep sharks
and other dangerous creatures out.

The safe ocean pool was called La Concha, and
Francesca had learned to swim underwater here, drawn
by the colorful flashes of tropical saltwater fish too
small to be restrained by the nets. She saw them swimming lazily by her now, some so tame she could stroke
them with her fingers.... Ah, there was one that was
bolder than the rest...rubbing lightly against her
arm...gliding along her breast...even nibbling at one
of her nipples—

Her nipples?

Startled awake by the incongruity of the image,
Francesca opened her eyes, instantly aware she'd been
dreaming. But before she was able to shed the lethargy
of sleep to think clearly about where she was, a shim-

mer of incandescent pleasure rippled through her. Its
source was at the nipple where the nibbling of her dream
continued unabated, and there was an answering chord
of unbelievable pleasure in her woman's core.

Recognition came swiftly when her hands went to the
damp curls covering Rafe's head as his mouth worked
its magic on her breast. She smiled and parted her lips
to say his name. But then his finger, subtly tracing the
wetness high between her thighs, had her moaning instead.

"Finally awake, sleepyhead?" Rafe's voice was low
and husky as he moved up to nibble and whisper at her
ear. But his finger hadn't ceased the devastating work
below, and when she said his name, it emerged as a
throaty tremolo.

Rafe felt himself go hard as a rock. God, how he
loved the low, vibrant sound of her voice, the sexy little
noises she made when he aroused her. He smiled against
her ear, kissed it, then touched the tip of his tongue to
its center.

"It's been a long time since I've made you purr,
querida," he murmured, feeling her quiver. "And
there's gonna be a lot of that—and other things—before we're through...."

Francesca felt the heat of his hard body against her
naked flesh, dimly recalled his undressing her when he'd
carried her to this bed. She'd been too tired to do anything more than smile at him then, but now...*oh, Dios,
now—!*

"Ra-a-afe..." she moaned as his finger slipped inside her and his mouth trailed liquid fire along her neck
and shoulder. She was ready to climax, yet the muzzi-
ness of sleep still clung to her. She wanted to tell him
that it was too soon, that she hadn't even had time to

pleasure him in return, but the things he was doing to her body...

"Don't hold back, love," Rafe told her in a rough whisper. "I want you to come first, *querida*. Right now, like this. Then you'll come again, with me inside you...I promise...."

He'd no sooner said the words than he felt the first trembling begin, and the tightening of her slippery core around his finger. She mewled like a kitten and dug her nails into his shoulders, then sobbed his name before letting out a high, keening cry.

"Yes," he encouraged her as she shuddered beneath his hands. "Oh, yes, sweet baby, yes!"

When the last convulsive tremor had claimed her and she began to settle, he pulled her against the length of him, stroking her naked back. Her head was tucked beneath his chin and she was still breathing rapidly.

"You okay, kitten?" he queried softly.

She didn't speak, merely nodded, the silent affirmation sending the silk of her hair gliding along the underside of his chin.

"Good," he murmured thickly, "because we've just started. Only—" he reached for something on the bedside table "—this time, when we love..." She heard the crinkle of something wrapped in foil. "It's gonna be deliberate, sweetheart...with nothing accidental."

Francesca pulled away to see what he was doing. She blushed beneath her tan. "Is...is that a...?"

"A condom, yes," said Rafe, kissing her lightly on the lips. He wasn't worried about disease; he'd always practiced responsible sex. But if she wasn't already pregnant from that surprise in the mountains, he wasn't about to impregnate her now.

She saw him start to open the package, well aware of the straining hardness of his sex as it pressed against her belly. Shaking her head, she placed her hand over his, and the packet.

"No," she murmured, looking up into his face to see his reaction.

"No?" Rafe's expression held a mixture of perplexity and astonishment. "Sweetheart, if you're saying what I think you're saying..."

"I am," she said.

"But—"

"I want your baby, Rafe. Our baby. I want to feel your child growing in my womb as soon as God wills it."

Rafe sighed. "I suppose this has something to do with the Church and—"

"Only indirectly." Francesca's eyes were a clear, translucent green, and Rafe thought he'd never seen them look more intent and purposeful.

"Mostly," she went on, "it has to do with love. I love you, Rafe. I want to bear your children. It is as simple as that."

As simple as that. Rafe's head was spinning. How could he forget maybe the most hellish part of those moments when he'd tried to force her to hate him? When he told her that, in the unlikely event of pregnancy from that accidental deflowering, she could pass the kid off as Pagnani's.

It went in the face of his deepest personal convictions. There were too many carelessly conceived children in the world, unwanted innocents who never knew their fathers. So he'd always—even when engaging in the most casual sex—taken careful measures to prevent fathering such a child himself.

Not that he'd thought, in their unusual case, the child would lack for maternal love. Everything about 'Cesca said she'd love a child she brought into the world. Even what she was telling him now... *Hell!*

Carefully he phrased what he wanted to say in his mind. "Sweetheart..." His eyes held hers as he voiced the words. "Does this have anything at all to do with—with that unspeakable blasphemy I uttered on our way out of the mountains? Because you know—you've gotta know now—I'd cut out my tongue if that would unsay it. I don't know... it seemed like the right way to go at the time, but now I think I must have been out of my mind.

"But 'Cesca," Rafe went on as he searched her eyes, "if your saying you want a baby now has anything to do with what went down then... well, I just think it might not be the best reason to bring a kid into the world, that's all."

Francesca thought of those terrible hours when the pain had been so unbearable—the thought of losing Rafe, of his not loving her, of having to wed another man, and finally, the possibility of being pregnant with Rafe's child and needing to pass it off as a stranger's. Was that what was influencing her now? Was she so traumatized by what had almost happened that she was trying to ensure a stronger bond existed to keep Rafe by her side?

No, she found herself answering at once. If that were the case, she could argue that the possibility of such a bond had existed before, and it had done little to hold him when he'd thought her welfare overrode all other considerations.

No, the simple fact was, she wanted children, Rafe's children. And she saw no reason to wait now that they were planning to be married.

Married! Dear God, is it really going to happen? I'm not still dreaming?

Rafe saw her face grow anxious as she asked him, "You . . . do you still want to marry me, *querido?*"

Rafe's smile was like sunshine lighting up the night. "More than anything in the world, love." *That is, if your brother doesn't decide to—* He buried the rest of the thought, unable to deal with its implications. He'd have to cross that bridge when he came to it. "More than anything in the world," he repeated.

Some of the anxiety left her eyes, but not all of it. "Then . . . then I need only ask you this," she went on. "Do—do *you* wish to have children, Rafe?"

His blue eyes reached into hers, and the depth of feeling in them nearly staggered her. "I would mortgage my soul to see one day your belly beautifully swollen with our child," he whispered thickly.

"But—but not just now?" she whispered as tears began to swim in her eyes. "Is that what you're trying to tell me, *mi amor?*"

Rafe was beginning to feel like an ogre as he kissed away the threatening tears and pulled her close. Hell, she really did seem to want a baby now. It was just that—

Releasing her enough to cup her chin and look at her, he voiced his thoughts. "I want a baby anytime you're ready to give us one, *querida*. But I was thinking about *you*. After those years in the convent, this marks the beginning of the first real freedom you've ever had. Married or not, you could be ready to explore all kinds of things. What about a career? What about—"

Francesca's radiant smile stopped him, and then she began to chuckle. "Is that all that is troubling you, my darling?" she managed to say as tears competed with the mirth. She wiped them away with shaky fingers and went on. "Haven't you heard of the modern woman? Who says I can't have both?"

"Both." Rafe was stunned. Why hadn't he thought of that? In some ways, for all her sheltered life, she was light-years ahead of him.

"*Sí,* you goose!" She was laughing now.

Slowly, Rafe stroked his chin. "Well...to do it right, we'd need enough money.... Day care, from what I've heard, is problematic. A live-in nurse and maybe a housekeeper would be best, and maybe I could arrange my teaching hours to be there when you couldn't be, and—"

"Teaching hours?" It was her turn to look stunned.

"Well, yeah. You didn't think I was gonna keep doing what I've been doing, did you?"

Francesca looked as if she'd been poleaxed. "We— we spoke of *my* teaching career, b-but...teaching *what? You,* I mean."

Rafe looked sheepish. "Guess I never mentioned it, but you see, I've got this standing offer to teach engineering at UCLA. The head of the department's, uh, somewhat high on me...has been, ever since I finished my degree and..."

Francesca was grinning at him. "Go on...don't stop now!"

"Well, it's about this disgustingly, uh, high grade I managed to get on something called the GRE, and—"

"The Graduate Record Exam." She knew all about it; at one time, before her engagement, she'd planned to

take the entrance exam for graduate school herself.
"You had such a high grade, they *solicited* you?"

Rafe looked more embarrassed than ever. "Uh, yeah.
You know, do a doctorate and teach at the same
time...that sorta thing."

Francesca let out a whoop and hugged him. "*Un
genio!* My *novio* is a genius!"

Rafe hugged her back, laughing. "Hey, cut that out!
You're embarrassing the hell out of me."

Francesca laughed with him, but suddenly she pulled
away and gave him a serious look. "We can both do the
teaching, I think, but Rafe...teachers...they do not
earn the sort of money you spoke of—to raise the *ni-
ños* with the proper help."

Rafe grinned at her. "I have a little put away...a
coupla bank accounts, some stocks and bonds. We
might be able to do it okay...."

The look he gave her suddenly made her breath catch
in her throat. "So if you really want this baby now..."
he finished in a voice that had instant liquid pooling
between her thighs.

Her answer was a purr that melded into a growl as she
pulled his head down and kissed him hungrily.

Rafe shifted until she lay beneath him, never breaking the kiss that was a promise between them. He shut
out Ramón Valera and his imminent arrival. Hell would
freeze over before he let Ramón or anything else come
between him and this woman. Between them and the
future they held in the palms of their hands. 'Cesca and
he belonged together, and nothing—*nothing* would stop
them now!

They clung to each other, rolling and shifting on the
large bed. Greedily they took from each other, and

gave, their passion at full throttle now, secure in what lay settled between them.

When at last they separated, their bodies were covered with a fine sheen of perspiration, despite the air-conditioned room. Rafe ran his tongue along the inside of her arm, tasting it...tasting *her,* then found the dampened flesh at the inside of her elbow and pressed a kiss against it.

Francesca shivered, then experimented with the process, bending her head to taste a slick, muscular shoulder. She found it faintly salty...and redolent of him.

Rafe shuddered, fighting the throbbing heat in his loins that made him want to bury himself inside her that second. She was all his now, really his, and he loved her with a force as great as the fire storm she sent rolling through his body.

But, long familiar with the process, he held back, making them both wait. Those faraway days in the mountains had been both hell and heaven for him, and he would use them to make it better for both of them now. But now he knew he could take the heaven and leave the hell behind.

He stretched out beside her and laced the fingers of both hands through hers, then slid them upward until he held her hands pressed against the mattress on either side of her head. He took a long moment to gaze down at her, drinking in the beauty of her face, the silken tumble of auburn hair catching the lamplight in a shimmering wealth of copper and gold.

He met her eyes. They were heavy-lidded with passion, smoldering like a hundred fires trapped in green agate. He smiled at her and saw an answering flare in the emerald depths. The smile remained as he let his eyes roam over the fine-boned nose, the sculpted cheekbones.... But when his gaze dropped to her mouth, his face went serious, and he felt his pulse quicken. Her lips were parted, and now she ran the tip of her tongue along them. He could see it, wet and glistening in the soft lighting.

Slowly, his eyes never leaving her mouth, he lowered his head to capture it with his own. The kiss was unhurried...indolent...a promise and a beginning. His lips covered hers and tested their pliant softness with a lazy, undulating motion while he traced their edges with his tongue.

After a while...a long, long while...he began to delve deeper, increasing the pressure by degree, letting his tongue graze her teeth, and almost meeting her tongue...but not quite...

Francesca shifted restlessly as Rafe's tongue darted deftly away from hers for the third time. Her mind told her what he was doing...the waiting game he was playing, but her body wouldn't listen. He was driving her slowly mad!

She tried to voice her protest, but Rafe forestalled it by increasing the pressure of his mouth. And when she tried to shift her body again, he eased his thigh over hers to prevent it and—

Dios! Now his sex was pressing against her thighs and— *Dios!*

Rafe felt her strain and try to free her hands, but he held them pinned to the bed as his tongue finally dipped inside her mouth, meeting the eager touch of her own. He allowed the intimate mating of tongues briefly, then slid his mouth to her ear.

"Want me?" he questioned lazily.

Francesca's voice was a rasping explosion in the quiet room. "*Want* you? *Dios,* you are driving me insane! I cannot— Ohhh..."

Her moan echoed across the bed as his mouth found the upthrust tip of her nipple. He began to tease it, grazing it with his teeth, flicking it with his tongue. Again she tried to free her hands, but Rafe ignored her—and was treated to a furious string of Spanish that told him what she thought of his callous behavior.

"*Insensible,* am I?" he questioned with a grin, then shifted to the other nipple. The Spanish became a tortured groan.

Francesca thought she might die. She well remembered his control from the time in the mountains. His ability to prolong the love play had been expert—and delicious. But this was going far beyond what he had ever done then. This was bringing her to the brink again and again, yet never letting her go over.

She ignored the niggling voice that insisted he'd already brought her to completion once while denying himself. She was hot and ready for him ten times over, and that was all she could think of now! Didn't he have any compassion for her plight? Didn't he need to come into her as much as she craved it?

But of course she knew the answer to that. She could feel the heat coming from him in waves... feel his answering shudder every time she moaned or cried out... feel the swollen hardness of his shaft as it throbbed between her thighs...

"Rafe!" she cried. "Rafe, you devil! I want you— now!"

"Do you, *querida?*" he asked as he drew her hands to the mattress on either side of her hips, keeping them lightly pinned. "Do you, truly?"

"*Sí!*"

"Good" was all he said as his mouth blazed a trail across her belly.

Francesca tried to use her legs to twist out of his grasp, but she only succeeded in parting them before he anchored her to the bed again with his big, muscular frame.

"*Why* are you doing this?" she demanded breathlessly. She knew she was open to him, that his mouth was achingly close to her quivering flesh. *Dios,* if he only teased her there, and didn't—

"Don't you know, *querida?*" Rafe responded solemnly.

She didn't answer, but a sob escaped as she felt his warm breath on the insides of her thighs, the whisper of a kiss grazing the tiny nub that signaled her passion.

"It's because I love you more than life itself," Rafe declared softly.

And then his mouth found her and she thought she was dying.

Rafe reveled in the heat of her, the slick, swollen flesh that told him she was hovering on the brink. He wanted to linger there, giddy with the musky woman's scent that was hers alone, but he knew he couldn't. He, too, had reached the edge of his resistance, and there was no way he was going to let it break without being deeply encased in her warmth.

"You win, sweetheart," he said thickly as she began to sob his name. He shifted until he was above her, at last freeing her hands and holding her head between his while he branded her with a hot, demanding kiss.

Francesca returned the kiss with a frenzied passion, her nails raking his flat but tightly drawn nipples. Then her hand found his sex and she stroked it with trembling fingers.

There was a fleeting instant of smug satisfaction at his answering groan, but it fled like mist in the wind when he twisted and lay with his body covering hers, his sex poised at the entry to her melting core.

"I love you, 'Cesca," he rasped as the thick shaft began to push slowly into her. "As my body loves you—" he inched deeper "—my mind loves you...." He paused, shuddered, and added, "...And my soul..." And he drove home.

Francesca gasped and closed her eyes, feeling the prickle of tears behind the lids, even as a vortex of pleasure began to spiral through her. *"Mi amor,"* she cried, *"mi vida!"*

He brought them to a shuddering mutual climax, and then again, a short time later, without ever leaving her pulsing warmth. The third time took longer, but the pleasure was just as keen.

"I STILL THINK YOU COULD have told me he was coming," Francesca grumbled. Rafe stood behind her and their eyes met in the suite's full-length mirror. He nuzzled her neck and felt her shiver.

"More aftershocks?" he questioned with a teasing grin.

Francesca closed her eyes and nodded. "You would think," she offered in a half-embarrassed murmur, "there would be little stirring...inside me, I mean, after..."

Rafe chuckled and finished closing the back zipper of her hopelessly wrinkled silk sheath. He wrapped his arms around her from behind.

"The more we 'stir' it, love," he whispered against her ear, "the more, I suspect, it takes on a life of its own."

"Humph!" she groused. "Well I certainly hope it doesn't decide to 'stir' while Ramón is here! And I still think you should have told me about his call."

"What, and have you worrying about what would happen when he got here instead of keeping your mind on...more important things?" Rafe answered with a grin. He placed a kiss at the nape of her neck, felt her shiver again, and grinned at the face she made at him in the mirror.

The kiss, like his grin, was playful, belying the tension he felt. Despite his resolve to deal handily with Ramón Valera, he wasn't looking forward to the encounter.

"I told you," she said as she turned to face him, "I have nothing to worry about with Ramón. I have him—"

"I know, I know—wrapped around your little—"

A knocking at the door of the suite's sitting room made them break apart.

"How do I look?" Francesca asked as she took a last glance in the mirror.

Like a woman who's been well loved, dammit! Ramón would have to be blind not to see it. Why the hell didn't I think of that when I—

"You look fine," he told her as the knocking came again. Rafe clasped her hand and they went to answer the door together.

Ramón Valera looked very little like his half sister, Rafe thought. Except maybe for the tall, clean-muscled leanness of his frame. Rafe studied him as Francesca made introductions after an effusive exchange between the siblings. He was dark—black hair and eyes, olive complexion—with a narrow, angular face that was good-looking in a way, but was maybe too harsh to be considered all-out handsome.

And he had his half sister's intelligence, too, Rafe decided as Valera's eyes met his across the coffee table when they were all seated.

"I don't have to tell you this has been one of the blackest times of my life," Ramón told them, then glanced at his sister. "I am taking Papa's body back to the *estancia* for burial, Francesca. As soon as they will let me. It was his wish to be buried there... beside your mother."

Francesca nodded but said nothing. The ambivalence was faint now, but she imagined it would always tug at her. She was grateful for the warmth of Rafe's hand as it reached for hers, beside her on the sofa.

Rafe watched Ramón's eyes follow the gesture, then lift to meet his.

"It is clear to me, O'Hara," said Ramón, "that you have guarded my sister well. I would like to hear, from both of you, the details of what happened since the plane crashed in the Sierra Madre, although what I have already learned makes it obvious it was an ordeal. But before you begin, let me say simply that I have never seen Francesca looking healthier... or happier."

This last was said with a warm smile for Francesca, and for the first time since meeting Ramón, Rafe began to relax. He told him, then, the same basic story he'd given Jason Cord, although he mentioned nothing about being on an assignment for the agency. But he didn't have to: Ramón did it for him.

"I would have thought you might have wished to bring the killer of Brad Holman back alive, for...uh, questioning," Valera said.

Rafe quirked an eyebrow, but said nothing.

"Brad...who is this Brad Holman?" Francesca asked.

"Holman was Señor O'Hara's closest friend when he was with the Central Intelligence Agency," said Ramón. "He was murdered by one of the men whose bodies have been found buried under heavy rocks in a certain camp in the Sierra Madre."

Francesca nodded and smiled softly at Rafe. "Rafe killed them when they would have—"

"*Sí,*" Ramón cut in. "He sacrificed his true mission to protect you, even when it meant giving up his only chance of bringing justice to Ezio Morano's son—" he looked pointedly at Rafe "—because we both know, do we not, O'Hara, that there are worse fates than death for a creature like Tony Morano."

Rafe still said nothing, but there was a complete understanding between the two men.

Ramón reached into the inner pocket of his expertly tailored suit jacket. He withdrew a gold pen and what looked like an embossed leather checkbook.

"I owe you a quarter of a million dollars, O'Hara," he said as he began writing out a check on the coffee table.

Francesca gasped and looked wide-eyed at Rafe.

Ramón went on as if she hadn't made a sound. "It is what our father promised you for bringing Francesca safely to Miami, and you have certainly earned it."

He tore out the check and held it out to Rafe. "Take it," he prompted when Rafe made no move to accept. "It won't bounce, I can assure you."

Rafe shook his head. "I can't take the money, Valera. Not when I'm keeping your sister. I'm gonna marry her, Ramón."

Ramón lowered the hand with the check and eyed him quietly for several seconds, then looked at Francesca. "Do you love this man, *chica?*"

"With all my heart, Ramón." She looked at Rafe, who smiled softly at her and ran his knuckles gently along her cheek.

Her brother saw the love that shimmered between them for what it was and nodded, then picked up the check again. "I offer this to you again, with my blessings. You did manage to knock off my competition, O'Hara."

Rafe laughed, starting to shake his head, but Ramón was persistent.

"As a wedding gift, then."

Francesca smiled shyly and nudged Rafe's arm. "It will buy a lot of child care."

"Child care?" For the first time, a fierceness crossed Ramón's face.

Francesca blushed and thought she might have heard a groan from Rafe. Quickly she hastened to explain their plans to pursue teaching careers while giving him nieces and nephews.

"Really?" said Ramón, greatly mollified.

"Really," Rafe answered for both of them, adding that he already had money set aside to support a family, but that the wedding gift would probably allow them to buy a small farm somewhere, near where they taught.

"A place where our kids can play freely and there'll be space for 'Cesca to ride her horses, if she wants to," he finished.

"Truly?" said Ramón, genuinely interested now. "And what will you raise on that farm, besides kids?"

Rafe's adoring eyes fell on Francesca as he answered. "Well, the kids for sure, Ramón. But I was thinking of something else, too."

"Oh? What's that?"

Rafe grinned. "Cherries, *amigo*. Wild cherries."

HARLEQUIN SUPERROMANCE®

WOMEN WHO DARE
They take chances, make changes
and follow their hearts

#615 GONE WITH THE WEST by Dawn Stewardson

Paranormalist Alanna DeRain got more than she'd bargained for when she arrived in the old ghost town of Chester City, Nevada! She hadn't counted on having two money-grubbing thugs for company. Nor had she expected to fall in love with 1880s cowboy John McCulley, who insisted he was quite alive. But how could that be? If John wasn't a ghost, what was he doing in the year 2014?

AVAILABLE IN OCTOBER, WHEREVER HARLEQUIN BOOKS ARE SOLD.

This September, discover the fun of falling in love with...

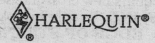

Harlequin is pleased to bring you this exciting new collection of three original short stories by bestselling authors!

ELISE TITLE
BARBARA BRETTON
LASS SMALL

LOVE AND LAUGHTER—sexy, romantic, fun stories guaranteed to tickle your funny bone and fuel your fantasies!

Available in September wherever
Harlequin books are sold.

❖ HARLEQUIN®

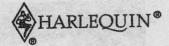

THE VENGEFUL GROOM
Sara Wood

Legend has it that those married in Eternity's chapel are destined for a lifetime of happiness. But happiness isn't what Giovanni wants from marriage—it's revenge!

Ten years ago, Tina's testimony sent Gio to prison—for a crime he didn't commit. *Now* he's back in Eternity and looking for a bride. *Now* Tina is about to learn just how ruthless and disturbingly sensual Gio's brand of vengeance can be.

THE VENGEFUL GROOM, available in October from Harlequin Presents, is the fifth book in Harlequin's new cross-line series, **WEDDINGS, INC.** Be sure to look for the sixth book, **EDGE OF ETERNITY,** by Jasmine Cresswell (Harlequin Intrigue #298), coming in November.

This summer, come cruising with Harlequin Books!

PORTS OF CALL

In July, August and September, excitement, danger and, of course, romance can be found in Lynn Leslie's exciting new miniseries PORTS OF CALL. Not only can you cruise the South Pacific, the Caribbean and the Nile, your journey will also take you to Harlequin Superromance®, Harlequin Intrigue® and Harlequin American Romance®.

- ◆ In July, cruise the South Pacific with SINGAPORE FLING, a Harlequin Superromance
- ◆ NIGHT OF THE NILE from Harlequin Intrigue will heat up your August
- ◆ September is the perfect month for CRUISIN' MR. DIAMOND from Harlequin American Romance

So, cruise through the summer with LYNN LESLIE and HARLEQUIN BOOKS!

HARLEQUIN SUPERROMANCE®

The O'Connor Trilogy
by award-winning author KAREN YOUNG

Meet the hard-living, hard-loving O'Connors
in this unforgettable saga

Roses and Rain is the story of journalist Shannon O'Connor.
She has many astonishing gifts, but it takes a near-death
experience and the love of hard-bitten cop Nick Dalton to show
her all she can be. July 1994

Shadows in the Mist is Ryan's story. Wounded in his very soul,
he retreats to a secluded island to heal, only to be followed by
two women. One wants his death, the other his love.
August 1994

The Promise is the story that started it all, a story so powerful
and dramatic that it is our first featured Superromance
Showcase. Laugh and cry with Patrick and Kathleen as they
overcome seemingly insurmountable obstacles and forge their
own destiny in a new land. September 1994

Harlequin Superromance,
wherever Harlequin books are sold.